Sarah blinked stupidly as she stared at the gun in Larry's hand. "No," she whispered, rising blindly from the sofa.

Her vision cleared. She turned and met Mike's turbulent gaze, then stepped deliberately between the two men.

Larry shouted. Mike reached for his holster and shoved her aside.

A gunshot exploded as Sarah fell, her head smacking the sofa's thinly padded arm. She slid to the carpet. Curled up and trembling, she faced the sofa. Her ears still rang from the gunshot or head blow or both.

"Sarah? It's over, sweetheart."

Mike!

Releasing her breath in shaky relief, she looked up. Visual details registered in telescopic clarity. The trace of dried milk above Mike's upper lip. The dribble of cheese on his sweatshirt. The tender regret in his brown eyes.

The slow-motion swing of his pistol barrel her way.

ABOUT THE AUTHOR

Why would a former bank vice president and advertising agency executive become a romance novelist? "Selling women a sense of their own self-worth beats hyping checking accounts or washing machines any day," Jan says of her newest—and third—career. "Plus I'm a sucker for happy endings."

Jan is proud to write in a genre that presents a hopeful view of life without diminishing its hardships. Her heroines are "strong, gutsy women who safeguard traditional values against all odds—sort of John-Wayne-in-panty-hose types."

Her debut novel, *Too Many Bosses,* won a *Romantic Times* Reviewer's Choice Award, Best Superromance of 1995. Her third novel, *My Fair Gentleman,* was nominated for the same award for 1996, as well as the Romance Writers of America RITA Award, the romance genre's highest award of excellence.

Jan is a native Texan and lives near Houston with her husband and two children.

Books by Jan Freed

HARLEQUIN SUPERROMANCE
645—TOO MANY BOSSES
676—THE TEXAS WAY
713—MY FAIR GENTLEMAN
741—NOBODY DOES IT BETTER

Don't miss any of our special offers. Write to us at the following address for information on our newest releases.

Harlequin Reader Service
U.S.: 3010 Walden Ave., P.O. Box 1325, Buffalo, NY 14269
Canadian: P.O. Box 609, Fort Erie, Ont. L2A 5X3

THE WALLFLOWER
Jan Freed

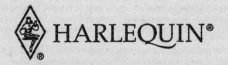

HARLEQUIN®

TORONTO • NEW YORK • LONDON
AMSTERDAM • PARIS • SYDNEY • HAMBURG
STOCKHOLM • ATHENS • TOKYO • MILAN • MADRID
PRAGUE • WARSAW • BUDAPEST • AUCKLAND

ISBN 0-373-70790-8

THE WALLFLOWER

Copyright © 1998 by Jan Freed.

Printed in U.S.A.

To my staunch and talented support team:
Kathleen McKeague, Kim Rangel and Bonnie Tucker, for
plotting and plodding patiently with me on this project.

Special thanks to Mica Stone and my husband, Gerald,
who were beacons in darkness.

Let's all go have a beer!

PROLOGUE

SHE WASN'T AFRAID. Not anymore. In fact, only the thought that John Merrit's killer wanted her dead kept her from dying of sheer boredom.

Sarah Davidson adjusted her flannel nightgown, tightened the belt of her terry robe and dragged herself from the steamy bathroom into the den. Drab and cheerless, despite the tinsel-draped Christmas tree shimmering in one corner. A black ski jacket lay in bloated rigor mortis on the flattened beige carpet potato chips tumbled out of an open bag on top of the water-stained coffee table.

She grinned and shook her head. Mike, her favorite of the two deputy marshals assigned to guard her in shifts, had returned from the grocery store. The industrious clatter of pots said he was whipping up something to feed his tapeworm. Larry must've gone straight to bed.

Sinking onto the worn sofa, she slapped a palm down on the end table and groped. "Hey, where's the remote control?" she called over her shoulder.

The racket in the kitchen stopped. "I dunno. Wherever you left it, I guess."

Grrr. This was why she lived alone. Or at least, used to live alone.

She wanted her life back, dammit! The one with an immaculate apartment in Dallas and rising star status at WorldWide Public Relations. Another four months out of the loop would make her loopy. She'd shoot *herself* by then and save some hitman the trouble.

The rumbling whir of the garbage disposal interrupted Sarah's mental tantrum. When the telephone rang seconds later, she let Larry pick up from the bedroom. It would only be someone from the department checking in. She wasn't allowed to make or receive calls.

Swallowing her lump of self-pity, Sarah probed between the couch cushions for the missing remote control. The kitchen door swung open and Mike walked in carrying a plate and glass of milk.

"I made a killer omelette," he said, tilting the plate. "If you're nice I'll let you have some."

She eyed the oozing butter and cheddar cheese. "Killer is right. *You're* the one who needs protecting—from a major heart attack."

"Spoken like a starved woman." The middle-aged marshal settled an annoyingly trim backside onto the seat of a nearby armchair, his leather shoulder holster creaking. "According to my last physical, I've got the body of a thirty-year-old stud."

"And the *brain* of a two-by-four," Sarah quipped.

Lively brown eyes contradicted his sorrowful tsk-tsk. "Starved women are always so cranky. Sure you don't want to split this?"

"Yes, thank you." The smell of buttery eggs, the

sight of cheese stringing between his plate and uplifted fork set off geysers in her mouth.

Leaning forward, he waved the plump morsel in front of her nose. "Mmm, looks good, doesn't it? One bite. What could it hurt?"

A man who ate like he did without gaining an ounce would never understand her fear that one taste might lead to another, and another, until she woke up one morning in the body that had caused her so much pain growing up.

"I'm not hungry," she insisted.

He popped the fork into his mouth and moaned in appreciation. Within seconds, half the omelette had vanished.

Scowling, she reached for the farthest cushion crevice and wedged her fingers inside. Aha! In one swift movement she extracted the remote control, aimed at the television set and zapped in rapid succession.

"Wait! Go back a station," Mike ordered.

Sarah paused midclick. "I refuse to watch another ball game."

"No balls in sight," he promised, drowning his juvenile smirk in a huge sip of milk.

Thumbing the Down button, she arched a brow. "I see what you mean. So, I guess not all home-shopping programs are 'foreign infiltration of American culture designed to bankrupt families and create anarchy,'" she quoted him dryly.

"Hey, *some* of the credit charges my ex ran up were worth the money."

Sarah studied the on-screen red satin peignoir modeled by a Claudia Schiffer look-alike. "And to think that all these years I could've been tall, blond and sexy by ordering a nightgown. Quick, pass the phone!" Half-serious, she wondered if Larry was off the line yet.

"Quit fishing for compliments." Stuffing the last bite of omelette in his mouth, Mike stabbed the fork at the TV. "You'd look great in that little red number," he mumbled.

Her bubble of laughter was as much for his milk mustache as his outrageous flattery. "I'd look like a kid playing dress-up, and you know it."

Makeup and sophisticated clothes helped, but she still couldn't order a beer without having to show her ID. What had been annoying at twenty-one was humiliating at twenty-seven.

Setting his empty plate and glass on the floor, Mike regarded her thoughtfully. "Trust me, sweetheart, you'll thank the powers that be for that baby face when you're my—" His gaze lifted sharply to a point beyond her shoulder. He flashed a startled smile. "Hey, Larry, what's up?"

Sarah twisted toward the red-haired man standing in the hall doorway behind the couch. Wearing a rumpled flannel robe, his ginger freckles stark against skin drained of color, he looked as if he'd just awakened from a nightmare.

"What's the matter, buddy?" Mike prodded. "Couldn't you sleep?"

"The phone woke me."

To her left, Mike stiffened. Tension crackled between the two men, raising the hair on Sarah's arms. Larry pulled a hand from his robe pocket and withdrew a dull black pistol.

She blinked stupidly. Was this some kind of joke?

His two-handed marksman's stance appeared deadly serious. "Raise your hands slow and easy, Mike. You even twitch funny and I'll shoot. Sarah, don't move."

She couldn't breathe, much less move.

"You're making a big mistake," Mike warned, his voice grim. "C'mon, buddy, put the gun down and let's talk. Nobody needs to get hurt."

It's happening again, Sarah thought. A fog of horror blurred the boundaries of time, distorted her perception. Larry's pistol melted into a glittering knife. His red hair became blond, his blue eyes a colorless reflection of moonlight. She was once again in John Merrit's backyard, knowing her client was in danger yet cowering behind the ligustrum bushes to watch a blade pierce his chest—and bloody her conscience for the rest of her life.

"No," she whispered now, rising blindly from the sofa.

Her vision cleared. She turned and met Mike's turbulent gaze, then stepped deliberately between the two men.

Larry shouted.

Mike reached for his holster and shoved her aside.

A gunshot exploded as she fell, her head smacking the sofa's thinly padded arm. She slid to the carpet. Curled and trembling, she faced the sofa's box-pleated skirt. Her ears still rang from the gunshot or head blow or both.

"Sarah?"

She suppressed a moan and tightened her fetal position.

"It's over, sweetheart."

Mike!

Releasing her breath in shaky relief, she looked up. Visual details registered in telescopic clarity. The trace of dried milk above Mike's upper lip. The dribble of cheese on his sweatshirt. The tender regret in his brown eyes.

The slow-motion swing of his pistol barrel her way.

As her mind reshuffled the cold facts, blessed numbness cloaked her emotions. "The phone call," Sarah said evenly. "It was for you, wasn't it?"

He nodded in a friendly manner. "A day earlier than I expected. Larry's been acting suspicious for a while. He must've pretended to be me on the phone, and the idiot on the other end believed him. *Damn,* I hate working with amateurs."

"You professional bastards have your standards, huh?"

His friendly expression vanished. Sarah couldn't find the strength to care. She'd be dead soon, anyway. She pushed up awkwardly into a sitting position.

"So how much is my carcass worth?" she managed to ask, fighting a wave of nausea. "Enough to cover home-shopping charges?"

Affronted ego glittered in his eyes, more dangerous than anger. "Ah, Sarah, I'm gonna miss that sassy mouth. Actually you're worth a small fortune in gambling debts, not to mention my neck. I'm afraid my book's not a very…understanding operation." He offered a charming, apologetic smile to absolve his deceit…and his unhesitating earlier decision to snuff out Larry's life.

Deep inside Sarah, a last vestige of innocence died.

"Now be a good girl and stand up." Moving forward, Mike hauled Sarah to her feet and thrust his pistol barrel against her temple. "The bullet has to come from Larry's gun, but I promise it'll be quick and painless if you stay right here. Close your eyes, sweetheart," he said almost pleadingly.

"No." She held his gaze. "I want you to carry this memory all the way to hell."

Blanching, he released her arm as if stung and stepped away.

A gunshot cracked. Mike's head snapped back. He crumpled in a graceless heap at Sarah's feet, a round bloody hole between his surprised eyes. Behind the sofa, a second heavy thud sounded.

She was cold. So cold.

"Sarah," a weak voice whispered urgently.

Larry!

Her movements sluggish, she made herself stumble around Mike and the end table to the young deputy marshal sprawled faceup.

Oh, dear Lord, there was so much blood. And more pumping out with his every heartbeat. She ripped off her robe, fell to her knees and pressed the makeshift bandage against the bubbling wound on his chest.

"You'll be just fine," she murmured, praying she was right. "Hang on, Larry. I'm calling 911, then I'll be right back." She started to rise.

He grabbed her wrist and squeezed with surprising strength. "No time," he croaked, his chest lifting and falling in great labored breaths. "He's coming—" wheeze "—trust no one—" wheeze "—hide... until...trial." His gaze intensified along with the pressure around her wrist. *"Run!"*

It was snowing outside. She had two hundred dollars and some traceable credit cards in her purse. "Run where? Hide how?" Panic sharpened her voice. "Who's coming, Larry? Answer me!"

His breath rattled out, then stopped.

In the terrible silence, a baritone voice urged shoppers to take a look at the new item coming up. A sterling silver friendship ring, delivered to your best pal in time for Christmas if ordered now. Turning, Sarah stared at the toll-free number blinking at the bottom of the screen.

She was cold. So cold.

CHAPTER ONE

STUCK-UP RICH KIDS. That's how the students of Roosevelt High School appeared to most Houstonians—at least to the ones without servant's quarters behind their pools. Jack Morgan was quick to call the generalization unfair.

Usually.

Right now he found it hard to put himself in these kids' shoes and be objective. Especially when the combined cost of new Dr. Martens and Air Max Triax footwear shuffling through his classroom door would fund a semester of college for his sister Kate. If Kate had wanted to attend college. Which she most definitely and stubbornly did not.

Frowning, he scooped up a pencil from his scarred oak desk and focused on his fifth period lesson plan. The word *quiz* stood out in red letters. He doubted anyone but Elaine Harper had read *The Grapes of Wrath* over the Christmas break, but what was he supposed to do? Blow off the assignment because it was the first day back? That's what every other teacher had done, or so his first four classes had assured him.

Doodling in the margin of his lesson plan, he absorbed snippets of conversation from incoming students. The skiing in Vail had been awesome. The new

Jeep from Mom and Dad was "kickin'." Kevin had finally replaced his piece of shit stereo using cash sent from aunts and uncles.

Jack grew still. Kate had asked for a combination stereo CD player last Christmas. He'd said maybe next year, then promptly forgotten until now. A prickle of guilt increased his irritation.

"Cool Hilfiger shirt, Danny."

"Love the new jacket, Kim."

"Ohm'god, Jessica, you got the purple Docs!"

Jack's pencil tip snapped against paper. He brushed a tiny cone of lead from the scribbled word *brats,* then plucked a new pencil from the dozen sharpened replacements filling a black coffee mug. White letters on the curved ceramic stated, Bad Spellers of the World…Untie! Staring at the Christmas gift from Beto Garcia, an atrocious speller and the fifth period class clown, Jack felt his lips twitch. He needed, as the gift card had advised, to "lighten up."

These kids on the verge of adulthood weren't necessarily brats. Just normal self-centered teens who possessed resources others didn't. If they would hit the books with half as much persistence as they'd obviously hit up their relatives for gifts, he might not have to teach Responsibility 101 as well as English. And *somebody* had to, dammit, before the oblivious seniors were thrown to demanding bosses or impersonal professors. Before they joined the increasing pool of underachievers in a disillusioned post yuppie generation.

Before they relinquished their dreams and settled for less.

Glancing at the wall clock, he reached out and tapped his one-minute warning desk bell. The four football jocks lounging next to the blackboard sent him disgruntled looks, but broke apart and ambled toward their desks as if it had been their idea to sit down. Books hit wood laminate in staccato rhythm all around. Obedient rumps slid into assigned seats.

Trapped in the middle of one aisle, "Elaine the Brain" hugged her textbooks tighter, walked forward three steps and waited behind Jessica Bates, who stood chatting and oblivious to her shy classmate's dilemma. Turning, Elaine retraced her steps and faltered to a stop behind Tony Baldovino, who'd better sit his hot-shot quarterback butt down and let the girl through, Jack thought grimly, else he'd make sure the Italian heartthrob never passed English—or a football—in the near future.

Jack's tip-of-the-tongue reprimand turned into a silent plea. *Oh, honey, not through there.*

But his best student was already trying to squeeze her extra large Levi's between the petite space separating two empty desks on her left.

Metal ground against metal in protest. Elaine grabbed for a tilting chair back with one hand, clutched at her sliding textbooks with the other, and lost her grip on both. One desk toppled sideways, the other forward, while books thudded open-faced against the thin blue industrial carpet. In the sudden silence, the fifth period bell sounded shrill and jarring.

The bell's echo faded into snickers.

Elaine stooped over to gather the fallen books, her

long brown hair not quite screening her mottled red flush and mortified dark eyes.

Jack had risen halfway from his chair before he remembered Wendy Johnson. He sank back down. After the popular cheerleader's accusation of sexual harassment last semester, he didn't dare risk comforting a female student. Thank God Wendy had transferred to another class for the spring semester. The admissions office had notified him of a replacement; a transfer student from California who apparently wasn't going to show up today.

"Kim, would you shut the door?" he asked the tall brunette sitting in the first row. "Tony, Jessica, pick up those desks and then take your seats, please."

Tony's killing glance spoke volumes about what Wendy must have told him. Still, Jack couldn't fault the boy for siding with his girlfriend.

"All right, the rest of you get out your holiday reading assignment for a quick review before the quiz."

As intended, the swell of groans successfully diverted attention from Elaine. She walked unobstructed to her desk and slipped into her seat, her relief palpable.

Jack waited until all nineteen gazes watched him warily before beginning his "welcome back, the party's over" spiel. "First of all—"

The door burst open. A petite girl with shocking red-orange hair swooped inside and stopped short. She adjusted her books, her lime green sweater and her yellow vinyl shoulder bag in graceful fluttery movements, then cocked her head; an exotic little parrot come to roost among wrens.

"Sorry I'm late, Mr.—" she yanked a card from between her books and peered at it closely "—*Morgan*. But this school is really huge, and some *idi...* some person scheduled me for P.E. before your class."

She walked forward and extended her schedule card for him to sign, as if disrupting his class was no big deal and her explanation settled everything. The closer she got, the more outrageous her skirt became. Made of some clingy fabric in a purple and lime green geometric print, the hem would rise above dress code regulations if she so much as sneezed.

"Would you sign this, please?" The surprisingly mature voice commanded, rather than asked.

Too late, Jack realized he wasn't staring at the card she held out. Heat burned slowly up his neck along with his rising gaze. He looked deep into black-fringed violet eyes...and forgot what she'd asked.

Those eyes could pass for a young Liz Taylor's. And Liz's eyes were a one-time phenomenon—or so he'd *thought* during his ongoing study of film history and screenwriting. He couldn't get over the resemblance.

She lifted a single brow, its dark color confirming that the color of her tousled chin-length hair came from a bottle. "They told me to get this signed today by every teacher. Is there a problem, Mr. Morgan?"

"No problem." He cleared his throat and reached for her card. Dashing off his signature, he noted her name. "Welcome to Texas, Sarina. I'll cut you some slack for being late since this is your first day here. But I'll expect you to be on time to my class from now on."

A slight furrow marred her pale smooth forehead. "I'll do my best."

She'd do her best?

A wondering murmur broke out among the students Jack had forgotten. He hastily closed his mouth, then straightened in his chair. "I know you're new to this school, and maybe things were different in California. But the first rule of behavior in my class is to be on time. No exceptions. If you're late, you'll accept the consequence." He lowered his brows in a toe-the-line expression. "Do I make myself clear?"

"Not exactly."

Unbelievable. "What don't you understand?"

"Well, the consequence is a little murky. My English teacher in California always said clarity is the basis of good communication. Could you be more specific?"

The murmur broke out again. Beto Garcia's unmistakable bark of laughter prompted several nervous chuckles. The faintest hint of a dimple appeared in Sarina's left cheek. She cast a mischievous glance at the class.

Could this girl possibly be *making fun of him?* Jack wondered. "The consequence of not arriving on time is clear and simple. For every minute you're late, you'll spend fifteen minutes in detention."

The dimple vanished. "Are you serious?"

He didn't dignify the question with an answer.

"Do you *realize* how far the gym is?" Her eyes flashed amethyst fire. "It's a five-minute walk *without* fighting through two crowded hallways and two flights of stairs on the way. I'll do my best to be on time, Mr. Morgan. But it may be physically impossible."

"Then you'll spend a lot of time in detention, won't you?"

"That's unfair!"

The knot in Jack's chest grew colder and tighter. He held the girl's frustrated gaze, no longer dazzled by the sight. "Are you quite finished?"

She glanced at their riveted audience, tightened her mouth at their damning silence, then nodded mutinously.

He forced his voice to remain neutral. "There's a great deal in the adult world that is unfair, Sarina. Some people—the people who form the backbone of our society and economy—learn how to cope with challenge and adversity. Others continually blame circumstances for getting a raw deal and then ride the rest of us piggyback throughout their lives."

Watching her expression register which type of person he'd pegged her for, he reached for an extra copy of *The Grapes Of Wrath* and extended the book along with her schedule card. "Please take your seat in the fifth row and read chapter one. We've wasted enough of the class's valuable review time." He turned pointedly to their avid audience. "Unless you're all prepared to take the quiz now?"

About a third of the students squirmed and avoided his gaze. Another five or six grumbled cowardly beneath their breaths. The rest slapped Steinbeck's masterpiece onto desktops with less care than they would hamburgers onto a grill.

Not that Jack cared. He'd made his point. If he'd had to sacrifice popularity to do it, at least he hadn't compromised his standards.

Sometimes those standards were all that stood between him and the restless stranger inside howling for release.

SOMETIMES SELF-RESPECT was all that stood between Sarah and the emptiness inside mocking her brave facade.

But blending smoothly into Mr. Morgan's class should've been her first priority. If only the self-righteous prig hadn't said "Do I make myself clear?" in that combination Darth Vader-Mount Sinai tone of voice, she wouldn't have felt the need to take him down a peg. But he had. So she did. And now she'd given him a reason to watch her closely.

"Keep those eyes on your own paper, Beto," a cavern deep voice advised. "If you'd done the assigned reading, you wouldn't need help from your neighbors."

Sarah cast a speculative glance at the tall broad-shouldered man passing out quiz questions in the second aisle. Everyone hid something behind the front they presented to the public. What would rattle if she dug around in his closet? Pretending to read the open book on her desk, she watched him hand out the last quiz and move to the front of the class.

The image consultant in her approved of his conservative haircut. But his wardrobe needed a serious overhaul. His white dress shirt, boring navy tie and off-the-rack navy slacks didn't do justice to a body made for European-tailored clothes.

"All right, ladies and gentlemen, you've got—" he glanced at the wall clock and back "—twenty minutes to answer five questions. If you finish before then, bring your paper to me and then begin reading chapter four." Rounding a huge oak desk, he sat and faced the rows of bleak expressions. "Good luck," he added wryly.

Sarah swallowed a snort. What kind of teacher expected kids to read Steinbeck over the Christmas holidays? A very unpopular one, she'd bet. At least, unpopular with the boys.

He probably flipped more than a few young female hearts with those intense hazel eyes, that short dark hair left long enough on top to spill just so over his forehead, that strong square jaw shadowed with beard, making the patchy scrub on several male chins in the class seem endearing at best. She looked up and met his mocking stare.

"Finished with the chapter so soon?" Mr. Morgan asked.

Jerking her gaze down to page one, Sarah cursed her adolescent blush. How this man cracked her usual composure she didn't know. What she *did* know is she would never, ever make it through four months in his class without getting expelled...or exposed.

And exposure would threaten not only her life, but

also Donna Kaiser's job as associate principal of Roosevelt High. Sarah's former college roommate had argued that disguising a twenty-seven-year-old career woman as an eighteen-year-old student was brilliant. A week ago Sarah had agreed.

Funny what terror did to a person's good judgment.

The quiver started in her legs and shimmied its way up, gaining force along the way. By the time it reached her shoulders she could barely breathe, barely focus on the printed words returning her stare. Images flashed with snapshot speed in her mind, each more sickening than the last.

An empty glass and plate edging the pool of blood beneath Mike's head. The compelling gleam of urgency dying in Larry's eyes. His bright scarlet blood staining the terry robe, her hands, the carpet, her *soul,* until she'd wanted only to empty her stomach, then scrub the sticky warmth and cloying smell from her skin.

Unconsciously hugging her stomach now, she bit back a moan.

"Sarina...are you feeling all right?" Mr. Morgan asked.

Her head came up. The unexpected concern in his green-brown eyes was almost her undoing.

She blinked rapidly, unfolded her arms and nodded. When he continued studying her in a thoughtful probing manner, she forced her attention back to the book on her desk. But the words were too blurred, the allure of sympathy—even from a stranger—too strong. Slowly, reluctantly, she peeked up through her lashes.

He was writing in a spiral-bound notebook, his concentration so intense she wondered if she'd imagined that instant of compassion. A feather of disappointment brushed her heart. She listened to the scratch of pencils, the squeak of desk chairs beneath fidgeting bodies, and drew a strengthening breath. His disapproval was good, she assured herself. It hindered his ability to see through her flamboyant disguise. Not that he had that much imagination.

For the first time, she noticed what her awareness of the teacher had obscured: the windowless classroom walls. Orderly and serious, with absolutely no sense of humor or style. In other words, exactly like him.

Papers marched across a large bulletin board in precise alignment. The blackboards were actually black, as if they'd been washed rather than erased clean. Displayed prominently beneath the clock, where restless young gazes were sure to drift, a poster board provided the only spot of color in the room.

No way, Sarah thought, her gaze widening on the bold red letters.

But apparently there was not only a way for this guy to confirm his anal retentive mentality, but *ten* of 'em—all listed in a chiseled typestyle under the heading Morgan's Ten Commandments. Amusement nudged her last trace of horror aside.

"Thou shalt not be late to class," she read silently, hearing his authoritative voice resonate in her head. "Thou shalt not talk out of turn. Thou shalt not steal the concentration of fellow students by wearing inappropriate clothing, jewelry or hairstyles."

Uh-oh. No wonder his jaw had dropped during his thorough once-over of her getup. A smile tugged at her mouth as she continued reading. "Thou shalt not covet thy neighbor's test answers, nor his homework, nor his term papers, nor any thing of thy neighbor's that does not rightfully belong to you. Thou shalt not kill the English language."

Ha! Good one. Maybe he had a touch of humor after all. "Honor thy Teacher: that thy days be long upon the classroom which the Teacher thy superior giveth thee."

Sarah laughed out loud.

She might as well have belched in church from the shocked looks turning her way. Gesturing helplessly to the poster board, she caught one pair of dark merry eyes among the stares. Beto, Mr. Morgan had called him. The small Hispanic boy flashed an engaging grin. Sensing a kindred spirit, she grinned back.

Ding!

She whipped her head around as Mr. Morgan lifted an index finger from a small domed service bell on his desk.

"No laughing during the quiz," he warned, his stern gaze censuring.

Sarah laughed again.

Not on purpose. It just sort of popped out before her brain could say, "Don't laugh, stupid, he's serious."

Mr. Morgan leaned back in his creaking chair and tented his long blunt-tipped fingers. "Would you like to share what's so funny with the class, Sarina?"

She always advised her clients at WorldWide Public Relations to meet hard-line questioning with unwavering eyes, unflappable politeness and unfailing honesty. "No, thank you."

His fingertips whitened.

"It's not that funny," she assured him hastily.

"Why don't you let us be the judge of that?"

Wonderful. "I was laughing at your...bell, Mr. Morgan."

A minnow of warning flashed silver-green in his gaze. "My bell?"

"Yes." Like he didn't know what she meant. "That little dinging noise..." *Don't be stupid, Sarah.* "Caught me off guard," she finished judiciously.

He looked pleased. "That's what makes it effective for stopping inappropriate behavior."

Grrr. "That's what makes it more distracting than laughter during a quiz."

The room grew unnaturally still and quiet. She listened to herself breathe and realized too late the gravity of her error.

Mr. Morgan pushed back his chair and rose, his slow deliberate movements more unnerving than a show of anger. "Come outside with me a moment, please, Sarina." His quelling gaze swept the wide-eyed students, who'd dropped all pretense of working on their quiz. "You're on the honor system, class. Don't disappoint me."

Sarah unstuck her clammy legs from the metal desk and stood. Whatever this control freak dished out would be trivial compared with facing the wrong end of a pistol and watching two men die. Still, walking confidently to the door he held open required all the skill she'd learned in assertiveness training.

Somehow she managed the charade. Somehow she passed by Mr. Morgan without stumbling and entered the hallway. The scent of his aftershave followed. Citruslike, familiar…sheesh, it was Old Spice! Her *grandfather* used to wear that stuff.

Turning, she met his fuddy-duddy glare and clamped down on a highly inappropriate urge to laugh.

ELAINE STARED in awe through the classroom doorway. She glimpsed Sarina's spreading grin an instant before the door closed.

"Awri-i-ght," Beto breathed softly, breaking the stunned silence.

Whispers buzzed around the room, collecting reactions to the new girl that would pollinate the entire senior class by the end of the day.

As usual, Elaine kept quiet. With teachers there was always a "right" way to act and dress, a "correct" answer to questions. But with her classmates, she would never act, dress or talk right as long as she was fat, smart and shy—a combination that was social suicide.

When she'd knocked over the desks earlier…

She shuddered, violently rejecting the memory and substituting a less painful one of the new girl. Sarina. Even her name was cool. Small but curvy, wearing clothes normally reserved for *Seventeen* magazine models and a few girls like Wendy Johnson, Sarina had the confidence to look and act outrageous. Elaine had never seen *anyone* stand up to Mr. Morgan like—

"Shhh!"

Tony's fierce command stopped the whispers and Elaine's thoughts instantly. Alarm riveted her motionless until she remembered she hadn't said a word.

"Quiet, you morons. I wanna listen," Tony explained, cocking his ear toward the door.

Elaine found herself straining along with everyone else to hear the conversation in the hallway. Now that it was quiet, she understood every tension-filled word.

"...and if you expect to stay in my class your attitude has got to change. Do I make myself clear, Sarina?"

She paused a fraction too long. "Yes, Master Morgan."

"She's nuts," Jessica murmured.

"She's awesome," Tony corrected, and gestured to keep quiet.

"You want me to come, sit and stay on command. If I salivate when you hit that bell, do I get a doggie treat?"

"That's enough!"

Every spine in the classroom stiffened. Mr. Morgan had *never* yelled at a student. Not even at Wendy Johnson, who'd accused him of horrible things and almost cost him his job.

"Look," he said in a more subdued tone. "This is your first day in a new school and I'm sure the transition has been difficult, especially enrolling midterm as you did. But antagonizing me isn't going to make your life any easier. I have rules in the classroom, yes. I made them to establish the best learning environment possible in an imperfect world. The attitude I want you to have requires following those ten simple rules. Do you think you can do that, Sarina?''

Three beats of silence pulsed. "I'm sure you've learned that honor and respect can't be bullied, bribed or even belled from another person." She matched his solemn tone. "But I do apologize for disrupting the quiz, Mr. Morgan. Please don't take my behavior out on the kids."

The kids? Elaine marveled. As if Sarina wasn't one of them herself. Gazing down at her completed quiz, Elaine knew the transfer student had already earned more respect from classmates than she had during three years at Roosevelt High. Not that she blamed them.

How could she expect them to admire her when she didn't even like herself?

CHAPTER TWO

AT 5:35 THAT EVENING, Jack shifted into Park, listened to the stuttering engine of his old Volvo, and fought an overwhelming urge to back out of the driveway and keep going until he reached Los Angeles. That's where he needed to be. Near the film industry professionals in search of promising new screenplays. Far, far away from here.

Having his own place would've helped ease this restlessness, he knew. But his modest salary wouldn't cover a mortgage payment, apartment rent *and* living expenses for three people. The house would be paid off in two years, though. His sister would graduate in three. The future possibilities made his heart beat faster now.

He leaned his head back, closed his eyes and succumbed to his favorite fantasy. Sleeping as late as necessary to recharge his brain. Reading the morning newspaper cover to cover. Doing lunch with his face-less-nameless agent to review his newest action thriller movie treatment. Then heading back home to sit at his computer long into the wee hours, the time the prank-ster god of creativity had seen fit to make Jack most productive.

Heaven. Pure nirvana.

Tap-tap-tap. "Jack?" a muffled voice called.

He tensed against a stomach spasm, then lifted his head and opened his eyes. Outside the passenger door, Vera Morgan stood in the dusky twilight, her knuckles raised as if to knock again. She met his gaze and lowered her hand while he rolled down the electronic window.

"Dinner's ready," she said, irritation sharpening her voice and hazel eyes. "What are you doing out here?"

Only years of practice kept his own voice even. "I was listening to the engine idle. It needs a tune-up." That much was true enough.

"Oh. Well. I'm sure you'll take care of it later. Hurry on inside before the pot roast gets cold. Your sister hasn't had the courtesy to come home on time, so we might as well start without her."

Before he could speak, she turned and headed for the front door of the modest house they'd moved into after his dad had died. Her shirtwaist denim dress flattered a trim figure, her short dyed brown hair appeared freshly combed and sprayed. From the back she looked more like a girl than a fifty-three-year-old widow.

It was only from the front that her deep frown lines marred the illusion of youth.

Jack rolled up the window, cut the engine and reached for his spiral notebook. Where the hell was Kate, and why wasn't she home yet? A fifteen-year-old girl should be safe inside by dark.

Just then a deep rhythmic rumble vibrated the air,

the Volvo's dashboard, his very bones. He opened the door as a souped-up engine roared somewhere blocks away. Sliding from behind the steering wheel, he stood and shifted toward the sound, kept shifting as the source traveled closer and closer. High shrieks and laughter joined the dissonant pounding, the whole cacophony growing louder by the second, tensing his muscles, drawing his reluctant gaze toward the cross street fifty yards away.

A black Chevy pickup burst into view, its bed sprouting fluttery arms and swaying torsos and a familiar white ski jacket that narrowed Jack's gaze. Overshooting the corner, the truck nearly turned on two wheels and teetered. Startled screams of terror competed with the squeal of rubber tires against concrete.

Miraculously, the pickup righted itself. Incredibly, nobody fell out. Unbelievably, by the time the Chevy braked to a stop in front of the Morgan house, the three girls and four guys in back were bragging in the hyperactive way of kids at the end of a roller-coaster ride.

As Jack's breathing returned slowly to normal, he singled out a pair of wary eyes and slammed shut the Volvo door.

"Shit, it's Mr. Morgan!" someone warned.

Glowing cigarette butts arced from the truck to bounce against the street. In the sudden absence of voices, the deafening boom of a rap song rattled the truck windows.

"Get inside, Kate," Jack commanded.

Kate's mutinous gaze captured the waning light and glittered a challenge. She scrambled quickly over the side of the truck to the curb, called out, "Thanks for the ride, Tony," to the shadowy driver, then whirled to run up the front walk. The sight of Jack's purposeful stride toward the truck stopped her short.

For an instant her face changed from a sullen stranger's into the little girl he loved and had raised like his own daughter. *Please, please, don't embarrass me,* she begged him silently.

His heart twisted. He slowed his steps.

"C'mon, Tony, get your ass in gear. I've gotta be home in five minutes," an aggressive male voice yelled.

Jack threw Kate a silent plea for understanding before loping out to the street and slapping a staying palm on the hood. Holding the driver's surprised gaze through the windshield, he rounded the bumper and motioned to roll down the window.

The glass lowered, releasing four hundred watts of subwoofer bass that nearly blasted his eyebrows off. So much for Tony's upper register hearing range as an adult.

"Turn it down," Jack mouthed, slicing the air near his throat with an index finger.

The rap song cut off midboom.

His ears ringing, Jack peered inside the cab. Whew! It reeked of cigarettes, but at least not the unmistakable fumes of pot. No sign of alcohol. The boy's dark brown eyes were clear, alert—and defensive as hell.

Obviously Tony Baldovino hadn't expected to run into Jack. And Roosevelt High's star athlete wasn't happy.

That makes two of us, kid. Curling his fingers over the lip of the window, Jack adopted a neutral tone. "Hi, Tony. I didn't know you and Kate were friends."

"We're not," Tony said, lifting a broad shoulder.

Jack glanced over the cab roof at Kate's stricken expression, then returned his gaze slowly to the person responsible.

After several seconds Tony's casual slouch straightened, his olive skin growing a shade paler. "Hey, I've seen her around school, okay? She asked me for a ride home from the mall."

Perfect. "She asked you for a ride?"

"Yeah. Her and Pam."

"She and Pam," Jack corrected absently, turning toward the back of the truck. He recognized and dismissed the four boys as part of Tony's entourage at school. The girls were strangers to him. All three went into high alert under his appraisal.

It used to fluster him; young girls preening and posturing for his attention, testing their budding sexuality on a male old enough to be forbidden, yet young enough to make the experiment exciting. Wendy had flirted so aggressively and persistently he'd resorted to cold rudeness in order to stop her advances. He'd never encouraged Wendy or any young girl. Never even been tempted.

Memory of a pair of violet blue eyes, shrewd and mocking, kicked the air from his lungs. Damn, he didn't need this!

He refocused on the three faces painted as garishly as any hooker's. "Which one of you is Pam?"

A blonde with dark roots giggled and raised her hand.

"Next time you're with Kate and need a ride home, you have her call me, okay?" To soften his uncompromising tone, he added a full smile.

Three pairs of heavily made up eyelids blinked. Three pairs of heavily glossed lips started to smile back. Four male snorts ranged from disbelieving to disgusted.

"What's the problem, man?" Tony asked, drawing Jack's narrowed gaze.

"The name is *Mister* Morgan. And the problem is your speeding. If you have a death wish, son, that's for you, God and your counselor to work out. But don't assume that eight other people want an early funeral, too. As the driver, you've got responsibility for everyone's safety."

Tony turned and stared through the windshield, his Italian James Dean profile defiant and brooding. No wonder half the girls in school were infatuated with him.

"We were havin' fun," he muttered. "Nobody got hurt."

"Nobody got hurt *this* time," Jack amended, making sure his voice carried to the kids in back who thought themselves immortal. "When I was your age I hopped in the back of a pickup with a couple of buddies of mine for a ride through the neighborhood. No hot-rod stuff, just cruising past girls' houses, honking and yelling our heads off and having 'fun.' The front tire hit a curb. Next thing I knew I was yelling again, staring at the bloody femur piercing right through my new pair of Wranglers.''

Tony's fascinated gaze swung slowly to Jack. The girls in back murmured, ''Eeuuwww.''

''One buddy got up without a scratch,'' Jack continued, his focus turning inward. ''The other one, my best friend, had landed on his head. We thought he was dead. He *should've* been dead.'' The horror of that surrealistic scene shuddered through Jack, but still he kept it graphic. The kids needed to hear the truth. ''Part of Jimmy's skull had cratered. We could see bits of bones mixed in with his brain. Like fresh roadkill.''

Swallowing hard, Jack forced himself to go on. ''A neighbor called Jimmy's mom. She got there right before the ambulances did. She and Jimmy were real close, you know? She took one look at him and made this…noise.'' After sixteen years, Jack still had occasional nightmares about that sound. ''She grabbed his hand and wouldn't let go. Not for the neighbors. Not for the ambulance technicians. Not for the emergency room staff—they wheeled me in minutes after Jimmy. I heard that the doctors had to sedate her before they could get him up to OR.''

Jack's own mother had been pretty hysterical, too, but his dad had still been alive then to soothe and calm her down. It was the last crisis Brian Morgan had ever handled for his pregnant wife and their teenage son. Two months later Jack had inherited his dad's role as head of the family.

"So, what happened to Jimmy?" one of the girls asked in a subdued voice.

Jack snapped back into the present. "Jimmy never came out of the coma. He weighs about seventy pounds now. His mom still visits him every day."

As he'd hoped, Tony looked distinctly uncomfortable. Jack held the boy's gaze. "Let your friends call you a loser. Let them call you a wuss. Believe me, Tony, anything's better than having their moms call you a murderer."

Registering the flicker of shock in deep brown eyes, Jack pushed off from the driver's window and straightened. "Promise me you'll drive these kids home safely."

Tony tried for a casual shrug, and failed. "Yeah, sure."

Nodding, Jack extended his hand and waited a long moment. Finally, the hand that spiraled the most accurate bullet passes in Roosevelt High's history crept through the open window and clasped his for a firm shake.

Satisfied with Tony's new air of responsibility, Jack stepped back and watched the Chevy roll forward to about twenty-five miles per hour, maintaining that speed until it turned out of sight.

Kate hadn't moved from the front walkway, he saw with a start. Even more surprising, she waited for him to join her before heading for the door.

"You never told me that story," she said, her upward glance curious. The straight dark hair bisecting the back of her white jacket to the waist slithered to one side. "I mean, I knew you broke your leg before I was born, but I never knew how."

"And why would I want to admit how stupid I was at your age?" he asked, slinging an arm around her shoulders and drawing her in close. When she didn't pull away, his spirits lightened a few tons. He'd save the lecture for later.

"You mean you haven't always been perfect? According to Mom and her friends, you have wings hiding under that shirt somewhere." The bitterness in her voice told him just how much the constant criticism *she* received hurt.

He stopped, gripped both of her shoulders and stared down at her dainty features. The thick eyeliner and bold lipstick failed to harshen a delicate beauty that would coil some poor bastard's guts in the future.

"Mother knows I'm far from perfect, Kate, but she's scared I'll leave her when you graduate. It's in her best interest to treat me nicely these days."

Kate's eyes widened, acknowledging the first adult confidence he'd shared with her. "Are you? Going to leave when I graduate, I mean."

Excitement flew aerial loops in his chest. "Maybe." He firmed his jaw. "Probably. I'm tired of trying to be perfect. It's damn hard work. I'm more than ready to break a few commandments." His sister's astonished expression was so comical he chuckled.

Her sudden devilish grin gave him pause. "I heard you had a new student today who broke a few of Morgan's Commandments," she said slyly, erasing his lingering grin. "What's the matter, big brother, are you slipping up already?"

How in hell had word spread so quickly about Sarina Davis? He'd spent a good part of the hours since she'd defied him wondering why he'd lost control of the situation; why he'd compromised one of his rules instead of marching her down to the administrative offices and letting her duke it out with Principal Miller or Assistant Principal Kaiser.

"I've got everything under control," Jack reassured himself as much as his sister. They resumed their companionable hip-to-hip stroll up the walk. "New students only get one second chance. Sarina used hers up the first five minutes of class. From now on, I treat her just like any other student."

There's only one problem, Teach, an inner voice jeered as he opened the front door. *Sarina ain't like any other student.*

LYING ON A PLUMP peach love seat, Sarah contemplated the whirring brass ceiling fan of her new safe house. Since anyone tracking her might eventually check out Donna's condominium, her grandmother's guest house behind the stately Kaiser home had been a more sensible hiding place.

This way, Donna could visit under the pretense of seeing her grandmother. And the guest house was close enough to the school for Sarah to walk both ways.

She rubbed her big toe absently against the blister forming on her opposite heel. "I'm telling you,

Donna, I blew it. Between my defense of Generation X feminism in social studies, and my lecture to Moses in English class, Sarina Davis must be a hot topic in the teacher's lounge.''

"Kids mouth off every day," Donna murmured from her matching position on the full-size sofa. "I'm sure it's not that bad.''

"This is me, remember? It's that bad. I've gotten used to speaking my mind and having adults *listen*. This subservient student act is going to be much harder to pull off than I realized. Oh, and can you please get my schedule changed so I won't be late to Mr. Morgan's class?" Sarah rolled her eyes. "He probably has a list of 'inappropriate' students tacked up by the lounge coffeepot, and I've been added in red pencil. I can't believe you actually like someone who's so, so…''

"Handsome?" Donna supplied.

The image of a darkly masculine face popped into Sarah's head.

"Hardworking?''

The image expanded to include broad shoulders huddled over a notebook, a tanned hand writing furiously.

"Honorable? Heterosexual? C'mon, Sarah, you've got to admit he's 4-H material," Donna persisted, using the term they'd coined in college referring to prime date prospects.

Sarah blinked, then narrowed her eyes. "Yeah, but two of those *h*'s stand for *hard-nosed* and *high-handed*.''

"Jack's a great guy."

Something in her friend's tone made Sarah roll her head toward the statuesque red-haired beauty. Despite having just arrived after a school day lasting until six o'clock, Donna looked morning fresh. Amazing. Her conservative navy blue suit wasn't even wrinkled.

Moses would heartily approve.

"Are you two dating?" Sarah asked.

"We've...had coffee a couple of times." The wistful gleam in Donna's blue-gray eyes said coffee wasn't the only thing she'd like to have with the man.

"Donna, the guy's a control freak. I swear I'll go to sleep tonight hearing that stupid little...*ding!*" Sarah mimicked the annoying sound. "I kept waiting for him to yell, 'Number eight, your order's ready!'"

Chuckling, Donna unclasped her barrette and massaged her scalp, creating splashes of wavy dark red against the peach fabric. The hothouse orchid blend of colors lent an exotic lushness to her classic beauty.

"Jack may be a little strict," she admitted, "But I admire his sense of responsibility. He's been like a father to his younger sister Kate, and from what I gather, he's pretty much supported his mother for years."

"Is his mother ill?"

"Not physically," Donna said, her dry tone implying an alternative. "Mrs. Morgan and I have had a few talks regarding her daughter. Kate is looking for trouble, but Vera refuses to deal with anything unpleasant. Any time I suggest that she take disciplinary action, she defers responsibility to Jack."

"Jack is—how old? In his early thirties?"

"Thirty-two."

"Hmmm." Sounded like Jack was a mamma's boy who came with a lot of extra baggage her friend didn't need. "Whatever happened to David what's-his-name? The banker."

"The gigolo?" Donna said on a laugh, flapping a dismissive hand. "He got married two years ago to another bank customer and quit his job to be her 'investment manager.' Good riddance." She toed off her navy pumps, wriggled her hosiery-webbed pedicure and arched her neck in a blissful sigh.

Sarah's focus blurred. When had her career become more important than keeping in touch with a treasured friend?

"I'm sorry I involved you in this mess, Donna. I just...didn't know where else to turn. Risking your job, buying me clothes, letting me stay here...it's more than I deserve." *More than anyone else would've done for me.*

Even if her parents' home in Fort Worth hadn't been the first logical place a hunter would scope out, Sarah knew what she could've expected from Denise and Bob Davidson. Fierce hugs, followed by irritation because Sarah had inconvenienced their lives, finishing with escalating arguments between husband and wife over what their daughter should do. At which point Sarah would slip away and they wouldn't even know it. She'd lived the same scene over and over during her childhood.

A light touch on her arm brought Sarah back to the present.

Donna crouched beside the love seat, her expression gentle. "That first semester after Mom and Dad died, I was on self-destruct. But somehow you put up with my hatefulness and crying. Somehow you got me to laugh in spite of all that anger and pain. I would've flunked out if you hadn't shamed me by example into caring about my grades."

Her gaze intensified and she squeezed Sarah's arm. "You pulled me through one of the worst times in my life, Sarah. I'm grateful to have the chance to repay the debt."

Sarah stared blankly at the beautiful woman fate had assigned to be her dorm roommate at St. Edward's University. "Debt? If anything, I owe *you* for turning a fat social misfit into someone who could actually get a date by her senior year."

"Don't be an idiot!" Donna's patrician nostrils flared. "It was your shyness—not your weight—that kept boys from approaching you as a freshman."

A part of Sarah longed to think so, but the pragmatic majority of her brain accepted the truth. After four years of living with Donna, Sarah had assimilated the girl's social poise, her stylish taste in clothes—even her good eating habits—with dramatic physical and social results. People acted as if weight loss and fashionable clothes had somehow made her smarter, wittier and more worthy of respect than before.

The power of her "improved" image to influence

others' reactions to her was the main reason she'd focused her studies in that area.

Rising abruptly, Donna smoothed her crepe wool skirt and sniffed. "Any improvement in your dating calendar was due entirely to you, Sarah Davidson. You don't owe me a thing."

Not true, Sarah thought, watching her friend walk toward the small kitchen visible beyond a three-stool eating bar. After the trial, she'd find a way to show her gratitude. If, God willing, her luck continued and she lived that long.

Several grocery bags sat on the counter where Donna had heaved them thirty minutes ago. She reached for the lumpiest bag and began unloading produce into the refrigerator, her back to Sarah. "I think Gram is almost glad this happened. Oh, she hates that you're in danger, but she knows I have to visit her, for appearances' sake, before I can slip out back to the guest house."

"She's a sweetheart to let me stay here." *Guilt, guilt.* "Mrs. Anderson has been nice, too. She's already baked me cookies twice."

"Ahh, I knew she'd take you under her wing once she heard your story. She does love kids."

The housekeeper thought Sarah was a great-niece needing a quiet place to finish out the school year. Her parents were supposedly hashing out a nasty divorce.

Donna's teasing grin faded. "That call you made to the D.A.'s office stirred up a hornet's nest, I'm sure. Nobody's come buzzing around yet asking questions, but we can't let our guard down."

They'd decided to let Tom Castle, the prosecuting attorney, know Sarah was safe and would arrive for the trial—but not before. Tom had pleaded with Sarah to come in for safekeeping right up until the calculated second she'd hung up.

"I'll try to bring groceries every weekend," Donna said brightly, switching the subject. "But if you run out sooner or want something special, give me a call. Oh, and I hope you're still a Diet Dr Pepper addict. I have a case in the car."

She moved to another bag, pulled out a stack of frozen dinners and turned to open the freezer compartment. "I read the back of all these and didn't buy any entrees with over six grams of fat. Was that okay?"

Okay? To feed, clothe and house Sarah for almost four months? Sure, Donna wouldn't miss the money. She'd become independently wealthy the instant her parents had crashed into a concrete pillar on their way home from a fund-raiser. But her generosity of spirit, her unhesitating support...her example of friendship in its truest form gripped Sarah's heart and squeezed.

Donna spun around and met Sarah's eyes across the bar counter. "Don't you dare go getting all guilty on me, again. I'm keeping every grocery and department store receipt and I expect you to pay up when this emergency is over, so *forget* the idea of freeloading. Is that understood?"

Sarah nodded tremulously.

"Good. Because helping you is not charity. In fact, it gives me an opportunity to put one over on that know-it-all Linda in the admissions office.'' Donna grinned smugly at some inner vision.

She's enjoying all this, Sarah realized in surprise.

"I accessed Washington High School's records after only three tries! It would've taken Linda all day, *if* she managed to figure out the password at all.'' Tossing her glorious auburn hair, Donna huffed. "She acts like she's God's gift to hackers—but I'm better than she ever thought about.''

"She's not fit to wipe your keyboard,'' Sarah agreed loyally.

"Damn right she's not. She's lazy, too. Never even checked the records envelope, after I went to all that trouble to get one with a San Diego postmark and district office return address.''

"The *nerve*.'' Grinning, Sarah rose and headed for the kitchen. "I don't know how you accomplished registering me at Roosevelt High with a new identity. I don't think I really want to know.'' She reached her friend's side and looked up. "But I'm in awe of your talent. Thank you.''

"You're welcome. I'm in awe of your talent, too. The image makeover, I mean.'' A sweep of Donna's hand encompassed Sarah head to toe. "You were right about going the outrageous route instead of trying to blend in as an upscale suburbia student. You would've looked too much like yourself in Guess jeans and a Polo shirt.''

"I think I've been insulted, which means you insulted yourself. You're the one who taught me how to dress preppy.'' Sarah nudged aside the taller woman and began unloading the remaining full grocery bag. "Did you remember to get the hair color?"

"It's in there somewhere. Your hair, by the way, is divinely inspired."

"Too bad it's hell on the eyes." Sarah glanced wistfully at her friend. "I wish I could've gone auburn instead of pumpkin."

"No, your instincts were right on target. Even I wouldn't recognize you at first glance. Still, I can't quite decide how it makes you look."

Elbow deep in the bag, Sarah paused. "Like one of those shaggy sock thingies men stick on their golf clubs?"

"Funny. No, Sarina Davis is more like..." Donna tapped a finger against her chin, then plunged her hand into the bag as Sarah withdrew her arm. "A sexy rock diva, maybe. Not sleazy by any means, but tougher, more in-your-face than Sarah Davidson, politically correct career woman."

Stacking cans of tuna in the pantry, Sarah cast a startled glance over her shoulder. She *had* felt less inhibited by rules, freer to speak her honest thoughts while impersonating Sarina in school than she did working at WorldWide Public Relations. What would Mark think if he saw her now?

"Who's Mark?" Donna asked sharply.

Sarah blinked. Apparently she'd spoken his name aloud in the shock of realizing she hadn't thought of him before this moment. Not once in the two weeks since watching Larry bleed to death.

"Honey, you're as white as a sheet. Is Mark the man who's trying to kill you?"

"No, no." Sarah managed a wan smile. "He's the man trying to marry me."

CHAPTER THREE

THE NEXT DAY Sarah crammed her Spanish and government books into her locker, shoved *The Grapes of Wrath* and her physical science notebook into her backpack, then slammed shut the metal door. Built-in combination locks were just one of the improvements this modern building offered over the forty-year-old high school she'd attended. A cafeteria designed like a mall food court was another. And if she didn't get there fast, the long lines would mean another lunch gobbled down in ten minutes.

Shaking her head, she plunged into the stream of noisy teenagers. Wouldn't Mark be amazed to see her practically running to get an assembly line meal? The handsome young city councilman had seen her order nonmenu specialties—prepared and delivered personally by the chef—at the finest restaurants in Dallas.

The preferential treatment she'd received had impressed him, she knew. Made him aware of the PR clout she'd developed in the city, and how a woman with her media connections and image-maker savvy could benefit a politician on the rise. She'd sensed his imminent proposal of marriage and been flattered. After all, his pursuit was a tremendous coup for a former wallflower.

But hardly the basis for a good marriage, an inner voice warned.

Adjusting her backpack strap, Sarah frowned and picked up her pace. She refused to feel guilty. Maybe she and Mark weren't madly in love, but that was all romantic fairy-tale stuff, anyway. Games, appearances, hidden agendas—that was real life. Nothing was as it seemed. But what *seemed* was what counted in American culture.

"Sarina! Wait up," a feminine voice cut through the din.

Jessica, the tall sandy-haired girl who sat one row over in Mr. Morgan's class, jogged up and fell in step. "Great dress. I haven't seen it in the stores around here. Where do you shop?"

"Anywhere I can," Sarah said truthfully, earning a laugh. "But there's this boutique in San Diego I like a lot."

"You're from San Diego? I visited my aunt and uncle there last summer. I love that city!"

Uh-oh. "Yeah, me, too. But speaking of clothes..." And changing the subject. "Where's the best place to buy cool stuff?"

Jessica took the bait, rattling off a list of stores Sarah wished she could visit to pick up something in basic black. She appreciated Donna's efforts deeply. But the woman had gone a little overboard selecting outrageous colors. Today's lavender crushed-velvet dress against red-orange hair was the visual equivalent of chewing tinfoil.

"So, Sarina," Jessica said in a get-down-to-business voice. "You wanna sit together today? I talked to Wendy, and she's saving you a chair at her table."

"Thanks, I'd love to. Who's Wendy?"

"Wendy *Johnson*."

O-okay. "Should I know her?"

Jessica did a double take, as if nobody could be that dense. "Head cheerleader, Tony Baldovino's girlfriend, most popular girl in school? Anyway, she wants to meet the person who stood up to Mr. Morgan. Wendy hates him, too."

Sarah's conscience twinged. "I'm sure he's not as bad as I thought."

"Trust me, he's worse. He tutored Wendy privately last semester and came on to her big time."

Moses?

"Yeah," Jessica confirmed as Sarah gaped. "Mr. Ruler-Up-His-Ass Morgan offered to change Wendy's grade if she'd sleep with him. Wendy reported him to the principal. But since nobody else actually heard or saw him try anything, the superintendent let him off the hook— Oh, good! The lines are still pretty short. Want some pizza?" Jessica yelled the last question above the background noise of clinking utensils, chattering voices and an Aerosmith song playing over the loudspeaker.

Blinking, Sarah realized they'd entered the cafeteria. "No, I'm getting in the deli line."

"Okay. Meet me back here when you're finished. Then I'll take you to Wendy's table."

Sarah nodded distractedly and headed for one of six

food lines. Something didn't jibe. No matter how much she disagreed with Jack Morgan's rigid teaching style, he'd seemed...*honorable,* for lack of a better word. Besides, in this lawsuit happy society, only an idiot would risk professional suicide by messing with a student. An idiot—or a truly sick man.

"Hey, look alive!" a boy called from the back of the line.

Snapping to, she moved up next to the girl ahead. Beautiful hair, Sarah thought, automatically envisioning a shorter, wavier style for the chestnut tresses. More volume up top would balance the girl's pear-shaped body. And that huge flannel shirt over jeans would have to go. Instead of disguising extra pounds, it added weight that wasn't there.

Sarah had hidden in the same uniform as a teen, not knowing how to choose flattering styles that were also *in style.* But she doubted this girl would welcome fashion advice. Especially from a complete stranger.

As if on cue, the girl turned slightly, revealing a familiar profile. What was her name, again? Oh, yes.

"Elaine?" Sarah said, prompting a startled glance and blush.

"Hi. You're in my English class, I think. I'm new. Sarina Davis." *Damn.* Too late to withdraw her hand, extended from habit for a businesslike shake.

Elaine performed the gesture awkwardly, her shy brown eyes revealing intelligence—and amusement. "I remember who you are."

Sarah grinned. "I guess I did make quite an impression. But I shouldn't be late for class today."

"You got your schedule changed already?"

"Yes—yeah." Would she ever loosen up?

Elaine's dark brows arched. "It usually takes longer than that to switch classes."

Uh-oh. "Guess I got lucky," Sarah bluffed. Luck was all in who you knew, of course. But mentioning that her best friend was the assistant principal was out of the question.

She settled for a diversionary tactic. "You have beau—awesome hair. I was admir—checking it out earlier." Sheesh!

Slanting a suspicious glance, Elaine shuffled forward into the direct beam of an overhead skylight.

"See? Look at that color. It's so cool!" Sarah exclaimed, watching the red-brown strands catch fire in the sun. "You could be in a shampoo commercial. I'm serious."

Elaine smiled hesitantly. "Thank you. But I'd rather have your hair any day."

"Yeah? How 'bout Wednesday? Wear something beige. Give everybody a break." Good, Sarah thought. She'd banished the lingering trace of sadness in those laughing brown eyes.

A swell of feminine shrieks turned all heads to the left.

Girls at a distant table began popping up in sequence, passing something—a snake!—hot-potato style to the adjacent person. Since laughter was mixed in with the shrieks, the thing must be made of rubber, Sarah decided.

From opposite ends of the cafeteria, two men

headed toward the commotion. One of them, rotund and balding, pulled up short at the sight of the other. Relief flashed across his face and he turned back around.

Jack Morgan continued on, his broad-shouldered body dodging kids and tables with athletic ease. Today he wore brown slacks and a beige dress shirt. A blah tie in the same dull shades. The thought struck Sarah that, dressed in Mark's wardrobe, Jack would win votes just by *walking*. His presence was that commanding, that purposeful.

That undeniably masculine.

A moth wing of awareness fluttered low in Sarah's belly. She ripped her gaze away and muttered, "What's *he* doing here? I thought the teachers stayed up there."

"There" was a separate upper level eating area, where about twenty adults sat ignoring the chaos.

"Mr. Morgan and Mr. Williams are cafeteria supervisors for this lunch period," Elaine said. "They usually stand along the wall, unless somebody gets out of hand."

Sarah resisted a full five seconds before looking at Jack again.

He stood at the offending table lecturing the girls, his expression stern and forbidding. Reaching for the snake, he intercepted a skylight beam, his brown hair kindling—not into red embers—but sun-kissed golden streaks. The girls stared at him wide-eyed, appearing more subdued than intimidated. As if all that masculine TNT were overwhelming at close range. She supposed it would be, at least to teenage girls....

Have you lost your mind? she asked herself. It would be stupid, not to mention disloyal, to develop a personal interest in Jack. Donna liked him. A lot, if Sarah was any judge of human nature, which she was.

She focused on the small brunette gesturing to a nearby table of grinning boys. Jack turned. The grins vanished.

"I wouldn't want to be in their shoes," Sarah muttered, rolling her eyes at Elaine.

"Mr. Morgan will be fair."

Interesting. "Sounds as if you actually *like* the ty—hard-ass." She should've stuck with *tyrant*. It'd been years since using street language held any thrill.

Elaine's desire to be cool obviously struggled with her conscience. "I...think he's a good teacher. Strict—but good." She lifted her chin. "And yes, I *do* like Mr. Morgan. He cares about kids learning."

The girl rose a notch in Sarah's estimation. "Can you sit with me at lunch today, or do you have a regular spot somewhere?"

"You want me to sit with you?" Elaine's astonishment would have been funny, if it weren't so sad.

"If you can, yes. But you'll have to get something to eat, first." Laughing, Sarah pushed the girl gently up to a short counter, then followed behind.

Another meal, another battle. Sliding her plastic tray along a metal ledge, Sarah scanned her options.

A fat corned beef sandwich waved a little toothpick flag for attention. A container of potato salad teetered on the verge of tumbling onto her tray. Dark gooey brownies wept caramel as she bypassed them to reach for a bottle of spring water. She added an apple and a premade turkey sandwich to her tray, paid the cashier, then tilted her head in a follow-me motion to Elaine.

Jessica was waiting at the designated rendezvous spot. "Good timing, I just got here. Are you ready?"

"Is there room at the table for one more?"

"Yeah, probably. Why?"

"I asked Elaine to sit with us." One look at Elaine's face told Sarah how much she'd botched the situation.

Jessica appeared to see the other girl for the first time. It was hard to tell who was the more dismayed. With an inscrutable glance at Sarah, Jessica turned and headed off to the left.

"I'll sit somewhere else," Elaine said hastily. "It's no big deal. Really." She backed away.

"Wait," Sarah ordered. There was nothing to do but brave it out and protect Elaine as best she could. "There's room at the table for both of us. It'll be cool."

They wove through the rectangular tables, each seating about twelve kids. Teens called out greetings to Jessica from all sides. Evidently she was very popular. Sarah hoped the girl was also kind. She glanced back and smiled encouragingly.

Shoulders slumped, her expression grim, Elaine walked as if headed to her execution.

Sarah kicked herself again for her stupidity. For not remembering that high school social hierarchy was as structured and inflexible as an Elizabethan royal court. Her guilt and dread increased as she neared what could only be "Wendy's table."

Eight girls picked at their lunches, too engrossed in looking Sarah over to eat. All were attractive, or downright beautiful. All were slim and fashionably dressed. But only one radiated the supreme confidence and charisma that proclaimed her queen of Roosevelt High.

The most popular girl in school was stunning, of course. Silver-blond hair and a porcelain complexion to match. Emerald green eyes and perfect symmetrical features. A body that, in a tight green sweater, was more womanly than girlish.

Wendy Johnson had the looks and bearing of someone much older than eighteen. Stopping in front of the royal table, Sarah resisted a devilish urge to curtsy.

Jessica put down her tray and turned. "Wendy, this is Sarina Davis. Sarina, Wendy Johnson."

Sarah didn't catch the seven other names. She was too busy holding a challenging green gaze and seeking the nature behind the beautiful mask.

"Tony told me what you did in Mr. Morgan's class." Wendy broke the silence first. "I'm impressed. I only wish I could have seen the bastard's face."

Sarah stiffened. "Actually, I was out of line. He was pretty decent about the whole thing."

Surprise flickered in shamrock eyes, followed by a gleam of annoyance. "The last thing you can call Mr. Morgan is decent. He should've been fired last semester."

"Then why wasn't he?"

Annoyance deepened into something nastier. "Because I was the only one who had the *guts* to tell the superintendent what kind of pervert he is." Wendy's gaze swept over her squirming table companions, then narrowed on Sarah. "You don't believe me."

A statement, not a question. The girl was perceptive. But then, people in power usually were. The trait helped them manipulate others.

"I believe that every story has two sides," Sarah hedged. "And that this tray is getting *really* heavy."

Several girls laughed.

Wendy offered a tight smile. "Jessica, move your tray over so Sarah can sit in front of me."

Jessica obeyed, then glanced nervously behind Sarah.

Elaine!

Stepping back guiltily, Sarah nudged the blushing girl forward with her tray.

"I invited someone to eat with me since there's enough room. Y'all know Elaine, don't you?"

Incredulous glances were exchanged. A few snickers broke out.

"You've *got* to be kidding," someone muttered.

"Sure, everybody knows Elaine The Brain," another girl joked.

"Yeah, we know Pork Dork, don't we, Wendy?" a third girl added, prompting giggles all around.

Smiling indulgently, Wendy caught Sarah's gaze. "Eating at this table is by invitation only. Elaine understands—don't you, Elaine?"

But Elaine had gone someplace deep within herself, a place Sarah knew well, where the pain of the moment couldn't immediately cripple. No, that would come later. Her eyes glazed, the girl turned around and walked away.

"Don't look so worried, Sarina. She'll be fine," Wendy insisted. "C'mon and sit."

Sickened, Sarah looked at each girl one by one until all but a glittering green gaze had faltered, then dropped. "I don't get it. Do you think hurting Elaine makes you smarter? Or more popular? Or makes this table more 'special' in any way? Are you *that* clueless?"

"Lighten up," Wendy said, rolling her eyes. "Elaine's a loser. We have a reputation to think about."

"Yeah. For being callous and cruel."

"Callous?" Wendy jeered. She glanced around at her sidekicks, obviously puzzled at their silence, then snorted. "Are you for real?"

Damn. "On the West Coast, everybody says 'callous,'" Sarah ad-libbed. "As in, 'He dumped you? That's so-o-o callous.' It'll probably get to Texas by next year."

"Texas is so-o-o lame," somebody muttered.

"Shut up, Pam," Wendy snapped. "You're such an airhead."

Sarah tsk-tsked. "Now, see? There you go being callous again. Oops. You don't like that word, do you? Hmm, let me think...I've got it!" Sarah's triumphant smile faded into a stare as cold as her voice. "How does *vicious bitch* grab you?"

Right by the throat, if Wendy's red face and choked sputters were any indication.

"Gee, it works for me," Sarah said.

"Who the hell do you think you are, talking to *me* like that?" Wendy finally managed to sputter. "You're pathetic and stupid. This table *is* special. You could've sat here and had it made the rest of the year, you *loser*."

Sarah gentled her gaze. "But if I sat at this table, people would think I'm like all of you. I believe I'll go sit with Elaine, instead."

Turning, she paused and looked back over her shoulder. "I have a reputation to think about, you know."

Walking away, Sarah knew she'd kissed off any chance of friendship with the most popular girl in the senior class, a fact that would have devastated her nine years ago. But hard-won knowledge and maturity put a whole new perspective on things.

Her smile started small and grew with every step. High school might not be so bad the second time around.

ARMS CROSSED, his back braced against the cafeteria wall, Jack watched Sarina impart a final word to eight prima donnas, then walk away. Expressions at the table she'd left behind ranged from stunned to ashamed to furious. But *no one* was indifferent.

Sarina Davis wasn't a girl easily ignored or dismissed.

He'd completed that silly business with the rubber snake just as Jessica and Sarina had approached The Table Of The Chosen. The sight of Elaine dragging at their heels had snagged his attention, and he'd watched the action unfold. A riveting scene worthy of a D. W. Griffith silent film. High visual drama. Dastardly deeds and wrenching pathos. He hadn't needed subtitles to interpret the dialogue.

Wendy's table of vipers had struck at Elaine. And the transfer student from California had struck back! Amazing. Also extremely satisfying, after witnessing the dazed misery on Elaine's face.

Studying Wendy's expression now, Jack couldn't recall her ever looking so insulted. Or venomous. Not even that disastrous evening after he'd unpeeled her arms from around his neck. The blond beauty could be a dangerous enemy. Especially to the unwarned.

Frowning, he located Sarina—and straightened away from the wall. Her smile was feral, her walk the sated glide of a cat leaving a fresh kill.

This fierce little female with the flamboyant hair was apparently more than a match for his nemesis. Who would've thought? He watched her pass by twenty yards ahead and continue on toward the opposite end of the cafeteria. Several seconds later, the charged tension humming through Jack's body registered in his brain.

He wrenched his gaze away.

What was he *doing*, staring at the cup and release

of crushed velvet against a curvy bottom? A *student's* curvy bottom, for God's sake, when the whole damn school—kids and faculty alike—still watched him as if he breathed heavily into phones for kicks. Their subtle suspicions hurt. And made him cautious in the extreme. He rarely smiled at female students any more. Never touched or hugged them. Never spent time alone with them for *any* reason. Hell, he never even looked below their necks if he could help it...until now.

Groaning silently, Jack forced himself to lean back against the wall. He scanned the cafeteria for disapproving stares. The only eyes he met were Kate's, who arched a speculative brow from a table near Wendy. Suppressing a blush, he looked pointedly at Bruce Logan, then back at her. Jack had been searching for an excuse to run off the rich bad boy, a womanizer he didn't want near his sister.

Message received. Kate scowled and turned away. She'd made it clear his slightest attention in school was unwelcome. But if she wanted him to ignore the creep she chose to eat with, she'd keep her speculations to herself.

Muscle by muscle his body relaxed. He'd been lucky this time. There wouldn't *be* a next time, he vowed grimly. With Kate still in high school, he couldn't jeopardize his tenure. And despite being cleared of Wendy's charges, Jack knew he walked a career tightrope until he regained everyone's trust.

The safety net he'd planned for the future currently sat—three weeks and counting—somewhere on Irving

Greenbloom's desk. Response time on unsolicited screenplays ran from six to twelve weeks, according to the agent's secretary.

Unfolding his arms, Jack set out to patrol the cafeteria's perimeter. He wasn't naive. Even if the top agent in L.A. chose to represent him, the odds against *Free Fall* selling were astronomically high. He was prepared for rejection. What he hadn't counted on was losing his joy in teaching. A joy he'd never realized brightened his days until recently, when only a feeble glimmer remained.

Across the room, a flurry of airborne potato chips erupted. He changed direction, then stopped. Tim Williams could damn well cover his assigned territory for once. Jack was tired of always being the bad guy.

Two tables to the left of the food fight, a flash of red-orange hair caught his eye. He didn't at all like how his pulse reacted. Or the fact that he couldn't seem to turn away. He chalked it up to concern for Elaine, and saw that the two girls sat facing each other, their profiles clearly visible from his angle.

They appeared to be deep into a conversation. At least, Sarina was conversing. Elaine was listening, her gaze suspiciously bright. She nodded, and to Jack's dismay, a single tear broke loose and trailed down her plump cheek.

Speaking fast and earnestly, Sarina grabbed the other girl's hands, every line of her body conveying, "Heed my words." Elaine nodded again. Swiped at a second tear. Even managed a tremulous smile.

And then she laughed. Not a token effort, either, but the genuine light-up-your-face-with-happiness article.

Looking at Sarina's brilliant answering smile, Jack felt something inside him...shift.

He turned abruptly and headed back toward his post against the wall. Only ten more minutes and he could eat his own lunch. Leftover pot roast, packed in a Tupperware container by his mother the night before. His mouth twisted. She needed to "do" for him, he'd learned, in order to feel useful.

But he would gladly cook and wash clothes for himself if only she'd spend more time with Kate. His sister needed a gentle guiding hand right now. His gaze wandered halfway back to Sarina before his mind caught up and yanked it forward.

Jack decided he would slip outside and eat his lunch in blessed peace and quiet. He needed some time to think. To examine his emotions. To remind himself of the inviolate code of ethics he'd accepted along with his teaching certificate. He needed to regain his composure and inscrutable expression.

And he needed to do it all by fifth period.

CHAPTER FOUR

SINCE HER RETURN to high school two weeks ago, Sarah had blamed her poor performance in home economics class on lack of previous training.

After all, her mother hadn't needed, required or wanted her inept help with household chores. In college, she'd managed quite nicely with the aid of microwave dinners and—courtesy of Donna's inheritance—a weekly maid. Sometime during those four years Sarah had become hooked on sparkling toilets she hadn't scrubbed, a habit she gladly supported after graduation. What was skipping a few meals until her salary increased? A trivial inconvenience. Inconsequential compared with giving up Molly Maid.

But she wasn't addicted, Sarah had assured herself then. She could stop the service any time and clean her own apartment. Or for that matter, learn to sew frilly curtains and bake chocolate chip cookies. The question was, why on earth *would* she when she had more important things to do? She was a career woman. She was a mover and shaker. She was a nineties kinda gal.

She was a domesticity-impaired convenience junkie, Sarah admitted now, forty minutes into Mrs. Dent's home economics class.

The latest proof sat cooling before her on the red Formica countertop. Covertly, she scanned the other four kitchenette counters in the high-tech classroom. Vanilla sponge cake layers, perfect golden circles six to seven inches tall, destroyed her last faint hope. It was official. She'd screwed up the worst.

Poor Fred Adler, a fledgling home management computer software designer, no doubt wished he'd passed on taking home ec for research purposes. As the only other senior in a class full of freshmen "fish," he'd been assigned Sarah as his kitchen partner.

"Let's think positive, here," she told him gamely. "It *smells* good, doesn't it?"

"If you like the smell of burned toast."

She'd grown quite fond of it over the years, actually. She tried again. "Maybe we can say it's a new Cajun breakfast recipe. You know, blackened pancakes?"

"What'll we call *that?*" He nodded toward a bowl of fudge frosting.

"Well...I hear Cajuns like their syrup re-e-ally thick." Nothing. Not even a token smile. "Oh, c'mon, Fred. Lighten up. I'm sure it will taste good, even if it's not pretty."

He rolled his eyes—a startling sight behind Coke bottle lenses—then reached for a toothpick and stabbed one of the cakes. Wood splintered. "I'm just guessing, Sarina, but I think this is overcooked."

"I followed the recipe." A daunting task from scratch instead of out of a box.

"Well, you must've left something out."

I must've been crazy to take this class.

"You should've let me measure the ingredients."

I should've signed up for art.

"We're going to get a bad grade."

Sarah bristled. "*You* set the timer, bud."

He pushed up his Buddy Holly glasses and glared. When the kid grew into his shoulders, hands and feet, he'd be a force to be reckoned with. "Hey, I got the pans out of the oven right on time. If the batter had *risen,* it wouldn't have burned."

Drooping, Sarah stared at the two pens hooked over his plaid shirt pocket. "I know, you're right. I'm worthless. I'm dust on Paul Prudhomme's blackened redfish. I'm bacteria on Julia Child's cutting board. I'm mold in Martha Stewart's food processor." She peeked up through her lashes.

His dark blue eyes *finally* gleamed in amusement.

"I'll tell Mrs. Dent this is all my fault," Sarah promised.

The teacher would be back shortly from checking on the rest of the class next door. The computers there were Sarah's friends. But the sewing machines were aliens yet to be faced and conquered.

"No, I should've paid attention to what you were doing instead of—well, I just should've helped you more, is all." Flushing to the roots of his dark shaggy hair, he firmed his jaw.

A nice square jaw, in a much too serious—but very nice—face. Not that Kate Morgan, the reason for his lack of attention to the recipe, had noticed his longing glances.

Patting Fred's bony shoulder, Sarah moved up to the stainless steel sink. "Why don't you ice the cake while I wash the dishes?"

"Yeah, okay. Just make sure you don't *burn* yourself."

"Sarcasm doesn't become you," she said haughtily. But she grinned while sliding the bowl of frosting within his reach.

Staring down at the pans and mixing bowls in the sink, she hitched up the sleeves of her lime green mock turtleneck. She could handle this. Her cleaning service in Dallas didn't "do" pots and pans. As she and Fred worked in companionable silence, her thoughts drifted to the object of his unrequited crush.

Ever since realizing Kate was Jack's little sister, Sarah had watched the girl closely, although they'd never exchanged a word. Kate seemed determined to break the rules her older brother held so dear. In the past two weeks alone, Mrs. Dent had sent Kate to the principal's office twice. Once for visiting Internet chat rooms on a class computer instead of working on her family budget spreadsheet. A second time for arguing that she'd get the "no-brainer" assignment done, because she wasn't "computer illiterate like her teacher."

Sassy little snot, Sarah had thought at the time. Yet the more she observed Kate, the more her rebellious I-don't-give-a-damn attitude didn't ring true. Even the army surplus clothes she favored didn't seem…natural. Sarah would bet the sloppy G. I. Jane look was a new one for Kate. It must drive Jack nuts, combined with her discipline problems. Donna had mentioned his mother deferred all parental responsibility to him.

Suppressing an unexpected twinge of sympathy, Sarah placed another mixing bowl on the drying rack. She glanced at Fred's progress. He was icing the last bare section on the pitiful cake. She'd seen him hover over a keyboard with that same intensity. The quintessential computer nerd absorbed in his work.

One day, after he made the cover of *Forbes* as a featured software company mogul, Sarah suspected Kate would remember Fred Adler. Right now, she didn't know he was alive. Maybe if he killed the geeky clothes and glasses, she would see his 4-H man potential.

"What's so funny?" Fred asked.

Sarah's affectionate smile vanished. "Um, a joke I heard," she bluffed.

"I could use a good laugh before Mrs. Dent sees this cake."

Sarah's mind scrambled, then stopped. "Okay, but you didn't hear it from me." She met his gaze impishly. "How does Wendy Johnson screw in a lightbulb?"

He was already starting to smile. "I dunno. How?"

"She holds a bulb up to the socket while the world revolves around her."

His laugh rang out, surprisingly masculine and infectious. Female heads turned, including Kate's, Sarah noted with interest. The girl's eyes were greener than Jack's, but much the same shape, and fringed with the long thick lashes so startling on her brother. Her bemused expression dissolved into a smile.

Good heavens, no wonder Fred was smitten!

"She's ba-a-ack," Fred murmured under his breath for Sarah's ears alone.

A snow-haired bunny of a woman bustled into the middle of the room and stopped, her uplifted nose twitching. "Oh, doesn't it smell marvelous in here! The freshmen dance committee will be thrilled. You've all worked so hard, I've decided four cakes from each class is enough to fill the refreshment table." Tapping a finger against her round little chin, she cocked her head, her blue eyes twinkling. "Any ideas on what we should do with the extra cake?"

It took a second for her meaning to register. Then shouts of "Eat, eat!" and "Aw-right!" and "Hroo-hroo-hroo!" echoed from all around.

Smiling, she clapped her hands sharply. "Settle down. We have just enough time to sample a slice before the bell. Melanie, bring me the paper plates, please. Thomas, the plastic forks are in the cabinet above your stove. Quickly, quickly! Now, whose cake should we cut?"

It was Friday. Spirits were high. Regressing to childhood birthday party silliness, teens too cool to walk faster than a casual stroll jumped up and down, waving their hands, vying to be chosen. To be picked *first*.

Amid the hyperactivity, Sarah and Fred stood rock still shoulder to shoulder, united in dread.

Mrs. Dent zeroed in on them, of course. Teachers had radar about these things. She smiled knowingly and headed their way. "What are you two hiding back there, hmm? Move aside—" she made a shooing motion "—and let me see your— Oh! Oh, dear."

Not since a rubber band ejected from her braces to hit Jeff Miller—the crush of her life—on the forehead and stick, had Sarah seen such astounded revulsion on another's face.

She looked at their cake as it must appear to Mrs. Dent.

Fred had tried, bless his heart. Sarah could see his effort to create the illusion of a level surface by using alternating thicknesses of frosting. But he wasn't Houdini. The thing still looked like something best avoided in a cow pasture.

By now the class had crowded around to stare.

"I was in charge of mixing the batter," Sarah explained in the heavy silence. "Please don't blame Fred. I'm sure the frosting tastes great. He mixed that. Maybe you can grade us separately—"

"I'm as much to blame as Sarina," Fred interrupted. "Whatever grade you give, Mrs. Dent, give it to us both."

Sarah revised her earlier thought. Fred wouldn't *become* 4-H material as a man. He already was.

Obviously searching for words, the ancient teacher adjusted the pink cardigan sweater covering her matronly bosom. She cleared her throat, looked from Fred to Sarah, glanced at the cake and then down at her stout white nursing-type shoes. Her mouth twitched. A tiny chuckle escaped. Then another, this one rising in volume and scale.

That's all the encouragement the class needed to laugh as if Jim Carrey cavorted on that cake plate. Suggestions for what to do with the disaster flew fast and furious. Donate it to the track team for discus throwing practice. Donate it to the metal shop for a new grinding stone. Leave it on Principal Miller's office chair, sort of a whoopie cushion without the whoop.

Sarah herself offered a suggestion just as the shrill bell rang. They should freeze the cake for the next *senior* dance, and sneak it onto the refreshment table with the note, "A token of our esteem. Signed, The Fish."

While the others hooted their appreciation and collected their books, Sarah ignored Fred's disapproving glance. Hey, she had no loyalty to the graduating class. And she'd kept these fish from sampling any cake. She owed them.

Retrieving her backpack from a storage shelf, she wound up walking beside Kate to the doorway.

"I liked your idea the best," Kate said, her smile friendly, but curious. "Why would you help freshmen play a joke on seniors?"

"I remember what being a fish feels like." Miserable. Especially if your own class scorned you.

"You have Mr. Morgan for English, don't you?

Sarah's antennae shot up. "Yes. How did you know?" Had he talked about her to his sister?

"You've broken Morgan's Ten Commandments and lived to tell about it. The whole school's talking."

Of course. The *kids* were talking. "I don't know why. Since that first day, I've been a model student." Jack was a stickler for rules, true. But he was also, as Elaine had said, an excellent teacher who cared about his students. Sarah actually enjoyed his class now.

Kate paused at the doorway. "Hmm. That's not what my brother says." With a mischievous glance, she entered the crowded hallway.

Sarah's heart lurched.

"Heads up, Sarina," a voice behind her snapped.

Realizing she blocked the doorway, Sarah stumbled after Kate, intending to grill her for specifics. But the girl had been intercepted and pulled aside by a boy. Tall. Good-looking. Hair as black as his expensive leather jacket.

Closer to a man than a boy, really. His heavy chin stubble and brawny build said he'd been held back in his school career more than once. Sarah had seen him sitting with Kate at lunch, come to think of it. Jack was always frowning their way.

Sarah could see why, now. The look of fascination and fear on Kate's upturned face was disturbing. He spoke a few words, fondled a strand of her hair possessively, then slipped something into her pants pocket. Sarah might have missed the move altogether if his fingers hadn't wandered on their way out. A shadow of distress passed over Kate's features.

To hell with this. "Hey, Kate!" Sarah called, weaving through jostling bodies toward them.

They jerked apart, Kate with a look of relief, the boy with a scowl of irritation.

Ignoring him, Sarah stopped beside the girl. "Can you sit with me at lunch today? There's plenty of room." Actually, the empty table Elaine and Sarah had started out with was filling up fast.

"Kate sits with *me*, beautiful."

Turning, Sarah stared into ice blue eyes. Her blood drained straight to her toes.

Time raced backward in a dizzying rush. She was watching the downward arc of a knife, moonlight glinting off a blade and icy colorless eyes—

"Sarina! Are you all right?" Kate asked.

Sarah blinked and drew shaky breath. Her surroundings came into focus. "Yeah. Yeah, I'm fine." She managed a small smile. "Just hungry, I guess."

"Shit, I thought you were trippin' out there a minute," the man-boy said.

Sarah met his eyes again and forced herself not to shudder. "I don't do drugs."

His smile was half sneer. "So you're a good little girl, huh?"

"Just a smart one," she corrected, her instinctive dislike of this boy intensifying.

From his expression, she wasn't making any points with him, either. "I'm Bruce Logan. You're that new girl from California I've been hearing about, right?"

"Guess so. Sorry. I've never heard of you." Bull's-eye. His puffed up self-importance deflated a little.

Her gaze moved to Kate. "You never answered about sitting at my lunch table."

"Yo, Bruce!" Tony Baldovino strutted through the hallway traffic, his dark gaze taking in both girls curiously. He stopped near the trio and looked at the older boy. "I need to talk to you, man. I'm almost out of— Well, we need to talk."

Bruce slung an arm over Kate's slender shoulders. "In a minute." He thrust his jaw at Sarah. "I told you before, Kate sits with me unless I say so. You're asking the wrong person."

Sarah arched a brow. "No, I definitely want Kate— not you—to sit with me. And she can answer herself. Right, Kate?"

Blushing, the girl glanced nervously at Bruce and Tony, and finally, at Sarah. "Maybe we can sit together some other time?"

Triumph flashed in Bruce's icy blue eyes.

"Sure, we can do that," Sarah agreed.

Bruce smiled insolently. "You can always sit at my table. The chairs are full, but there's room on my lap."

"Good plan," Tony said, grinning.

Bruce's leer deepened. "How 'bout it, beautiful? I'm sure I could…squeeze you on."

Good grief. "Be still my heart," Sarah said evenly.

"I think that means no, pal," Tony said.

Bruce's icy gaze, bent on intimidation, never wavered from Sarah's. "You sure? Think *hard,* babe." He adjusted himself at the crotch. "You don't know what you're missing."

Sarah flicked a dismissive glance at his zipper. "I

think I do. And if both heads were as big as the one holding that giant ego of yours, I might be more tempted.''

Ignoring Tony's loud bark of laughter, she looked at the blushing girl beneath Bruce's arm. ''Sure you don't want to walk with me to the cafeteria?''

Wide-eyed, Kate shook her head no.

''Okay, but that was a standing lunch invitation. Any time you want, come on over to our table.'' *You don't have to sit with that jerk,* Sarah conveyed silently.

The halls were thinning. The feel of Bruce's hostile glare sent a shiver of fear over her skin. But she held Kate's gaze until the girl nodded, then she said goodbye to Tony, turned and walked away.

Behind her, Bruce demanded, ''Who does that bitch think she *is,* anyway?'' Kate's murmur was indistinguishable.

Too bad. Sarah would have liked to hear the answer. Lately, she didn't know who Sarina was, either. She only knew it wasn't the old Sarah.

TWO HOURS LATER, Jack watched the last of his fourth period class leave the room, then pulled fifth period's graded quiz papers from a file. He'd resigned himself to the anticipation heightening his awareness this time every day. But he didn't have to acknowledge its presence.

If he ignored the fact that one particular student walking through that door any minute would bump up his heartbeat, then he didn't have a problem. He wasn't out of line. He remained responsible and honorable, like his father had been.

Brian Morgan's footsteps were hard to follow, but Jack did his best. He always had. Giving up his scholarship to USC, which offered the finest School of Cinema-Television in the country, had been the first step. Supporting his mother and sister the past eleven years had taken him closer to his role model's standard.

He'd only stumbled once. At least, in the way his mother saw things. As she so often pointed out, he could have taken business courses in night school, something practical and potentially lucrative. But he'd earned a degree in English Literature, then *chosen* to teach. Vera Morgan couldn't to this day understand why. She considered the "hobby" teaching enabled him to pursue during long holidays and summer vacations a waste of time.

Maybe it was. Five weeks and counting since he'd mailed *Free Fall.* And still no word from Irving Greenbloom.

Students began trickling in. Some, like Elaine Harper, walked quietly straight to their desks. Others, like Beto Garcia, came in laughing, but sobered right away. Very good.

Tim Williams had once asked for the secret of Jack's disciplined classroom. "My kids know the rules," he'd told the chemistry teacher. "And they know the consequences of breaking them. It's as simple as that." *And unlike certain wimpy teachers around here, I never make exceptions to the rules,* he'd added silently.

Life wouldn't make exceptions, either, once these kids graduated.

Jessica Bates wandered in, together with Tony Baldovino and his four shadow jocks. Almost time for the bell, now. Two empty seats left. But he'd seen her in the cafeteria earlier. She wasn't absent.

The bell jangled.

Sarina slipped in under its fading echo. If he'd been a cop, he would've ticketed her for charging through yellow as the light changed. But she threw him a dimpled grin and his heartbeat ker-thumped. By the time he recovered, she was in her seat, her hands folded demurely on the desktop.

Who was he kidding? He was so goddamn out of line if he'd been a cop, he would've arrested himself.

Without Jack asking, Kim got up and closed the door.

"Thank you, Kim." He looked out over the class. The natives were restless. Fridays did that to kids. And teachers. "Okay, I know you all couldn't enjoy your weekend without finding out what you made on the review quiz, yesterday. So I stayed up late last night grading them."

Rising from his chair to the sound of groans, he rounded the desk and began passing out the multiple choice quiz results. The questions weren't difficult— *if* you'd read chapters one through eight in *The Grapes of Wrath.* Which only about two-thirds of the class had managed, judging from the grades. He sighed.

"Kathleen—" he handed down her high B score "—review chapter two. Otherwise, keep up the good work. Beto—'' he met the Hispanic boy's guilty gaze ''—the Noah I was referring to is Ma and Pa Joad's oldest son.''

Taking his paper, Beto grimaced at his grade. ''Aw, ma-an. Don't I get some credit for reading The Bible? It's a *lot* thicker than *The Grapes of Wrath*.'' He grinned unrepentantly amid the giggles and snorts.

The kid was bright, but more interested in getting laughs than good grades. ''I'm glad you've read it. You're going to need to do some serious praying to pass this class unless you start taking assignments seriously.''

He leveled a stern look before moving on to Elaine. ''Very nice. As usual. I wish all my students were as conscientious as you.''

Flushing, she darted quick looks at her classmates, then shrank deeper into her seat. Go figure. He continued up and down the rows until he reached a red-orange mop of hair.

She'd read the chapters. Still, she hadn't followed directions on one of the questions. Trust her to be different.

''Sarina—'' her upraised Liz Taylor eyes kicked his heart into that extra beat ''—read over chapter three again and you'll be fine,'' he assured her, then moved out of the danger zone.

''Bonnie, good job. Tony, whichever athletic scholarship you accept will be worthless unless you actually graduate from high school. Do you think—''

''Excuse me, Mr. Morgan?'' Sarina called out.

Jack stopped. *Why am I not surprised?* Composing

his expression, he turned to see her frowning at her quiz. "Yes?"

She met his gaze. "I don't understand why I missed this question."

He didn't pretend not to know what she meant. "Because you didn't answer it correctly. In case you didn't notice, there is no multiple choice option called 'other.'"

"Of course I noticed. Did you *notice* my explanation?"

God grant him patience. "The turtle in chapter three is an analogy to man's struggle against his uncontrollable destiny."

"Says who?"

"Sar-ina," he drawled warningly.

"I'm not being disrespectful. I honestly want to know why that's the 'correct' interpretation." Her violet eyes were clear, intelligent and inquisitive. As if she really did want to learn.

His brain shifted into a higher gear. "Academia agrees that Steinbeck was a master at symbolism posing as realism. Think of the passage with the turtle. It's written in such accurate detail, we *are* that turtle. Hindered by ants, hills, oat seeds under our shells... and finally, the dangerous highway traffic. Just as man is a victim of a hostile universe."

"I don't dispute the symbolism. But I saw that turtle as courageous, always continuing on despite one setback after another. A symbol of man's fortitude, not his victimization. There wasn't a multiple choice for my interpretation, so I added one."

What an astoundingly articulate answer. Still... "You can't just go *adding* on answers when the interpretations by recognized experts in American literature don't suit you."

"Says who?"

"Sar-ina."

"I'm *not* being disrespectful. I simply object to being forced to think like the 'experts.' This is America. Freedom of speech and thought is my constitutional right. I'll bet John Steinbeck would've been glad to knock back a couple of cold ones with me and listen to my opinion of his work."

Jack crossed his arms, enjoying himself immensely. "I doubt it. John was probably so sick of public opinion he would've thrown you out of the bar. When the book first came out, the majority of Americans thought he was a liar and a Communist."

She looked startled, then intrigued. "I can see they might not have known migrant conditions were that bad until his facts were investigated. But calling him a Communist? I'm assuming that was because of Jim Casy's outlook," she said, referring to the former preacher character traveling with the Joads. "But his philosophy was more...I don't know, Emersonian than Communistic. At least, that's my *opinion*." The glint of challenge in her gaze was unmistakable.

Inordinately pleased, he conceded her point. "It's taken the distancing of time for Americans to arrive at that rational conclusion."

"Well, there, you see? The experts at the time thought differently from how they do now. So, what's to say my interpretation of the turtle won't become accepted in the future?''

She had him there, dammit.

Sarina cocked her head. ''I would think you'd want to encourage students to think for themselves, to develop their own opinions.''

''And you think I don't?'' Her answer was suddenly way too important to Jack.

''Based on this quiz, I have my doubts. I gave you a well thought out answer that took a lot more time than circling letter *a*. But it wasn't straight out of *Cliffs Notes,* so you counted it wrong.''

Unbelievable. ''Did your previous high school teachers let you make up your own multiple choice answers?''

''Milburn High School is very progressive,'' she said primly. ''The English teachers there know the difference between Steinbeck and algebra.''

He narrowed his eyes. ''Oh, *do* please enlighten me.''

Her eyes narrowed to match his. ''There are no wrong answers in evaluating literature.''

Jack threw a huffing glance at Beto and back. ''Excuse me, but Noah Joad did *not* build an ark and fill it with animals.''

She laughed, a rich chesty sound that exposed two deep dimples and small white teeth. ''Touché. But you know what I mean.''

He found himself smiling. ''I think I get the picture.''

She really was very lovely, even with that ridiculous

hair and glow-in-the-dark lime green turtleneck. He wondered if her pale skin was as soft as it looked. The deepening rose in her cheeks intensified the color of her eyes...

Jack started, aware of his surroundings for the first time in lord knew how many minutes. His arms were crossed, his butt propped nice and comfy on a student's desk. Snapping to a stiff, military stance, Jack cleared his throat.

Twenty-eight students were staring as if he'd just beamed down from the mother ship. What the *hell* had he been doing?

Frowning, Jack turned to pass out the last few quiz papers. He'd been staring into pansy purple eyes like a besotted fool, that's what he'd been doing. Yet it wasn't the beauty of those eyes that had enthralled him, but the excellent brain behind them.

Oh, God. He had a definite problem. He was out of line big time. And he wasn't anywhere close to being the responsible and honorable man his father had been.

CHAPTER FIVE

PLUCKING THE LAST fat-free donut from a plate on the bar counter, Sarah examined the marvel of culinary science in her hand. "You think they'll ever learn how to take out the calories, too?" she asked Donna. "I probably shouldn't eat this."

Her stomach growled a protest.

"Oh, c'mon, you've only had one." Perched on the next stool, Donna flapped a hand. "Live a little, it's Saturday."

Thank goodness, Sarah thought.

She needed a quiet weekend in the Kaiser guest house to recover from that…episode in English class the day before. That interval when she'd carelessly debated with Jack on an adult—instead of student-teacher—level. That moment when he'd stared into her eyes and everyone else had simply…disappeared. Had she imagined something that wasn't there? A sexual awareness that made her heart pound erratically even now?

"That donut was fresh when I stopped by the bakery this morning," Donna pointed out. "Don't blame me if it's stale when you take a bite."

Flustered, Sarah focused on the treat poised inches from her mouth. "I really shouldn't. But—"

"Then don't torture yourself, hon." Donna pat-patted Sarah's knee. "Give it to me."

Sarah did. Slowly and grudgingly. "Funny how un-pleasant memories have a way of blurring over the years. I'd forgotten how you can eat five donuts—"

"Thicth," Donna corrected around a huge mouthful of calories.

"Pardon me, *six* donuts and still manage to look like *that*."

Popping the last bite into her mouth, Donna rolled her eyes and crossed her legs. She looked elegant and shapely in formfitting black pants—size five, Sarah knew because she'd asked—and a white cashmere sweater. Her dark red hair shone with health, her slate blue eyes with an inner glow.

Sarah glanced down at her new gray sweat suit, bought by Donna at Sarah's request, and knew John Steinbeck would've had a field day with the symbol-ism. She would always be cotton fleece, and Donna, one hundred percent cashmere. Yet their interwoven lives had formed the fabric of a strong and lasting friendship. The thought made Sarah get a little misty.

Oblivious, Donna brushed crumbs daintily from her lap, reached for her Diet Coke, then took several long sips. "I don't eat like this all the time, you know. Only—" she ducked her head and burped "—when I'm happy."

Maybe *eighty* percent cashmere, Sarah thought, laughing.

She sipped her own coffee du jour, Diet Dr Pepper, then studied her friend closer. "You do look pretty chipper for someone stuck delivering groceries on a beautiful morning. So, what's the good news? Tell me everything.''

As if a switch had flipped on, Donna lit up from within. "Oh, Sarah, you'll never believe it.''

Intrigued, Sarah leaned forward. "Yeah?''

"Yesterday in the teacher's lounge...''

"Yeah, yeah?''

"I'd really given up hope on anything happening...'' Wedgwood blue eyes grew dreamy and distant.

"Snap out of it, Kaiser, and *tell me*.''

Donna blinked. "Jack Morgan asked me out.''

Sarah's stomach slid to her toes. And stayed there. "As in, out for coffee?''

"No! As in, out to dinner with him. Last night. After all this time he finally asked me on a date!'' Donna broke into a beatific smile.

Well, there's my answer to whether or not I misinterpreted his interest in class. I was probably wrong about the damn turtle, too.

"Well?'' Donna appeared eager for a reaction.

"A little late notice, wasn't it? Asking on Friday afternoon for a date the same night?''

"He apologized,'' Donna said, bristling. "His previous plans fell through at the last minute. I know you don't like him, but I thought you'd be happy for me.''

Sarah mentally cringed. Even if Jack was attracted to her, she could hardly expect him to act on inappropriate feelings for the eighteen-year-old Sarina. Sarah felt guilty enough about John Merrit's and Larry's deaths without adding the destruction of a teacher's career to her list of regrets. "I *am* happy for you. Really. So, tell me where you went and what you did." *I don't want to hear this.*

Brightening instantly, Donna launched into a play-by-play description similar to what she'd shared after dates in college. Sara had wanted to know every detail then. Now, the details twisted a knife of wistfulness deeper and deeper in her chest. She didn't even want to *think* about what Steinbeck would make of that.

At the end of an hour, Sarah knew Jack's tweed sport jacket made his eyes look more brown than green, but they reversed color when he felt strongly about a subject. She knew he liked going to the movies and playing basketball. Browsing in bookstores and fishing in Galveston Bay. Also T-bone steak, a good vintage merlot, and pecan pie à la mode.

His favorite color was purple, his favorite book *To Kill A Mockingbird,* his favorite movie a tie between *Fargo* and *Terminator II.* Sarah had questioned that last tidbit. But Donna had said, no, she'd heard him right. She'd then proceeded to describe his wonderful smell, the thrilling feel of his hand on the small of her back, the way he'd seen her safely to her condominium door—

"Look, Donna," Sarah interrupted, unable to stand another second. "I feel like a voyeur. It's okay to keep some things private." Although nothing had been sacred information in the past.

Sarah squirmed under the dawning comprehension in her friend's slate blue eyes. Perfect. Just dandy.

How would she explain her irrational jealousy when she didn't understand it herself?

"Oh, Sarah, I'm so sorry. I've been so selfish. Rambling on about going out with a sexy man, when you're virtually a prisoner outside of school. You must miss talking and...you know—*being* with Mark, terribly."

Sarah's face heated. She was *worse* than mean and petty. She was pond scum.

Donna bit her lower lip. "Now I've embarrassed you, and I didn't mean to. Forgive me?"

"Sure, forget it." Sliding off her bar stool, Sarah carried the empty plate and glasses into the kitchen, then took her time putting them into the dishwasher. No way could she admit her confused feelings for Jack. But she could correct the impression she'd given about Mark.

Turning around, she leaned back against the lip of the sink. "I do miss Mark, but we've never actually...done the deed."

Over the bar counter, Donna's eyes were wide and alert. "I thought you said you two were serious."

"You know me. Cautious to a fault about letting people get close." The debacle with a handsome office colleague a year and a half ago had been Sarah's last serious relationship. One-sided, she'd learned. All on *her* side of the bed. "Mark made no secret of the fact I was top candidate for his wife. But now..." She brushed a nonexistent crumb from her sweatshirt.

"Well, that's cryptic."

Sarah looked up. "I can think of at least two women

who will try to move to the top of the candidate list while I'm gone.''

Donna frowned. ''But if he loves you, surely he'll be faithful? You said the justice department explained to him why you had to disappear. He must be crazy with worry.''

''I'm sure he is.'' Sarah's gaze faltered. She spun around, grabbed a sponge and wiped the spotless countertop. ''But he's being groomed to run for mayor in a few years. There are charity functions, high-profile events he has to attend—preferably with a woman on his arm. I can't expect him to put his agenda on hold until I get back.''

She scrub-scrub-scrubbed as the tightness in her chest increased. The truth was, no one was crazy with worry about Sarah Davis. Not her parents. Not her almost fiancé. Not her so-called friends at WorldWide Public Relations.

Oh, the justice department cared about her safety. Also, both sets of attorneys in John Merrit's murder trial. The former wanted answers to the bloodbath she'd left behind. The latter reassurance that she would—or would not—be able to testify as key witness.

A gentle hand on Sarah's arm stopped her mindless repetitive motion.

''Sarah. Hon. I know this is a hard time for you, being ripped from your job and the people you care about, being treated like a high school kid again. Not to mention the homework, the hassle from Wendy's crowd, the boredom of sticking close to school and

Gram's guest house all the time. But our plan is *working*. You're safe, and that's what's important in the long run. We'll get through these next months just fine, you'll see. Before you know it, this will all be a bad memory.''

Sarah had been wrong. Someone *was* crazy with worry about her.

Turning, she gave Donna a fierce brief hug and pulled back. "Not a bad memory. A unique one, yes." Sarah laughed thickly. "But not bad. Thanks to you. You're the best friend anyone could possibly have. What can I ever do to repay you?"

Now it was Donna's turn to appear embarrassed. "Don't be silly. I told you I'm keeping track of my expenses. You'll reimburse me after the trial. Until then, don't give paying me back another thought." She started to turn, then stopped, a speculative gleam entering her gaze. "Of course, there *are* five more donuts around here somewhere, aren't there?"

Sarah huffed and, shaking her head, retrieved the bakery bag from the small pantry. "You'd better hope this happiness thing doesn't last too long. Jack might be one of those jerks who only dates women who wear size five pants."

If Sarah handed over the bag a little more readily than a good friend should, she had no ulterior motive, she told herself. Donna had stars in her eyes like Sarah had never seen before. She would never knowingly do anything to hurt her extraordinary friend.

That made Jack Morgan absolutely and positively off-limits.

HANDS PROPPED ON his ergonomic keyboard, Jack stared blankly at his computer screen. Saturday afternoons in his home office were usually the start of a marathon spurt of writing. He normally didn't slow down until the wee hours, then slept late on Sunday. Pure bliss. Something he looked forward to all week. But today he couldn't seem to concentrate on his latest screenplay.

Two red-haired females, as different as burgundy wine and orange soda, flooded Jack's thoughts instead.

He'd known one of them for years. Liked and respected her all that time. Donna Kaiser was beautiful and smart, a caring and responsible school administrator. A woman any man would be proud to date.

Just like Susan, a cynical inner voice reminded Jack. The last woman he'd been involved with hadn't wanted to "compete" with his mother and Kate. She'd forced him to make a choice, and he'd chosen to honor his responsibility as head of the household.

Bye-bye, Susan. Hello six months of healing. He'd only recently felt the need for female company again. *Casual* company.

Jack had vowed to keep his relationships light until Kate graduated and he was free. And Donna Kaiser wasn't a casual relationship kind of woman. He knew that.

Yet the day before, in his shaken condition after fifth period English class, he'd asked the assistant principal out on a date. He'd seen a hopefulness in her eyes at dinner he had no intention of fulfilling. And damned if he hadn't given her a chaste kiss at the door, then asked her out again for the following Friday! What was his problem?

Sarina, the answer echoed in his mind, mocking his head-in-the-sand innocence.

Everything about the girl spelled trouble. For his career. For his equanimity. For the honor he strove to uphold. During those few pleasant hours with Donna, Sarina hadn't poisoned his mind with inappropriate thoughts. So he'd opted to continue the antidote for as long as it worked. Not very gentlemanly, but he'd have to trust Donna to take care of herself. After all, she was a grown woman.

Sarina, however, was not.

Swearing, Jack focused determinedly on the computer screen and read his pitiful output for the day.

Night—Outside Senator Maxwell's Mansion
Dressed in dark camouflage, his face blackened, MIKE tosses up a scaling rope that hooks on a second floor railing. He climbs, pulls himself onto the small balcony, extracts a small tool from his pocket and fiddles with the terrace door lock.
PULL BACK…toreveal the scope and grandeur of the mansion as MIKE slips through the door and out of sight.

CUT TO…Interior Bedroom—Night
All is dark. *MIKE moves stealthily toward a bed where ANN MAXWELL sleeps, caught in a beam of moonlight.* Blond, thirtyish, modest white cotton nightgown. Angelically beautiful.

ZOOM IN...*on* MIKE'S *stern expression softening as he watches her sleep.*
WIDE SHOT...*as he places gloved hand over her mouth. Her eyes pop open. She jerks and stares terrified up at* MIKE.

MIKE: *Leaning over to speak in her ear* Don't scream. Jerry sent me. I'm not going to hurt you. Nod if you understand.
When she nods wide-eyed, he slowly removes his hand.
ANN: *Urgently* There's a guard patrolling the grounds. If you didn't see him outside, he'll be here soon. He comes in to check on me every two hours.
MIKE: Not tonight. *Smiles grimly* He'll have one helluva time explaining his little nap to your father.

Now what? Jack wondered. Originally he'd intended for Ann Maxwell to be a helpless victim of her father's corruption, dependent upon Mike Ransom to save her life. But recently, she seemed to want a more active role in the plot. Maybe he would make her a bit stronger....

An image of a fierce redhead defending Elaine at Wendy's lunch table sprang to Jack's mind. In Ann's place, Sarina would insist on helping Mike, despite the danger and personal pain of exposing Senator Maxwell....

Jack blinked. Damn, he was doing it again. With a

growl of frustration, he scrubbed his face in his palms. He was becoming obsessed with the girl.

Lowering his hands, he dropped his head back against the secondhand executive chair. Something had to change. Up until now, he'd tried to ignore Sarina as best he could. But maybe what he needed to do was learn more about her. In retrospect, the adultlike speech and demeanor that made him forget she was a student seemed more than unusual. How had she developed such confidence?

Monday, he would take a look at her permanent record and start the process of demystifying Sarina Davis. Hopefully, this unhealthy fascination would disappear.

Feeling better than he had in days, Jack resumed studying the computer screen. At last, his fingers moved over the keyboard in the steady clacking rhythm of peak concentration. Camera direction, action and dialogue came together in the craft he loved enough to treat as if it were a second job instead of a hobby.

Mike flashes a last grin at Ann, climbs over the balcony rail and slides—Jack stopped writing midsentence, his fingers poised.

Voices from the kitchen escalated in volume and agitation. He groaned silently. Please, no. Not another fight. He tried to regain his concentration, but the raging argument scattered his thoughts.

"Jack?"

Vera Morgan's near shriek deepened his dread. Just once he wished his mother would leave him out of her conflicts with Kate. He didn't answer, hoping they would resolve whatever had them in an uproar.

Minutes later the door burst open. His mother stormed into the spare bedroom Jack had converted into a study. "That's it! I give up. She doesn't care who she embarrasses or hurts."

"What is it now, Mother?" he asked wearily.

Hands on her trim hips, she pursed her mouth before speaking. "If you don't care what Kate is up to, fine. I'll leave you alone and call the police. Maybe they can handle her."

Jack swiveled his chair around. Behind his mother's bluster, he saw real worry in her hazel eyes. He stiffened. "What are you talking about?"

"I'm talking about finding *these* in Kate's room." She reached into her denim skirt pocket and withdrew something. "Your sister is a drug addict. What are you going to do about it?"

Rising, Jack moved closer and examined the two rolled cigarettes in his mother's palm. He picked them up and sniffed. Definitely marijuana.

He'd talked to Kate on more than one occasion about the danger of seemingly harmless recreational drugs. She knew the physical and legal consequences of using them. What would Tim Williams say about Jack's discipline theory now?

If only he could sit back down and work on Mike's and Ann's fictional problems. "Where is she?"

"In the kitchen, if she didn't sneak off to meet *that boy*. He used to wait for her at the end of the block sometimes. She thinks I don't know, but Phyllis Lowrey saw them out her kitchen window and told me.''

"She was meeting a boy secretly?" Jack's alarm increased. "When?"

"Over the Christmas break. Phyllis said he looked too old to be in high school. Tall, black hair, drives a red car, something sporty looking.''

Bruce Logan, Jack identified grimly. "Phyllis Lowrey needs to get a life," he muttered. "Why didn't you tell me about this when it started?"

His mother's eyes flashed defensively. "You were either buried in here working on that thing of yours, or sleeping late. I didn't want to bother you. Phyllis said she never saw them once school started again, so I let it drop." Her chin came up at Jack's aggrieved sigh. "You know Kate never listens to me, anyway. I do the best I can.''

Not trusting himself to touch that one, Jack headed for the kitchen, his mother at his heels.

He'd taught Bruce the year before and flunked his spoiled lazy ass. The kid had plenty of money and—rumor had it—weed to burn, but not an ounce of responsibility or self-discipline. It was a good bet he was using Kate to settle his score with Jack. First by eating lunch with his sister right under Jack's nose, which he'd allowed to save Kate embarrassment. Now by supplying her with a couple of joints, which Jack damn well *wouldn't* allow. He braced himself for a scene.

Kate was sitting at the dinette table, her head propped on one hand, her expression studiously bored.

Her long hair appeared uncombed and unwashed. She wore an oversize black T-shirt with some dead-looking guy on the front.

His mother nagged Kate constantly these days about her sloppy clothes. He secretly agreed. But he'd tried to reserve his energy for more important battles. Now, he wondered if maybe he'd had his head in the sand again.

Without preamble, he held up the lumpy cigarettes. "Where did you get these."

She shot him a surly look. "I found them under my pillow. The toke fairy left 'em."

His heart twisted. Where was the baby sister who'd tagged after him worshipfully? "I'm waiting."

Her mouth thinned. She looked away.

"I told you, Jack," his mother said, fingering the embroidered bluebonnets on her white shirt placket. "She doesn't care who she embarrasses or hurts. Thank God her father's not alive. He'd be so ashamed."

Jack didn't miss the flicker of emotion in his sister's eyes. "That's not true, Mother."

"Forget it, Jack," Kate said bitterly. "She'll never change her mind about me. It's pointless to try."

"All I know is your brother never hid drugs in his room," Vera snapped, drawing her children's attention. "Of course, he was a star on the basketball team and wouldn't have done anything so stupid as pollute his body. Maybe if you'd made the volleyball team—" She broke off at the screech of chair legs against linoleum.

Kate leaped up. "I can't listen to this anymore. Nothing I do is ever perfect enough, smart enough, responsible enough—you name it. I'll never be enough like *Jack* to please you, Mom, not if I tried for a hundred years." Her defiant gaze met her mother's and clung for a tense moment.

Tell Kate you love her, Mother.

"Seems to me like you never try at all," Vera said.

Kate looked away, her slow self-deprecating smile painful to witness. She raised her palms and shook her head. "I'm outta here."

"Kate, wait!" Jack called to her disappearing back.

Seconds later, a loud slam rattled her bedroom door frame.

Jack uncurled his fist and examined the joints, crushed and pungent, in his hand. He hadn't confirmed where Kate had gotten them. Or announced the punishment for her accepting them. She would have to be grounded, and forbidden from going anywhere near Bruce Logan. But Jack didn't have the heart to lay into her now.

He met his mother's gaze. A maelstrom of emotion darkened her eyes. She turned and walked to a large mixing bowl on the counter. Cooking had always been her joy…and her escape.

"I don't know why you're looking at me like that," she said, adding a cup of walnuts to the bowl. "If I sound tough, it's because I want her to live up to her potential." She picked up a spoon and lightly tossed the bowl's contents. "We're having Waldorf salad with our roast chicken tonight. Oh, and there's some mail for you over by the bread box.''

He didn't have the heart to lay into his mother, now, either. She'd loved Brian Morgan with all her soul. When he'd died, it had taken a year before she could function normally for a full twenty-four hours. Medication and cooking controlled her depression these days. But he could see her hands trembling. His concerns would have to wait for another time.

He walked to the sink and ground the two joints in the garbage disposal. What would it feel like to get high just because it felt good? With no thought of who might be affected by your actions, or what would happen to you later? The thought of such...such *freedom* almost made him dizzy. He washed and dried his hands, then went through his mail.

Bill, junk mail, renewal notice for *ScreenWriter* magazine, junk mail, bill—"*The Greenbloom Agency*" leaped out at him from a return address.

Jack's heart slammed against his ribs in great battering ram beats.

His forehead went clammy.

This was it!

Jeez, his hands were shaking so hard he couldn't get the damn thing open.

He finally ripped it all to hell and unfolded a somewhat mangled letterhead. His gaze skimmed frantically over the body copy, backtracking to reread two sentences again. Then again.

I believe your screenplay Free Fall *has great potential and would like to represent you on the project.*

Please contact me at your earliest convenience to discuss…

The words blurred. Jack closed his eyes and drew in a deep dizzying breath.

He'd wondered how it felt to get high with no thought for anyone else. Well, now he knew.

It felt pretty friggin' wonderful!

CHAPTER SIX

BY LUNCHTIME Monday, Sarah had convinced herself Jack had only shown the natural enthusiasm of a teacher for both a favorite subject and an informed student. But her stomach jumped a little as she entered the noisy cafeteria.

He was in here somewhere. She would be cool, remote and disinterested when she saw him. Heading for the deli line, irritatingly long because she was late, she scanned the room for his tall lean form....

There! By the pizza line. As if sensing her stare, he looked up into her eyes. His gaze sharpened. Intense. Curious.

Suspicious?

All sound faded. Only a muffled roar in her ears remained. When he looked away, she released her breath slowly. The clink of utensils and yammer of voices returned. Blinking, Sarah yanked her gaze straight ahead and moved into the deli line.

Well, gee, she'd handled that coolly. If she were any more disinterested, she'd need CPR. Taking several deep breaths, she managed to calm her runaway heartbeat.

Why had he looked at her like that? As if she were a doe in a rifle scope, examined, then found unworthy of shooting. Now that she thought of it, his dismissive look was more insulting than Bruce Logan's leer had been. The macho kid's lack of respect meant nothing, whereas for some bizarre reason, Jack's did.

Shaking off her uneasiness, she shuffled forward with the rest of the slow-moving students, spotting Elaine, who smiled and waved from their table. They'd shared a lot about themselves since that day Sarah had rejected Wendy's table in favor of sitting with Elaine.

So much about the girl reminded Sarah of herself at the same age. The good grades. The taunts about her weight. The unhappily married parents who reduced, instead of bolstered, her self-esteem. Elaine was quiet and shy, however, whereas Sarah had wisecracked her way through pain. Sting 'em first before they sting you, had been her motto. She'd never been *any* teacher's pet.

After joining WorldWide Public Relations, she'd adopted a wiser, more discreet attitude. One that had promoted her steadily within the organization. For six years she'd been savvy, circumspect and politically correct.

Now, as Sarina, she didn't seem to care who she angered in defense of her beliefs. It was a great feeling. Better than se— Well, it was great, anyway. And she was probably overrating the other. One and a half years tended to exaggerate the memory of most things...most sensations...

...Like the weight of a masculine body. Heavy, but welcome. Pressing her deep into a mattress. Warm bare skin. Hard bunched muscles. Long blunt-tipped fingers stroking slowly at first, building exquisite tension, then moving faster, keeping pace with her heartbeat. Whiskers rasping against her flushed cheeks, her tender breasts, her sensitive belly. A tousled dark head lifting up, hazel eyes burning— Sarah drew in a shocked breath, then glanced furtively at the boys behind her in line. No snickering looks. Thank heavens.

Where had *those* thoughts come from? Certainly not from any encounter with Mark or, for that matter, any other of her limited sexual experiences. Plucking up a bit of shiny brown fabric from between her breasts, she fanned the material in and out. Her shirt and jeans suddenly felt too hot. Too tight. Because of the humid air, of course, heavy with the smells of burgers, chicken nuggets and soggy vegetables.

Not because of a fantasy her abstinence had prompted, or the convenient leading man her brain had supplied. The cafeteria was always at least ten degrees warmer than the classrooms. She complained every lunch period. Today was no different. No different at all.

Finally, the line took her up to the lunch counter. Sarah made her selections, slid her tray next to the register and handed over her money.

The student cashier met her eyes and cleared his throat. "Don't you, uh, get tired of eating turkey sandwiches?"

She blinked. "You've noticed what I get for lunch?"

A flush evened out his complexion, spotted with a

teen's worst nightmare: acne. He looked down at the open cash drawer. "You always get the same thing. I was, uh, just curious."

"Hey, uhhh, you at the register," the boy behind Sarah called out. "Hurry it up. She doesn't, uhhh, want to talk to you." His three buddies—the last people in line—snickered obnoxiously.

The cashier's face grew even redder. He fumbled in the register drawer for coins.

Sarah threw a killing glance at the jerk on her right before extending her upturned palm for change. "I'm Sarina Davis. What's your name?"

He reached out and shook her hand. "Ro-ger." His voice cracked into falsetto on the last syllable.

The other boys hooted. "She wants her money, you idiot," one of them jeered.

Snatching back his hand, Roger dug once more in the cash drawer and extended her change. "Sorry," he mumbled.

Sarah smiled warmly.

Coins dropped beyond her fingertips to the red-and-black tiled floor. They both bent down to gather the money and knocked heads.

"What a spaz!"

"Way to go, pizza face."

"That's the only way *you'll* get a girl to lie down."

Morons, Sarah thought, grabbing the last twirling quarter. Roger's parents were morons, too. Modern dermatology had virtually eliminated acne. There was absolutely no reason for their child to suffer unnecessary teasing.

She rose with Roger and winked on the way up. "Actually, I don't get tired of turkey sandwiches. But I wish they sold fresher apples. Maybe they could put out some oranges once in a while, too? Do you know who I can talk to about that?"

"Uh." Roger glanced at the other boys and back. "I guess I can tell Mr. Crowley. He sets out the food and stuff."

"Would you? That'd be great. So, Roger, this seems like an interesting job. How long have you been a cashier?"

He swallowed hard. "Since I was a sophomore. I'm a junior now."

"You're kidding. You look more like a senior. Have you always worked at the deli counter, or have you—"

"Hey, man, what's going on, here?" the boy on her right protested.

Sarah turned. "It's called a con-ver-sa-tion," she enunciated slowly. "Something you haven't mastered beyond juvenile insults, yet. And you were wrong, before. I *do* want to talk to Roger."

"Well *we* wanna eat sometime today."

"You wanna eat? You apologize to Roger," Sarah stated.

"Yeah, right."

Sarah smiled coldly, then faced the cashier. "So, Roger, what electives are you taking this semester? I should've signed up for art—"

"Listen, bitch, you can't hold us up like this. *Move* it!"

A bony adolescent shoulder bumped her hard enough to make her stumble. She whirled on the balls of her feet, her hands upraised.

The boy cackled. "What are you gonna do, Grasshopper, some kung fu shit?"

"Cut the crap, Greg," the last kid in line called out. "Quit bein' so callous."

"Callous?"

Amazed, Sarah lowered her hands.

"Yeah, callous. Quit bein' an asshole," Greg's buddy defined. "It's a West Coast word, right, Sarina?"

She choked back a startled laugh. "Right."

"Is there a problem here, Roger?" a deep voice rumbled near her left ear.

"Uh...no, Mr. Morgan," the cashier said. "There's no problem."

Sarah twisted and looked up. Way up. She swallowed hard.

Jack had grown taller over the weekend. And his shoulders had broadened, too. They looked impressively wide beneath a boring white Oxford shirt. She inhaled the scent of Old Spice, which—granted—was sort of old-fashioned, but was growing on her fast. It didn't remind her at all of her grandfather any more.

"Are you waiting for change, Sarina?" Jack asked.

Those thick dark lashes of his could sell mascara with a single blink.

"Sarina?"

"Hmm?

"You're holding up the line. Are you waiting for change?"

It was a curse, having such pale skin. "No, no change. Just an apology."

His expression darkening, he glowered over her shoulder. "Is that so?" He obviously hadn't seen the earlier scuffle.

She turned to the boys in line, who seemed to have lost their swaggering cockiness along with their voices. "Yes, but we don't need to bother you with the details, do we guys? A simple 'I'm sorry, Roger' will do."

Jack looked surprised. "Roger?"

"That's right." Capturing Greg's gaze, she deliberately rubbed the shoulder he'd shoved. "Like I said, there's no sense boring you with specifics when all these guys need to say is 'I'm sorry, Roger.'"

Four gazes dragged reluctantly to the cashier. Four voices mumbled, "Sorry, Roger," with lukewarm sincerity.

Sarah nodded at them sweetly, then gathered up her tray. "Bye, Roger. See you tomorrow."

"Uh, bye, Sarina." He smiled for the first time, revealing a mouth full of silver.

"See you in fifth period, Mr. Morgan." She glanced up. He had that hunter-looking-through-a-scope expression on his face, again.

Turning, she made herself walk away slowly, despite the crosshairs centered between her shoulder blades. Oh, God, did he suspect something? If Jack found out her little secret, he'd pull the trigger and blow her cover for sure.

Sarah arrived at her lunch table feeling as if she'd hit the safety of the woods. She set down her tray amid greetings from six kids who were outcasts to the rest of the school. But at this table, they were simply friends.

Sinking gratefully into her chair, she smiled all around. There was Beto, the court jester. Fred, the geeky computer nerd. Janice, the six-foot painfully shy girl in Sarah's gym class. Derek, the loudmouth, whose habit of blurting out everybody's business could be funny or annoying, depending on whether or not the business was yours.

"Something is wrong," a soft voice on Sarah's right spoke. "Did you get in trouble with Mr. Morgan?"

And then there was Elaine. How anyone could not see this girl's inner and outer beauty was a mystery to Sarah. She met her young friend's perceptive gaze. "Nah, he was only asking about the holdup at the register."

Beto pointed an unpeeled banana across the table. "Hand over da pastrami on rye—and nobody gets hoit," he said in a low gruff mobster voice. He basked in several chuckles.

"Don't encourage him," Fred scolded, pushing up his glasses. "You know he'll only keep going."

"Your coleslaw—or your life," the gruff voice continued.

Fred rolled his magnified eyes. "Here we go."

"Hands oiff da garlic dill, wise guy, only unmarked pickles in da bag. Ya tink I'm stupid, or sumpin'?"

"Yeah, yeah, enough already," Fred pleaded, but he grinned while he said it.

"My cousin Randy was arrested for indecent exposure in a grocery store," Derek piped up. In the startled silence, he crunched potato chips.

Fred recovered first. "Thanks for sharing that, Derek."

Hiding her smile, Sarah took a big bite of her sandwich.

"Aunt Doris says she can never show her face in the produce section of Krogers again. That's where Randy did it. Unzipped his pants, I mean."

Sarah swallowed her half-chewed bite with an audible gulp. "Der—"

"Right next to a lady picking out fruit. She might not have screamed if Randy hadn't asked her to squeeze him instead of the cantaloupe. That was dumb."

Half laughing, half groaning with the others, Sarah shook her head.

Beto flung his partially eaten banana inside a paper bag. "Jeez, Derek, do you *mind?*"

"What'd I say?"

Sarah met the blond-haired boy's ingenuous blue eyes. "Do you suppose your aunt and cousin would want strangers to know about something that obviously embarrasses them?" They'd talked a little before about respecting people's privacy. "You've gotta *think* before you speak."

He flushed guiltily.

"It's okay, Derek," Janice said. "I usually think *too* much before speaking, and then I end up not saying anything at all."

Last week, Sarah had stood Janice before the gym mirror next to an open copy of *Seventeen* magazine and forced her to see how models made the most of their height. Sarah caught the girl's eyes now and straightened her own shoulders.

Looking sheepish, Janice uncurled from her habitual slump.

"Yeah, shyness is a big problem for Beto, too," Fred said, deadpan. "The guy just will not say more than two words—oophff!"

"*Damn*, Adler," Beto groused, massaging his right elbow. "I thought only your head was that hard."

"Sarina?" Elaine said, drawing Sarah's distracted attention. "I brought my stuff, today, if you still want to walk the track after school."

Sarah perked up. "Cool! Let's do it. I hate working out and could use the company." The past weeks of inactivity were beginning to tell on her thighs and her state of mind.

Elaine threaded a strand of chestnut hair behind one ear, her dark eyes hesitant. "Remember, I probably won't be able to keep up with you."

"Hey, I'm not out to win any races."

"If anyone's on the field, I'm going back inside."

"It should be pretty deserted out there until spring practices start up." At least, Sarah hoped so. Exercise raised her self-esteem as much as her heart rate. She wanted Elaine to experience the first benefit in particular. "C'mon, we can get some good gossip in. I don't get to see you enough during school."

"Hey, Adler! Look alive," Beto suddenly warned, his voice low and urgent. "Morgan's comin' to our table."

Jack? Sarah twisted in her chair and scanned the vicinity. No commanding figure walked their way. Her gaze backtracked to a slim dark-haired girl wearing dragging jeans and a ratty T-shirt. *Kate* Morgan, not her brother. And she looked more than a little upset.

Her color was high, her green eyes glittered, her chest rose and fell rapidly. She threw a defiant look toward someone in the distance before stopping two feet away.

"Hi, Kate," Sarah said, unable to keep the wariness from her voice. "What's up?"

"Well, I flunked my algebra test this morning, I got reamed out in the hall by Mr. Williams for chewing gum, my brother The Jerk won't let me sit with who I want, and my life totally sucks. Other than that, everything's hunky-dory."

Sarah zeroed in on the part she figured involved her. "The Jerk won't let you sit with Bruce?"

"Bruce is the jerk," Fred muttered fiercely.

Kate's outraged glance made him shrink in his chair. She looked back at Sarah. "You said on Friday that anytime I wanted, I could sit with you. Did you mean it?"

Sarah had, but not at the expense of Fred or the other kids at the table. "Sure. But why me?"

Despite Kate's guilty flush, her gaze was steady. "Because the only thing that will piss off my brother more than me sitting with Bruce," she explained, a satisfied gleam in her eyes, "is me sitting with *you*."

"Oh." Conscious of the collective tension at the table, Sarah managed a stiff, but credible, smile. "Well then, grab a chair and sit, already. I've got at least ten minutes left to corrupt you."

ROUNDING THE FIRST turn of the oval track, Elaine gasped as an icy head wind struck her full force.

This was horrible. She would never make it around the deserted football field four times, despite continual encouragement from the girl at her side. Sarina seemed as unaffected by the cold as Grandma and Grandpa Harper—and they were from Michigan!

Thirty-five degrees was tropical, Grandpa had insisted only that morning. Her teeth chattering, Elaine had bopped him on the head with the newspaper she'd just brought in. He'd laughed and tickled her ribs. Grandma had offered a stack of pancakes drizzled in butter and maple syrup to "warm her up." And Elaine had scarfed down every one, despite the disgust on her parents' faces.

For two weeks every January when her grandparents visited, her eating made *someone* happy.

Tucking her chin deeper into the hood of her parka, Elaine plodded miserably onward. Her face was numb, her thighs were chafed. Her lungs burned from the cold, her muscles from the unaccustomed exercise. She should've gone with her grandparents to Gulf

Greyhound Park like they'd asked that morning. She could be eating nachos from the enclosed grandstand and watching some other dumb animal fight this wind.

Elaine's parents had gaped at her explanation for turning down the invitation. After all, their constant nagging hadn't shamed her into using the treadmill in their bedroom. They naturally wondered why she would walk an outdoor track on a gray blustery afternoon.

Good question, Elaine thought now, gritting her teeth through a gust of arctic wind. This was worse than horrible. This was torture. Why did people do this voluntarily? Why was *she* doing this without a loaded gun pressed to her head?

"Hang in there, Elaine, I think we're going to make it," Sarina encouraged, slanting up a cheerful grin. Dressed in sweats and a hooded red jacket, her only sign of discomfort was a matching red nose.

Gladness burst warmly in Elaine's heart. Well, there was her answer. The "loaded gun" pressed to her head.

Sarina had invited Elaine to walk. Not Wendy, or Jessica, or any of the "popular" girls in class. But Elaine the Brain. The Pork Dork. The last girl picked for every team.

When she'd left Wendy's table that awful day at lunch, Sarina had apparently chewed out the other girls big time. Some people had called the red-haired Californian crazy. Others had said Sarina was brave. Elaine had only known the transfer student was kind and...older, somehow, than most eighteen year-olds.

She'd taken Elaine's hands and insisted the other girls had shamed themselves—not her. And that her day would come. She was a late bloomer. When Wendy was flipping hamburgers and reliving her glory days in high school, Elaine would be wowing the business world and its cocky men.

The fantasy had dried her tears and made her laugh. She'd vowed to stand by Sarina no matter what.

But after the latest buzz—Tony's version of her insult to Bruce—Sarina didn't need anybody's support. She was fast becoming a legend at Roosevelt High. Today people had called her "awesome" and "fearless" and "way cool." She sure didn't have to hang with a nobody, Elaine thought now, glancing nervously down at her friend.

"Pump your arms like this," Sarina suggested, demonstrating a controlled swinging elbow motion. "You'll get a better aerobic workout."

Mimicking the power walk motion, Elaine scanned the withered grass football field and beige brick outbuildings. A crushed Coke can scudded along a sidewalk. No other movement in sight. Whew. Talk about Pork Dork! She must look ridiculous.

"Good. Now synchronize your steps with your arms. There you go. See how it helps push you forward?"

It *did* help, Elaine realized in surprise. Not her aching lungs and protesting muscles, but her coordination. She didn't feel quite as awkward. Her sneakers didn't thud quite as heavily on the springy track. She began to feel warmer. Especially when they rounded the turn and put the wind at their backs.

"You're not even breathing hard," Elaine groused between wheezes. "I feel like such a spaz."

"Don't. You should have seen me the first time Do—a friend of mine took me out walking. I thought I was gonna die." She caught Elaine's skeptical glance. "Seriously. I barely made it half a mile."

"Well, at least you weren't fat," Elaine blurted, instantly vulnerable—yet oddly expectant. She'd never talked to anyone about "her problem," as her parents called her extra weight.

"Yes, I was."

Elaine's small bubble of hope popped. Skinny people sometimes made a big deal out of gaining five or ten pounds. Supposedly to make her feel better. But usually only to make themselves feel thinner by comparison.

"You don't believe me?" Sarina asked.

Watching their breaths plume side by side, hers fast and short, Sarina's slow and long, Elaine took her time answering. "I believe you wanted to lose weight, yes. But I don't believe you were, you know—" she indicated herself with a disparaging gesture "—fat."

Small fingers gripped her arm and jerked her to a stop. She met Sarina's beautiful eyes, an intense bluish purple against her tomato red hood.

"Elaine, I used to weigh almost two hundred pounds, and I'm shorter than you. I know what it feels like to walk past a guy and hear him say 'oink.' I know what it feels like to be treated as if you're invisible, or stupid, or worse—something to be pitied.

"I know what it feels like to be told a million times what a pretty face you have, and how great your life would be if only you lost weight. Like you can't possibly have a great life now, because, basically, you're unworthy. I know it's not fair. I know it hurts. And I know that's the way it *is* in this world."

The ache in Elaine's chest had nothing to do with the icy wind, and everything to do with her expanding wonder and pain.

"I know because I've *been* there," Sarina persisted. "Do you believe me, now?" The truth in her earnest voice and gaze couldn't be denied.

"Yes," Elaine said thickly. "How... What...?" Sniffing, she tugged down the hem of her sweatshirt below her parka, lifted the gray fleece and swiped beneath her eyes. Hard. Must she *always* act like a baby about this subject?

Sarina's gaze gentled. "It wasn't a miracle diet, if that's what you think. I'd been on all of those, and usually gained back more than I'd lost. In fact, it wasn't until I *stopped* dieting that I started losing weight." She smiled. "Close your mouth and let's keep walking. Then I'll tell you about the girl I used to be."

A small new bubble of hope rose from deep within Elaine. She clamped her jaw shut, opened her ears wide and lurched into motion beside Sarina.

SARAH STOOD beneath the spray of hot water and groaned in bliss. She'd only walked a mile two hours earlier, and a slow one at that. But for a while there on the track, everything had been cold and stiff. The wind. Her muscles. Elaine's expression while listening to Sarah.

The strain of battling on despite each resistance had exhausted her, both physically *and* mentally. But it was a good tired. The kind she hadn't experienced since well before the murder.

Grabbing a bar of soap, Sarah worked up a generous lather. Ahh, she loved the smell of peaches. So natural. So...wholesome, compared to the expensive perfume she'd worn with her professional wardrobe. A sophisticated image had been necessary to climb the management ladder at WorldWide Public Relations. Of course, she'd been very good at packaging clients, too.

A year ago, she'd coached a slick Dallas CEO to appear down-home for a job interview in Beeville. Hired, he'd drained the conservative company of working capital through a series of risky investments. Fired, he'd left with a fat severance check, none the worse for his experience.

She'd heard the company had had to lay off fifty employees, but she'd never checked, had never really thought much about her clients once they'd moved beyond her immediate area of responsibility. Now she found herself hoping the news was only a rumor. That was certainly possible. Rumors—good and bad—were easy to start.

Bumping up the hot water a notch, Sarah rinsed her skin and snorted. Six months ago, she'd steered a hotshot young NBA player's bad-boy reputation into safer, more lucrative waters. A strategic drugs-are-bad tour of high schools, culminating in an interview with Barbara Walters—and now the guy's face was on cereal boxes and sportswear tags. Packaging. The power of it was incredible.

Sarah had fostered deceptive images for so long, she'd almost forgotten what she'd loved about image consulting at first: the ability to help people achieve their personal goals and dreams. She'd almost forgotten what it felt like to work for a worthy cause. Nudging Elaine into the first step toward a better self-image was as worthy as it got.

And walking the track wasn't the step Sarah meant.

Turning off the water, she yanked open the shower curtain and stepped out of the tub. Only one clean towel left. Time to make use of the laundry room again. Donna had given Sarah codes to the burglary alarm and front gates, as well as a key to the back entrance of the big house so she wouldn't have to disturb Mrs. Kaiser. The sweetie would never admit that getting around was hard for her these days. And the housekeeper, Mrs. Anderson, got off at five o'clock.

Minutes later Sarah left the bathroom in a flannel nightgown and a cloud of steam. As she gathered dirty clothes and laundry supplies, her thoughts returned to Elaine. Hopefully she would take heart from "Sarina's" story. Sarah had changed necessary dates and names, but most of the facts were true.

She'd taken a New Age workshop with Donna,

who'd been told it might help her cope with the grief of her parents' deaths. It had. But the techniques had also taught Sarah to grieve for herself, for the person she'd never been. The person others thought she should be. Then she'd "buried" that girl and celebrated who she actually was.

The list of attributes she'd been forced to write down had surprised her. Made her recognize she'd focused on her flaws instead of her strengths. Amazingly, when she'd admitted to herself she *had* strengths, food was no longer her primary comfort and reward in life. Sarah had taken better care of the person she'd grown to like more. And she'd lost weight. A lot of it.

Snapping back into the present, Sarah tied on a pair of Nikes, slipped into her jacket, then hoisted the full plastic clothes hamper to one hip. At the front door, she unbolted the lock and paused. Six o'clock, dressed for bed and washing laundry for excitement. Pretty pitiful. Smiling, she opened the door.

And screamed.

CHAPTER SEVEN

SARINA'S BRIEF piercing scream skewered Jack to the
doormat, his fist still raised to knock.

Recognition flooded her deathly pale face. She
dropped a clothes basket. Her knees dipped.

He rushed forward and braced an arm around her
shoulders, his own heart hammering. "Whoa, Sarina.
It's me. Mr. Morgan. Take a deep breath. That's right.
Now another."

This was no fake swoon, but the aftermath of pure
terror. More terror than seemed warranted—even if he
had loomed unidentified and unexpected in the twilight. She felt small beneath his arm, but surprisingly
sturdy.

And she smelled like peaches.

He kicked aside the clothes basket with a boot,
shoved the door closed with his hip, then steered her
toward one of two sofas.

"I'm sorry I scared you," he said, helping her sit.
A strong waft of her scented skin jerked him upright
and two steps back. Why peaches? Of all things, why
his favorite? "I went to the main house first. Mrs.
Anderson said you lived here."

Her brow furrowed. "Mrs. Anderson leaves at five.
And she wouldn't send a stranger to my door."

"She stayed late to make sure Mrs. Kaiser was settled in her room. Your…great-aunt wasn't feeling
well, but she's asleep now." He sensed her renewed
tension. Concern for Mrs. Kaiser, or his telltale pause?
"And you're right about Mrs. Anderson. She wouldn't
send a stranger to the guest house. I met her at a
Christmas party that Assistant Principal Kaiser—or,
maybe you call her Donna?" He watched Sarina
closely.

No reaction but a blink.

"Anyway, Donna hosted this party at her grandmother's house for the teaching staff. Mrs. Anderson
remembered me. I told her that Donna was due to meet
me any minute, and I'd just wait in the living room
until she got there."

"Mrs. Anderson went home?" At his nod, she
looked shaken. "Then why aren't you still waiting in
the living room?"

*Because I reviewed your permanent record this
morning and learned something interesting. Because
I've become so obsessed with analyzing my obsession
with you I need answers now, so I can sleep tonight.
Because Mike Ransom wouldn't have waited to question you, and I'm tired of my screenplay children having all the guts in the family.*

He thrust a hand in his jeans pocket and said simply,
"Because Donna's not coming. I lied."

At least three different emotions sprinted across her
face before wariness skidded to a stop. "Why?"

"To make Mrs. Anderson leave. The sixty-four-dollar question is, why did *you* lie, Sarina? Where are you really from?''

''Wh-what?''

''According to your transcripts, you went to Washington High School in San Diego, but you said in my class that you went to Milburn.''

She blanched.

''There *is* no Milburn High School in San Diego. I checked. And where do the Kaisers fit into all this?''

''What do you mean? Mrs. Kaiser is my great-aunt.''

''Funny, Donna told me she had no family other than her grandmother, but you're Mrs. Kaiser's great-niece. Imagine my surprise when I saw her listed as your legal guardian. Wouldn't that also make Donna related to you? Your parents, too?'' He jingled the keys in his pocket and continued relentlessly. ''How *are* Paula and Todd, by the way?''

''N-not so great. They're going through a divorce. They wanted me to finish out the school year away from all the fighting, so they sent me here.''

The fingers in his pocket stilled. She was some little actress, he'd give her that. From the beginning she'd fascinated him. Now anger mixed in with his curiosity to form a hard knot in his chest.

''I tried to call your parents today, Sarina. The number on record is not a working number.''

''Mom got a new number. Under her maiden name,'' she said weakly. ''Dad moved out of the city.''

Good try, but no bananas. ''I thought they were still

together and fighting. Isn't that why you moved here?''

"Why are you asking these questions?''

"Why did you nearly faint when you saw me earlier?'' he countered, determined to get to the truth. "What's got you so scared? I've seen you in action at school. You're not exactly the timid type. I don't know *what* type you are. That's part of the problem I'm having with you. You don't act or talk like any high school student I've ever taught.''

Sarina pulled the open edges of her jacket together, an oddly vulnerable movement that gave him pause. Her long pink flannel gown clashed with her red coat and puddled endearingly over her sneakers. The ends of her rumpled chin-length hair curled damply, as if she was fresh from a shower. A far different image from the one haunting his thoughts the past two weeks.

Needles of guilt stung his conscience and goaded his temper. Why did everything about this girl get to him, no matter how she acted?

He yanked his hand from his pocket and crossed his arms. "Still not talking? Well *something's* going on, and I want to know exactly what it is before I drag Principal Miller into this mess.''

Sarina's chin came up. Her eyes said *how-dare-you.*

Jack's mouth thinned. "I guess I should've asked Donna first.''

"Leave her out of this.'' Her voice was fierce with warning. She rose and faced him, quivering with indignation. "You lie to the housekeeper to get inside, you scare me witless, you barge in here uninvited and start badgering me—one of your *students,* may I remind you—for answers like Perry Mason with a bad script. As if you have a right to pry into my life. Well, I don't *think* so, Mr. Morgan!''

Ah, yes. He liked this Sarina better. Much, much better. Too much better. The unwanted stirring of heat in his groin sent those stinging needles deeper.

She drew herself up to her full height, about his chin level, and glared. ''I suggest you turn around and leave, before this turns into a nasty little incident *I* have to report to Principal Miller. I'm not sure your reputation can stand another accusation of harassment, are you?''

He unfolded his arms slowly. ''Are you threatening me, Sarina?''

Her gaze faltered, then steadied. ''I'm stating the facts. I know you were cleared of Wendy's charges last semester, but that doesn't really matter, does it? Leave me alone, forget about all these questions, and I won't start another scandal by telling Principal Miller you came over here. Alone. At night. Then sent the housekeeper home.''

She'd slammed Jack's hot button so hard he exhaled smoke. He moved forward, boot tips to sneaker toes, invading her space, expecting her to retreat. ''Go ahead and tell him. There wasn't a first scandal, so you can't start a second one. You said yourself I was cleared of charges.''

Her world-weary expression held a tinge of pity. ''Get real. A beautiful girl like Wendy…a man like you tutoring her privately. Put the two in a room alone and you've got a scandal, whether you were guilty or not. It'll be twice as bad if I corroborate Wendy's claim with a new story. Which I will, if you don't leave me alone.''

Why, the manipulative little... ''A 'man like me' is exactly right. I've taught at that school for ten years. If it comes down to your word, or mine—I'll win. I don't lie, and people know it.''

She huffed in his face. ''Tell that to Mrs. Anderson.''

His neck heated.

''Besides,'' she continued. ''I wasn't talking about your sacred honor and sense of responsibility. That's only half of what a reputation's built on. Physical appearance is just as important.'' She arched a brow at his startled look. ''You may talk and act like Moses, but I've seen the way girls watch you. They're not drooling over your morals, that's for sure...''

Frowning at her revelation, Sarina looked away and swallowed hard, her cheeks growing pink.

A ray of speculation penetrated Jack's murky emotions. The following rush of male satisfaction was bright and purely sweet. He could see her fighting her need to step back, but she didn't budge.

''Would you like to explain that little comment?'' he asked.

Her head whipped around, her gaze resentful. ''And stroke your ego more? No, thanks. Go find somebody else to do it. In fact, leave now, or I'll call Principal Miller at home.'' She flicked a glance to the telephone on an end table two feet away. "I've had about all I can take of you and your harassment."

He refused to be railroaded again by another Wendy Johnson! "Well, I've had about all I can take of Lolita wanna-bes playing games with my career. I'll leave when you tell—"

"Lol*ee*ta?"

"You heard me." A thought occurred to him. "She's a teenager in an old movie who manipulates James Mason—"

"I *know* who Lolita is, I just couldn't believe your gall. Listen, buddy, I've never operated that way in my life. But if I did, I wouldn't be a wanna-be Lolita, I'd be the real thing. No, I'd be *better*."

God, her eyes were magnificent. "Okay, tell me how you *do* operate. What is your game?" He would damn well get some answers before he left, but—responsibly. Rationally. He drew a calming breath and asked, "Why are you staying with Donna's grandmother?"

She reached for the phone.

His hand flashed out, his fingers overlapping the delicate wrist bone above her padded coat sleeve. "Tell me what you're hiding, Sarina. Maybe I can help."

"Let *go!*" She pulled her arm once, twice, then suddenly went still.

The atmosphere shifted, quicksand beneath his feet. When her other hand came up he tensed for a slap. The feel of her gentle fingertips on his face sent a jolt of surprise to his boots. The Lolita gleam in her eyes sent a trill of alarm to his brain.

Her sigh was a calculated surrender. ''I guess it's useless to fight any more, since you've got me all figured out.'' She lightly scored the line of his jaw with her nails, the bristling sound loud in his ears, then curved her fingers and ran her knuckles the opposite direction.

''Shame on you, Mr. Morgan,'' she scolded, her voice a husky purr. Her nails retraced their original path. ''Not shaving before dropping by. I'm sure there must be a rule of etiquette against that somewhere.''

If she'd grown pointed ears and a snarling snout, he couldn't have been more shocked. Her body had softened. Her lids drooped, turning those dusky purple eyes into sultry weapons. Lethal within ten feet to a man's common sense.

His other brain rose valiantly to the occasion.

He released her wrist as if scalded. Big mistake, since her freed hand reached up and kneaded the back of his neck.

''All right, Sarina,'' he croaked, his heart clubbing his ribs in great thunderous blows. ''You've had your fun. Give it a rest.''

''Oh, but you're wrong. I haven't had my fun, yet.'' She pressed the pad of her thumb on his lower lip. ''Neither have you.''

He stumbled backward two steps, surrendering ground like the coward he was, but she rode his boots, her hands still busy. One read the braille of his features; the other did shivery things to his ear.

"Sometimes in class," she murmured breathily, "when you're talking? So stern and serious and responsible. I've thought about touching you like this."

Sweet mother of God! He grasped her arms and wrenched them down, not daring to look at her upturned face. "You win. I'm leaving."

"No, don't go."

He gathered up every ounce of his considerable willpower and started to move.

"Jack."

The sound of his name in that throaty whisper riveted his boots to the floor. Helpless to do anything else, he looked into her eyes.

Stunningly beautiful. Electrifying in their intensity. Naked with yearning.

All the blood in his body rushed to support his new command center. One touch, it ordered. To satisfy curiosity only. To confirm that her skin wasn't as impossibly smooth as it looked.

His gaze never wavering from hers, he reached up in slow motion and feathered his knuckles down one cameo cheek. Her lashes fluttered and dropped, allowing all his senses to focus on touch.

Warm smooth satin. Fine plush velvet. Dewy soft petals. None of the writer's clichés at his disposal did Sarina's skin justice. Beneath his fingers, her cheek flushed a rosy peach—to match her heated scent.

He couldn't ignore the fragrance any longer, couldn't pretend it hadn't been teasing him unmercifully since she'd opened the front door. Closing his eyes, he inhaled a deep reverent breath.

No custom-blended perfume could have been created to suit him better, to excite him more. She smelled lush and summery, wholesome and earthy, delicious with the promise of his favorite taste. Underlying the peaches was the her own unique scent. The one that grew stronger when a woman was aroused.

His eyes popped open.

She was staring at his mouth.

Forbidden fruit, his mind shouted from a great vast distance. He tried to remember why she was forbidden. But he was too dizzy, too hot, too hungry, too needy. He liked this Sarina much, much too much.

There was no room for anything else but the woman so near he could count every eyelash, yet too far from his starving body. As if reading his mind, she pressed closer.

"Sarina," he said on a groan, splaying his hands on her hips, pulling her the last forbidden inch. *Oh, yeah.*

His world narrowed to one purpose. His straining erection wept a grateful tear, despite the irritating barrier of her bulky jacket. Where to start? So many choices, all of them explored mentally the past two weeks. He looked down and watched the tip of her delicate pink tongue dart out to moisten her lips. Her mouth, then. That was at the top of his list, anyway.

He reached up and cradled her jaw, sliding his thumb inward to test the springy plumpness of her lower lip. Damp. Ripe for the tasting. He rubbed his thumb pad once. Twice.

She parted her upturned mouth.

Excellent. On the way down he changed his mind and made a detour to the base of her throat. His lips absorbed the frantic beat of her heart, then lifted in triumph. She was excited, which excited him more.

Cupping the base of her skull with one hand, gripping the jacket-padded curve of her bottom with the other, he found himself asking new questions. "Tell me what you like," he murmured in her ear. "Tell me what you want."

She grew still, as if possibilities whirled through her mind. They sure as hell did in his. He'd never been so aroused in his life.

"I don't know," she whispered. Her hands moved restlessly over his back. "I've never felt like this. I want…everything."

Jack fought through a wave of lust so powerful he nearly went under. Choking out a laugh, he said, "I think that can be arranged. Anything goes between consenting adults—"

He froze. Only one of them was an adult, consenting for the both of them.

In an instant of lucid clarity, he acknowledged the *wrongness* of this picture. A teacher, locked in a passionate embrace with a student. An older man seducing a young girl, no matter how seemingly mature, who was vulnerable to his greater experience. His ardor shifted to horrified self-disgust.

He grabbed her shoulders and thrust himself out of her clinging arms. She looked dazed, and he cursed viciously.

"Jack, it's okay," Sarina said urgently.

"It's *not* okay!" Whirling, he put a good eleven feet between them—out of the range of her lethal eyes—and paced back and forth in agitation. "Do you realize what I almost did? Jeez, another minute and you would've been flat on that sofa. Or the floor."

"Jack—"

"I swear, Sarina, I've never touched a student like that in my life. I—wanted to get some answers. I don't know how or why I let things get so far out of control. It was unforgivable."

"Jack—"

"Don't worry, I'll report myself to the superintendent tomorrow—"

"Jack!" Sarina bellowed, stopping him in his tracks. "Quit taking all the blame," she said in a calmer voice. "I started the whole thing. I could have stopped you any time, but I didn't. You're not going to report this to the superintendent and ruin your career. Now listen to me—"

"Why?" Spearing fingers through his hair, he glanced at the petite girl in her pink flannel nightgown and cringed inwardly. She wasn't much older than Kate, for God's sake. Wouldn't Brian Morgan be proud of his son, now? "There's not a damn thing you can say to me that will excuse my behavior, so don't even try."

Her chin came up in a now familiar gesture. She marched forward and planted herself two feet away, her eyes a brilliant blue-purple. Insistent. Compelling. And utterly, hopelessly mesmerizing.

He was doomed.

"My name is Sarah Davidson, not Sarina Davis. I'm from Fort Worth, Texas, not San Diego, California. And, for your information, I'm *twenty-seven years old,* not eighteen. A legitimate consenting adult, Mr. Martyr."

CUPPING HER HANDS around a mug of hot tea on the bar counter, Sarah wondered what Jack was thinking. He'd sat on the stool next to her virtually silent throughout her long tale. Now he appeared to be deep in contemplation.

She'd told him everything. Her background. Witnessing three deaths. John Merrit's, and then later, Mike's and Larry's. How the home-shopping sales pitch for a friendship ring had made her think of Donna, causing her to head from Omaha to Houston.

There were gaps missing from that nightmarish portion. Somehow she'd had the wits to use cash, a false name and a plausible sob story. She must've made a convincingly scared teen runaway on her way home to Mom and Dad. The gruff truckers had opened their hearts and cab doors readily enough. And Sarah, who'd feared and scorned hitchhiking her entire life, had felt lucky to get the privilege of a ride.

She'd told Jack about Donna's generosity and daring plan, then pleaded with him not to expose them both. Their fate was in his hands, now. That probably should make her nervous. But instead, she was comforted and relieved.

Just then, Jack lifted his cup of coffee and took an absentminded sip, his strong throat rippling. The arms beneath his moss green cable knit sweater were startlingly hard, she remembered. Sarah took advantage of his inner focus to study him with unabashed pleasure.

If, as an image consultant, she disapproved of the clothes he wore to school, she heartily endorsed this casual "look." She was Texas born and bred. What was not to like?

First there were those black Roper boots, the heels hooked over the lower brass rung of his bar stool. Their leather scuffed enough to prove he wore them more than once a year to a Garth Brooks concert.

Then there were his jeans. They were perfect. Faded and snug in a way stonewashed denim could never duplicate. Like if he stepped out of them, they'd lovingly hold his shape. Which was well worth holding, in her discerning opinion.

Maybe it was the legs that made the jeans perfect. They were long and muscular, the curve of his thighs twin temptations. She didn't know if she wanted more to touch them—to see if they were as hard as they looked—or sit on them, to feel what else might be hard....

She lifted her mug and sipped, hoping to cover her burning cheeks. What must he think? She hardly knew what to think, herself. Sure, she'd felt desperate. Yes, he'd angered and frustrated her. But she hadn't needed to come on to the man like Lolita after a raw oyster binge!

One touch of those long sensitive fingers on her cheek, and she'd been lost. Aching for his kiss—and more. She'd wanted just what she said. Everything.

Anything. As long as it was with him. Why *him?* Wrong place, wrong time, wrong man—Donna's man.

Setting down her mug, Sarah wondered where the pragmatic, undersexed woman she'd been had gone. The woman willing to settle for a marriage of convenience with Mark to fulfill the image of a perfect couple.

"Okay, backtrack for me to the man who murdered John Merrit," Jack said, capturing her guilty gaze.

"Hmm? Oh." Struggling for composure, she brushed the knee of the sweatpants she'd changed into, tugged down her white T-shirt. "What do you want to know?"

"I know he made bail. I know someone—someone he probably hired—put a bullet through your windshield the next day."

Sarah's stomach clenched. If she hadn't stretched at that precise instant to change the radio station...

"Tell me about the man and his motive."

Memory of icy blue eyes staring through a two-way mirror sent a delicate shudder through her body. "His name is Lester Jacobs. I didn't know that until after I described him to police, and they brought him in for a lineup. He owns a real estate development company. When the referendum to legalize casino gambling in Texas passed, he'd bought prime property in Galveston and San Antonio."

"I'm assuming he's wealthy."

"I think he's a high roller. Tom Castle—that's the prosecuting attorney on the case—said he's in over his head on the property he bought. He was betting everything on making a killing once gambling was legalized.''

''And Merrit's campaign for governor got in the way.''

Nodding, she reached for her mug but only grasped the handle, sliding her thumb back and forth along the rim. ''The campaign centered around an anti-vice theme. And he was so passionate, so charismatic that, against all predictions, he was beginning to affect public opinion. The latest poll indicated legalization wouldn't pass in the general election.''

''So, this Jacobs slime bag killed one of the few honorable politicians this country had left.''

She shot him a startled look.

''Merrit spoke at Roosevelt's graduation ceremony last year,'' he said, answering her unspoken question. ''He was great to the kids. Straightforward. Not patronizing at all. I liked the man.''

''Me, too. He was…very special.'' Her throat closed up on the last word. *Damn, damn, damn!*

''He was scheduled to come back this spring for a roundtable discussion with the senior student council. They were really excited about it. Couldn't believe he actually cared what they thought about the future.''

John had cared, Sarah knew. Biting her lip, she looked at the ceiling, drew a deep breath and fought the sting of tears.

She'd worked so hard to forget the huge loss John's death represented. Now memory of his larger-than-life personality, his optimism and belief in people and his government—despite a hundred reasons to be cynical—pressed down on Sarah with crushing weight.

He'd been cut down at age fifty-two, his prime leadership years ahead. He'd been her friend, a better friend than she deserved. A small strangled sound escaped her now.

Suddenly long fingers were cupping her knee, giving a little squeeze of comfort. She reached blindly for Jack's hand. It was large and warm, and completely swallowed her own to the wrist. And it gave her the courage to face what she'd shoved aside for months.

"Jack…" She looked up into his warm hazel eyes. "I killed John Merrit."

CHAPTER EIGHT

SARAH FELT a slight twitch in Jack's hand, otherwise he showed no reaction to the words festering inside her so long.

"That's ridiculous," he said soothingly, as one would speak to a jumper poised on a skyscraper ledge. "You watched Lester Jacobs knife John in the chest."

"Exactly." She would have to put it in words. Make him understand her contemptible behavior. "I *watched* him get murdered. I didn't *do* anything. I didn't run forward and bash Jacobs with whatever was handy. I didn't even scream like the idiot wimpy females I hate in movies and used to make fun of. At least that might've distracted him."

"It might've," Jack agreed, sinking her stomach lower. "It also would've told him he had an eyewitness. You did the right thing, Sari—Sarah," he corrected with a shake of his head. "You lived to identify him. The guy had a weapon. You had a wrapped present. It might've been a power tie, but it was no match for a knife."

Sarah had told Jack about delivering the good luck gift to John's home. She'd been in meetings all that day and had wanted him to have the Nicole Miller tie for an important chamber of commerce breakfast speech. No one had answered the front door. Raised voices had led her to the backyard.

She stared now at the pothos ivy on the kitchen windowsill because it was easier than meeting Jack's eyes. "I failed John when he needed me most. And I owed him so much. He was responsible for my promotion to account supervisor, you know." Rueful pride crept into her voice. "He'd seen the results I got for a pro basketball client, and specifically asked that I work with him until the election. He could've asked for one of the agency's officers, or a more experienced consultant. But he didn't. He believed in *me*."

"You were good," Jack said. A statement, not a question. "He didn't do you a favor. He wanted the best."

She laughed bitterly and met his compassionate gaze. "Oh, I was good, all right. I polished his rough edges and made the most of his charisma. I helped him sway public opinion. Maybe if I hadn't, Lester Jacobs wouldn't have had a motive to kill John."

"Sari—Sarah." Jack grimaced apologetically, then squeezed her hand. "Are you listening to yourself? The motive had nothing to do with the image you created for John. This guy Jacobs created his own hell, then went up in flames one night. Quit flaying yourself alive."

He was trying so hard to make her feel better. But facts were facts. "I'm a coward, Jack. I'm not proud of it, no. But at least I can finally admit it out loud."

And the admission lifted a burden so huge she would've floated to the ceiling but for Jack's anchoring support. She looked from their joined hands to his stern face.

Her best friend had been right. His eyes did change color with his mood. But Donna hadn't told Sarah anything she hadn't discovered on her own. When the brown flecks dominated his irises, like now, he was irritated. She much preferred the green-gold swirl of passion...

He released her hand and scowled. "So, let me get this straight. You're a coward for identifying the killer in a lineup instead of attending your own funeral. You're a coward for pulling yourself together after that slaughter in Omaha, and getting yourself hundreds of miles away and into safe hands without falling apart."

Sliding off the stool, he grabbed his mug and rounded the bar into the kitchen. "I guess assuming a new identity, plunging into an environment that most adults wouldn't last a day in—that was cowardly, too." He stopped at the coffeemaker, filled his mug and turned to lean against the counter. "Hell, you're hardly a coward. Even the teaching staff is impressed with the way you've stood up for Elaine against Wendy. There are a lot of words that come to mind when I think of you, Sarah, but *coward* is definitely not on the list."

What is on the list, Jack? Do you think of me as often as I think of you?

"And what you said to Bruce..." The hint of a smile curved his lips as he took a sip of coffee. He lowered the mug and shook his head. "I wish I could have seen his face."

She caught up mentally with the conversation and straightened. "How could you possibly know what I said to Bruce?"

"Get real," he quoted her earlier taunt wryly. "You slammed him in front of Tony. Those two have competed for head stud of Roosevelt High since Tony became a senior. Tim Williams overheard one of his students talking, then shared the story with me later in the teacher's lounge." His gaze sharpened, his interest suddenly keen and personal. "He said Kate was with Bruce in the hallway."

Uh-oh. "Yes. He'd pulled her aside."

"Did they seem...I don't know, like girl and boyfriend to you?"

Sarah shifted on her stool. She didn't want to put heat on Kate, but still, Bruce was major bad news. "He was acting pretty possessive, but I don't think Kate was comfortable with it. That's why I went over to talk with them." She took a deep breath, knowing she owed this man the truth. "And Jack—he slipped something into her pocket. Probably just a note, but I thought you should know."

In the space of a blink, Jack dwarfed the small kitchen.

"I *knew* it." His beard-shadowed jaw bulged, his brown-green eyes hardened to creek bottom stones. He looked dark, menacing and very masculine.

Sarah experienced an overwhelming craving to harness all that power, and a delicious feminine thrill at the prospect.

"It wasn't a note," he confirmed in a deadly voice. "Mother found two joints in Kate's room over the weekend. I suspected Bruce, but Kate wouldn't talk." He scrubbed his hair, the rumpled result increasing his dangerous appeal. "I thought when new zoning bussed her to Roosevelt, she'd might be safer from that kind of garbage. But most of these kids have too much money and freedom. How can they 'just say no' when they've never been told that by their parents?"

That obviously wasn't the case with Kate. "What happened after your mother found the pot?"

He blew out a frustrated breath. "I've forbidden Kate to eat lunch or have any contact with Bruce, and she's grounded from going out with her friends for a month. But I can't keep track of her twenty-four hours a day."

Kate had mentioned her dad had died before she was born. How many brothers would've taken on the role of father to an infant sister, much less played it heart and soul for all these years?

"She resents you," Sarah found herself saying, sympathetic with the difficulties for both siblings. "That's only natural at her age. It doesn't help that other brothers don't have the power to 'forbid' their sisters anything. Can't your mother do the grounding?"

His mouth twisted. "You'd think so. She's never had a problem dry-docking my plans for fifteen years...." He glanced away, as if embarrassed by dragging his problems into the conversation, then took a sip of coffee.

"Plans?" Sarah was intrigued.

Jack shrugged. "Forget it. I shouldn't have said anything."

But he had, and suddenly she wanted to know everything about him. "You're not happy teaching? But you're so good."

His startled gaze was almost completely brown. "I love to teach. That has nothing to do with..."

Your dreams.

Jack blew out a breath. "Forget it," he repeated.

Sarah pondered her new knowledge. This stern unbending man had dreams beyond what the world saw. Dreams, she sensed instinctively, he'd harbored unshared.

She knew about those. They'd gotten her through a painful adolescence, when she'd envisioned growing up to be admired and accepted...maybe even loved. But she'd often longed for someone to confide in, someone to validate the possibility of achieving her goal.

"So, pull out your biggest dream for me now," she said impulsively. "Let's go for a sail. A fresh breeze is just the thing I need right now to forget about John."

He eyed her incredulously.

"I know it's a very personal thing. I'll understand if you don't want to share. But I'm serious about needing the distraction. And I love to hear people's dreams."

"You're putting me on." He looked skeptical, and a little wistful.

She smiled. "Hey, it's why I chose to specialize in image consulting. That's *my* dream, Jack. Equipping clients with the right image to help them reach for the brass ring. Establishing a successful career for myself—not just working a job between having babies."

"What? No yellow house and white picket fence? No pitter-patter of little feet?" His tone was casual, but his expression was oddly intent.

Uncomfortable, she snorted. "Hardly. When the murder trial is over, I've got a lot of lost ground to make up. Twelve-hour work days don't leave much room for kids." Realizing she'd gotten off track, she steered back to the subject. "Okay, fair is fair. I told you my dream. Now you tell me yours. C'mon, we'll work out an image plan."

"You think I need a new image?"

"Well, maybe only an update." she said tactfully, slanting up a teasing glance. "I guess it all depends on your dream."

He pulled a wry face. "You're not gonna let this go, are you?"

"Not a chance," she confirmed, grinning.

"It can't leak to students and faculty," he warned.

"Like I can't keep a big secret? Gimme a break."

Raising his mug, he mumbled against the rim, "I want to sell screenplays." He studied her closely over a long slow sip.

Whoa! "Is that what you do in that spiral notebook you scribble in? Work on your screenplays?"

He lowered his cup and nodded warily.

"That is *so-o-o* cool!" She broke into a delighted grin, his obvious relief making her go soft and tender inside. "Have you completed one yet? An entire screenplay, I mean. Or are you still, you know, learning how to write one?"

"I've completed several. But I've only submitted one." Pushing off of the counter, he walked to his bar stool and sat facing her, his coffee perched on one thigh.

For someone hesitant to pull his dream out of dry dock, Jack was an enthusiastic sailer, once launched. The change in him enthralled Sarah. His expression grew more and more animated, he used his hands expansively, he looked happier than she'd ever seen him in class. The man had a big dream, and he'd worked years to reach the point of being accepted by a top agent for representation.

Thirty minutes later, she was genuinely impressed by his dedication and accomplishment. "But what happens if *Free Fall* sells? Will you still teach?"

His animation dimmed. He looked down and plucked at his sweater sleeve, hitched his wristwatch into position. "Yeah. I promised myself I'd be there for Kate until she graduates. Since she hit her teens, Mother's at a loss how to cope. Not that I do much better." His gaze lifted, filled with concern. "This drug thing really threw me. It's not like I haven't talked to her about the dangers of experimenting. I have."

"Do the both of you talk together, Jack...or do *you*

lecture?'' Oops. Wrong question, if his immediate stiffening was any indication.

"Sure I lecture her," he said coldly. "Then I lock her in her room and shove stale bread through the door once a week."

She offered an apologetic little smile. "No daily water ration?"

His expression relaxed a bit. "She's got a cup. It rains. Her hand fits through the bars on her window."

Sarah laughed, an unfettered natural sound she hadn't realized until now she'd suppressed for months. Sharing her burden of guilt had lifted a tremendous weight from her spirits. Sharing his dream had reminded her of the good things about her profession. Not all images she polished hid a tarnished soul. She reached for her tea, glanced at Jack and caught him staring.

Gone were the creek bottom stones. His gaze was the rushing water above. Glittering. Elemental. And swirling with *green-gold flecks*.

Her heart lurched into heavy ponderous beats.

"You should laugh more often," he said, his voice low and intimate.

"Yeah, well—" she lowered the hand still hovering over her tea "—I'll remind you of that in class."

He didn't smile, but then, neither did she. Her nerves were thrumming in awareness. Of the denim knees almost touching hers. Of the heat emanating from his big body. Of the eyes that made it hard for her to breathe.

This was not good.

"Thank God you're twenty-seven," he said fervently. "I was beginning to think I was depraved."

This was not good at all.

"You were so self-assured, so articulate—I knew there was more to you than the normal eighteen-year-old girl, and I couldn't stop thinking about you."

He couldn't stop thinking about her.

"I might not've dug for answers if you hadn't debated me in class on Steinbeck. You slipped up big time there."

Yeah, that'd been dumb. Dumb, dumb, dumb.

"What color is your hair?" he asked in a lightning switch of topics.

"Wha—?" She raised her arm and patted the stuff vaguely. "My hair?" *Du-uh.* "It's red. Well, red-orange. The package calls the color Outrageous Red and I thought that fit Sarina. I know it's pretty awful, but Donna agrees that I should try to look—"

"Sarah."

She stopped babbling, heat rising up her neck at the knowing gleam in his eyes, the smug cant of his lips. He had a gorgeous mouth. Sin in the flesh.

This was very bad.

"What color is your hair, naturally?"

Of course. She'd blushed more around this man in two weeks than she had her entire adult life. "It's dark. Like my eyebrows. I didn't dye them."

He nodded as if to himself. "Your hair is black, then. Liz Taylor black." His voice was rich with satisfaction. "You must get that comparison a lot."

His gaze traveled lazily, yet intently, over her face.

When it reached her mouth and stopped, so did her heart.

"Do you?" he asked.

"Do I...?"

"Do you get that comparison? Do people say you look like a young Liz Taylor?"

Sarah, Sarina, Liz Taylor, whatever. Who could think with those eyes making love to her mouth? But she was supposed to remember something. Oh, yeah. Almost four months left to face Jack in school and pull off a student-teacher relationship. This was the wrong time, the wrong place, the wrong man.

Donna's man.

She drew a shaky breath. "Sometimes Mark used to say that, if I was dressed up, or if he needed a favor."

Jack's gaze lifted alertly to hers. "Mark?"

"Mark Granger. A city councilman in Dallas. We're..." She couldn't quite make herself say engaged. "We're dating."

"Dating casually?"

Casually. Conveniently. He means nothing to me. His eyes do nothing to me. Sarah wavered, the green-gold creek promising to sweep her away to a place she'd never been, would never visit with Mark.

"No," she said tightly. "We're serious. We'll probably get married."

For a breathless instant she saw honor struggle with his fierce male desire to challenge another's territory.

Then his gaze shuttered. "You missed your calling,

Sarah. I'll keep you in mind when they cast my first movie."

It hurt. More than it should have on two weeks' acquaintance. Unable to answer past the regret clogging her throat, she stretched to hook both mug handles in one hand, then headed for the kitchen. The sudden shrill ring of the telephone made her glad the mugs were empty.

Her heart still racing, she changed directions and lifted the receiver. "Hello?"

"Oh, thank goodness you're all right," Donna said without preliminary. "I called Gram but got her message machine on the first ring. She's probably only asleep, but it worried me."

"She wasn't feeling well, so she went to bed early," Sarah confirmed, frowning. "You sound more than worried. What's wrong?"

"Sarah…did Gram mention anyone coming by the house to ask questions about you?"

Sarah's gaze snapped up to meet Jack's. How had Donna known? "No," Sarah hedged truthfully. "Why do you ask?"

"Because I just spent the last twenty minutes talking to some guy from the justice department. I'm pretty sure I convinced him he was on a wild-goose chase. But if he came snooping around for you…"

Sarah's grip on the phone tightened. "Then so will whoever tried to kill me," she finished grimly.

FOUR NIGHTS LATER, Jack tucked in his silk-blend charcoal gray T-shirt, an exact match to his double-pleated wool flannel slacks, then shrugged into his loosely constructed black three-button blazer. Funny, he'd always thought clothes were just clothes before talking to Sarah. Stepping back from the dresser mirror, he studied his expensive new reflection.

Too cosmo. He felt ridiculous. Like he was trying to be Don Johnson, or something. Jack never should've let Sarah's gentle comments about his outdated wardrobe get to him. But then, everything about her got to him. That was the problem. And the reason he was taking Donna to dinner and a play tonight.

He needed a distraction. The date gave him an excuse to attend The Alley Theater's new production with a pleasant companion. Jack met his eyes in the mirror and grimaced.

Right, pal. Showing Sarah you don't give a flip about her relationship with Mark Granger doesn't have a thing to do with this.

Frowning, he gathered up change, keys and wallet from the dresser and slipped them into his pockets. Sarah's unavailability was damned fortunate for his career. He'd decided to keep quiet about her "Sarina" scam, since it appeared to be her best option for safety. Donna had stayed away from her grandmother's house all week, and the deputy marshal hadn't returned for more questioning. The coast, for now, was clear.

Like it or not, Jack would see Sarah almost daily for the next four months. If he'd acted on his powerful attraction, he might've given some hint of their changed relationship at school. And wouldn't *that* have been great for his reputation? Talk about professional suicide!

The eyes in the mirror looked back with stark honesty. *Maybe so, pal...but what a way to go.*

For a minute he dropped all pretense of indifference and remembered how she'd felt in his arms. Her Lolita act had deserved a standing ovation, and part of him had sure as hell shouted bravo. Later, Sarah had tapped into something deeper than lust. A loneliness he hadn't realized existed until she'd climbed aboard his dream and encouraged him to hoist sail and head for the stars.

Warmed by the memory, he scooped up his wristwatch and fastened it slowly. During the past week, she'd even taken Kate under her wing, steering her clear of Bruce and easing Jack's mind and heart yet again. If only she weren't serious about this Mark character...

If only. The story of Jack's life. His gaze moved to the framed picture of his smiling father, a loving arm slung around a laughing young man. Cocky and carefree. Off to USC in five months...

If only the last words his dad had said weren't, "Promise you'll take care of your mother and baby brother or sister. I'm counting on you, son."

Sighing, Jack walked into his private bathroom. His final purchase the day before had been an impulse buy from the men's cologne counter. Dashing a little liquid gold on each palm now, he patted his cheeks and sniffed. It didn't smell forty dollars better than Old Spice to him. But hell, he liked the scent of peaches better than designer perfume. What did he know?

"Don't answer that," he told his reflection, then headed for the hallway. Donna would arrive any minute. She'd had to work late and had suggested meeting him here. It was closer than her condo to downtown, and the saved time would let them squeeze in an early dinner.

When he walked into the living room, the scene was surprisingly peaceful. His mother sat in her flowered chintz armchair crocheting her millionth afghan; Kate lay sprawled on the blue couch watching a loud sitcom on TV. Both of them looked up at the same time.

"Oh, my," his mother said, her crochet hook still, her hazel eyes full of startled pride.

Kate closed her gaping mouth and emitted a long low wolf whistle.

Maybe the bucks had been worth it, Jack admitted, his face heating. He walked self-consciously to the coffee table and its stacked newspapers.

Vera Morgan laid her afghan on the floor. "Let me just get the camera...." She struggled to rise.

"*No.*" Jack and Kate said simultaneously, startling their mother into plopping back down.

"Well, you don't have to shout," Vera said, her expression wounded. "It's not a crime to want a picture of my handsome son, is it?"

"Lookin' very fine, brother," Kate agreed, grinning. "I can almost see what the girls at school gush about."

Jack wasn't a vain man, but he was human. He picked up the business section. "They gush?" he asked casually, scanning the front-page articles.

"Oh, yeah," Kate said. "According to them, you're too strict, too hard, too mean, too uptight—" she met his chagrined gaze above the newspaper "—too fine, too hunky, too buff, too fly." Sitting upright, she laughed and smoothed her mussed hair. "If you ever relaxed a little, I'd have to go to another school. I couldn't stand for all the gushing to be good. I'd throw up."

"Your brother has a fine reputation, Kate," Vera scolded. "You should worry more about what people say about *you,* hanging around that awful boy, dressing like you have no decent clothes, using *drugs* for goodness sake—"

"All *right,* Mom, I get the picture." The teasing sparkle had vanished from Kate's eyes, twisting Jack's heart.

He turned to his mother in exasperation. "Mrs. Dent told me only yesterday she's noticed a big improvement in Kate's attitude." He laid down the newspaper and glanced at his sister. "I meant to tell you, Kate."

She rolled her eyes. "Thanks for the bone." Her stony gaze turned to their mother. "Do you think maybe for tonight you could act like you're not ashamed of me?"

Vera looked stricken. "Kate, I'm not ashamed—"

"We'll be in my room most of the time, so you won't be put out too much."

"Who's we?" Jack asked warily. "Is someone coming over?"

His mother shot him a surprised glance. "You don't

know? Kate said you gave her permission to have a friend over.''

As one, Jack and his mother looked at Kate.

She picked at a circle of worn threads on the couch cushion. ''You said I couldn't go out with my friends. You never said they couldn't come *in* to see me.''

As one, Kate and his mother looked expectantly at Jack.

Well, hell, now what?

The doorbell rang.

Kate sprang up to answer it, no doubt sensing a reprieve.

Jack decided to let her manipulation slide. He didn't have the energy or the time right now to deal with it. Which, of course, was exactly what she'd planned.

''Be careful on the road,'' his mother said. Her subtle way of telling him she had no intention of greeting Donna. The two had talked on several occasions about Kate's behavior. No love lost there.

''I'll be careful. Good night, Mother.'' He headed for the small foyer just out of sight and arrived as Kate flung open the door.

''Hi, Ms. Kaiser,'' Kate said politely. ''Come on in. Jack's right here.''

Lovely in a slate blue dress that matched her eyes, Donna stepped into the small foyer.

''Hey,'' Kate said to someone behind the tall elegant redhead.

''Hi,'' a feminine contralto voice answered.

Jack's smile of greeting faltered. One word, but he

knew. *Sarah?* This was Kate's "friend"? *No, say it ain't so.*

But it was. Sarah moved into view, wearing tight jeans riding low on her curvy hips, and a tight purple T-shirt stopping inches short of her jeans. Her rumpled "outrageous red" hair glowed beneath the overhead entry light, stealing the show from Donna's auburn shoulder-length waves.

Why was Sarah here? Could he *never* get away from her? It took Jack a minute to realize he wasn't the only one speechless.

Sarah and Donna were staring at him in a way that said the bucks had definitely been worth it.

Standing nearby, Kate snorted. "Then again, some of them don't gush at all. They just swallow their tongues."

Donna smiled, her eyes soft with approval. "You look wonderful, Jack."

She was his date. He owed her his attention. "Thank you. And you look beautiful, as always. No problems finding the house?"

"No. Your directions were very clear. And Sarina's a good navigator."

"Really?" Jack finally allowed himself to look into jewel-bright eyes, ignoring the kick to his heart. "Hello, Sarina. I didn't realize you were coming over tonight." *What gives?* he asked silently.

Play along, her gaze pleaded, the next instant flashing teasingly at Kate. "Blame your sister, Mr. Morgan. Here I was trying to keep the school from knowing Donna's my cousin, and darned if she didn't answer my phone when Kate called this evening. She recognized Donna's voice right off.''

"Hey, you gave me the unlisted number," Kate protested. "You said I could call."

"And I meant it. Really. I'm *glad* you called."

Donna spoke up. "I'd stopped by to change clothes since Sarina lives so close to school. Once the cat was out of the bag, we thought this might work out well. Now Sarina can drive my car home...if you don't mind taking me to Gram's house after the play."

"No, of course not." He frowned meaningfully. "But should Sarina be driving alone at night?"

"She really wanted to get out of the house, Jack."

"Yo, Mr. Morgan, Donna. You're not my parents." Sarah's chin was up. A bad sign. "I'll leave by ten and be tucked in bed safe and sound by eleven."

Kate giggled.

Jack's gaze lowered to the strip of pale skin beneath her skimpy T-shirt, then focused on the belly button peeking above her jeans snap. A sexy little "innie" that prompted a sudden image of Sarah tucked in bed. And she wasn't wearing a long pink flannel nightgown.

"Hey, Sarah. Want a Coke?" Kate asked, yanking Jack's gaze and thoughts to safer areas. "I think we might have Diet Dr Pepper and Sprite, too."

"Diet Dr Pepper? Yeah, that sounds great."

"Follow me. The kitchen's right ahead. G'night, Ms. Kaiser. Night, Jack." Her gaze turned wickedly mischievous. "Don't do anything I wouldn't do."

Tossing her long dark hair, she got while the gettin'
was good.

Sarah started to follow, paused, then looked over
her shoulder at Donna. "I'll be careful," she said
softly. "You two have a good time, okay?"

Donna smiled brilliantly. "We will. I'll use my second set of car keys, so don't wait up."

Sarah nodded, her gaze moving to Jack a lingering
instant. His stomach tightened. Then she turned and
walked after his sister.

Had he imagined that wisp of longing in her eyes?

"We probably should be leaving," Donna suggested.

"Hmm? Oh, right. Sure you wouldn't like a drink
before we leave?"

"No thanks. Maybe some wine when we get to the
restaurant. Or…after the play?"

Most men would've killed to hear that subtle invitation. Smiling noncommittally, Jack waved her first
through the front door.

Helluva thing, to leave the house with a beautiful
woman for a romantic date, yet want to turn around
and go back inside to the kitchen for a Coke.

CHAPTER NINE

TRUE TO HER WORD, Sarah said good-night to Kate and left the Morgan's house by ten o'clock. By ten-thirty, she was walking up the stone pathway to the Kaiser guest house. By eleven, she was tucked in bed like a good little girl. Safe—but far from sound.

Her body rigid, her gaze fixed blindly on the ceiling fan humming above, she replayed those first few minutes in the foyer over...and over...in her head. She didn't know which image made her more miserable.

The one of Jack, stepping off the pages of *GQ* magazine with a virility no narcissist male model could fake. Or Donna, his beautiful perfect *Vogue* match. Or herself, looking tacky and feeling like a selfish petty little worm.

Seeing them together had made her writhe on a barbed hook of jealousy. Slipping off to extend a civil goodbye to the couple had nearly ripped out her guts. But she'd done it. Then made the mistake of sneaking a final glance over her shoulder just as Jack had ushered Donna out the door. The sight of his big hand splayed on her lower back had promptly rethreaded Sarah on the hook. And there was no one to blame but herself.

Donna had warned against leaving the guest house.

But no-o-o, Sarah couldn't stay put. So here she lay squirming, victim of her own stupidity and stubbornness.

Rising on one elbow, Sarah punched her pillow into a new shape, fell back, twisted this way and that, rose and punched some more. She finally settled down with a huff and glared at the whirring blur of motion above her head.

She'd been so curious about the household Jack headed on tax forms and in fact. So curious about the mother who'd abdicated responsibility for Kate. So curious about the place where he'd pursued big dreams in solitude. Where he'd created fictional worlds that transformed his usual sternness to impassioned animation. She'd been curious, and so very eager for any excuse to see him again.

In her defense, which she found herself needing desperately, she'd also responded to the restless boredom in Kate's voice when she'd called. A dangerous mood for an "imprisoned" teenager. The kind of mind-set that might've sent her crawling out a window to seek excitement.

The same kind of rebellion against confinement that had made Sarah reckless enough to accept Kate's invitation. Allowing her to see Donna and Jack together. The perfect couple.

Back full circle to the foyer scene. As repetitious as the turning fan blades. *Think about something else,* Sarah commanded herself, and Vera Morgan popped into mind. Scary, but diverting.

Talk about a piece of work! She'd come into the

kitchen after Jack and Donna had left and immediately found fault with everything Kate did.

Use the good glasses for company, not the plastic Astrodome cups. Refill the ice trays. Don't leave the cans on the counter. Watch out, you're spilling it! Honestly, Kate, why can't you be more careful?

Sarah had bitten her tongue to keep from interfering. It would only have embarrassed the girl more. To turn the woman's attention away from her daughter, Sarah had commented admiringly on the counter full of baked goods.

Five minutes later she was sampling a plateful of treats. Heavenly. Truly outstanding. She refused to dwell now on why she'd pigged out when normally she exercised restraint. She would think, not about the foyer scene, but about the way her genuine praise had transformed Vera's irritated expression into one of delight. She'd spoken of experimental recipes as if they were beloved children.

Remembering, Sarah's heart ached for Kate, who hadn't received a loving word all night.

Wait…was that a car door slamming? Sarah strained in the dark to listen. Were those faint voices? Oh, hell, she couldn't hear. She'd parked Donna's car in the driveway outside the security gates a good distance from the guest house.

It was too early for them to be back, wasn't it? Unless Jack had driven her straight here from the theater. No, they were probably extending the evening at some romantic club, or hotel bar…or hotel room….

Aaargh! If she stared at the ceiling another second,

she'd go crazy. A cup of herbal tea might ease her restlessness. Yeah, that would do the trick.

She tossed back the covers, marched across the plush carpet and jerked open the bedroom door. Shadowy shapes in various sizes filled the dark living area. Her big toe unerringly found the end table as she passed by. Cursing, she hobbled toward the kitchen light switch.

A nice hot cup of tea. Just the thing to take her mind off car doors— *What was that?* Dammit, she was tired of safe walls and dangerous thoughts, outrageous red hair and nice hot tea, Jack's hands on Donna....

Veering away, she snatched her jacket off a bar stool and limped to the front door. She couldn't take the waiting another minute!

A breath of fresh air. That was what she needed. A brisk walk to clear her head of all these unwanted thoughts. She opened the door, slipped through, then eased it oh-so-carefully shut. No sense disturbing the elderly Mrs. Kaiser. Or Jack and Donna, if they were in the driveway. She would keep well away from that area.

Brrr. She yanked on her jacket and hugged her arms. Stars glittered against an inky backdrop; the sharp air bit deep in her lungs. Standing on the small porch, her bare feet shifting on the frigid concrete, she considered going back inside.

The sound of deep laughter rolled across the landscaped grounds to her porch.

Sarah moved toward the source, heedless of the rough stone walkway, the cold prickle of dead St. Augustine grass. Suddenly she was near the electronic driveway gate. She ducked out of sight behind the adjacent evergreen ligustrum bushes.

Déjà vu. She'd done this once before. Skulked behind bushes and watched two figures in the night. Then, she'd been gripped by horror and fear. Now, she battled a complex mix of guilt, jealousy and dread.

Jack and Donna stood by her parked car on the other side of the gate. Her bottom pressed against the passenger door. Her torso leaned slightly forward. Jack faced her a step away, one hand in his pocket, his stance relaxed. Their voices were low. The words indistinguishable. The tone hushed. And intimate.

They were building up to a good-night kiss. Observing date protocol with a little conversation first. A few soft smiles. Innocent touches. Laughing softly, Donna reached out and gave his lapel a flirtatious tweak.

In that moment, Sarah hated her beautiful friend—almost as much as she hated herself. She couldn't bear to watch. She couldn't make herself look away. Writhing on that hellish hook, she bargained with God.

If it's a long, passionate kiss, I'll be good and leave their relationship alone. But if it's short and sweet, he's fair game. I'll tell him Mark is history, and pursue this attraction I can't control.

The voices stopped. Sarah's breathing sounded loud in her ears.

Donna opened her arms and Jack moved up to fill them. Her head tilted up, his came down.

One-Mississippi, two-Mississippi, three-Miss—

His head lifted along with Sarah's gladdened heart. She'd been right! He'd felt this powerful thing between them and couldn't respond to another woman. She started to smile just as his head slowly lowered.

One-Mississippi, two-Mississippi, three-Mississippi, four-Mississippi, five-Mississippi, six...

Squeezing her lids shut, Sarah turned away, the sharp pain in her chest unrelated to the cold air. When she could breathe again, she opened her eyes and slunk away like the Peeping Worm she was. Moving low and silent, even if Jack and Donna were too engrossed in each other to hear beyond their pounding hearts.

Sarah reached her front porch, opened the door, slipped inside and locked herself in. Five minutes later she was tucked in bed like a good little girl.

Safe. But far from sound.

FROM HIS CURBSIDE Volvo, Jack watched Donna back her car out of the long pebbled driveway. Once in the street, she shifted gears, gave him a little smile and wave, then drove off out of sight.

Reluctantly, helplessly, his gaze turned to the fancy wrought-iron driveway gate. Beyond and to the left, in the guest house tucked out of sight, Sarah slept. Peaceful. Oblivious to his proximity. Untroubled by confusion or frustrated desire.

He ripped his gaze away and looked back at the empty street. Poor Donna. He'd used her as a guinea pig just now. Then tried to correct his mistake by warning he wasn't looking for a serious relationship.

What a tired old line. But one she'd accepted with grace. Too much grace.

All that benevolence made him damned nervous. As if she knew all men said they weren't serious at first but soon he would feel differently.

Cursing, he opened the car door, slid into the seat, then banged his forehead twice against the wheel. This mess was his own stupid fault. If he'd left well enough alone after the first kiss, Donna wouldn't have any false hope where he was concerned. Their first kiss tonight had matched the one they'd shared last week. Affectionate, brief and chaste.

But no-o-o, he'd decided to try again, this time giving it one hundred percent. Determined to prove that, given a chance with an attractive woman—*any* attractive woman—his body would respond with passion. That was the theory, anyway.

Well, Donna was drop-dead gorgeous. His body had gotten a helluva chance to respond. And he'd felt nothing more than a pleasant stirring of warmth. Not a fraction of what he'd experienced when Sarah had simply run her fingernail along his jaw.

Jack inserted the car key grimly and started the engine with a roar. Sarah had looked for and found a serious relationship. In Dallas. With a guy named Mark. Who was waiting right now for Sarah's fingernails to come home to Papa and work their magic.

In a little less than four months she would testify at the trial. Return to her life. Be out of Jack's for good.

And maybe, if he kept his distance in the meantime, they would *both* be safe and sound.

SARAH SLID her lunch tray along the metal bars and eyed the deli sandwiches. After six weeks of going through this cafeteria line, she could find her choices blindfolded.

She reached out, paused, and diverted her hand to the left. What were a few extra calories on a Monday that already sucked? At the cash register, she pulled out her wallet.

"Uh, Sarina, you realize that's not a turkey sandwich, don't you?"

"Yeah, Roger. See, turkey is white. But this meat is red. I figured out it must be something else." She handed over her money and sighed at the boy's fierce blush. "I'm sorry. It's been a bad day, but I shouldn't take it out on you." There were several other candidates, however, who deserved the brunt of her mood. Right now Bruce Logan was at the top of her list.

Roger handed back Sarah's change. "No problem. I have a *lot* of bad days," he said, smiling.

Sarah blinked, then broke into a grin. "*Roger,* when did you get your braces off?"

"Friday." He smiled wider, exposing at least twenty-four of his thirty-two straightened teeth, plus a subtle new air of confidence. "I was wondering if you'd notice."

"Are you kidding? Not notice a great smile like that? Lookin' good, dude!" She lifted her tray and turned. "Laurie's gonna have to guard you like a Doberman," she teased, referring to his new girlfriend.

Her steps were lighter as she walked away. Roger did look great. Especially with the dramatic improvement in his complexion. She'd talked to Donna, who'd talked to the school nurse, who'd talked to Roger's parents, who weren't morons at all. Simply stressed-out working parents trying to squeeze too many needs into a limited amount of time and money.

Somehow, bless their hearts, they'd managed to include dermatologist appointments in the budget. And Sarah's small part in boosting Roger's self-esteem felt great. Better than when she'd helped her NBA client land a huge cereal endorsement contract. Ironic. Possibly very important. But she'd have to explore the idea later.

Not while walking to her table. Not when she needed to begin her daily lecture. *Don't do it, Sarah. You've made it this far without cracking. Just go to your seat. You'll see him this afternoon in class....*

But somewhere to her right, Jack was standing against the far wall. *Now.* And her craving was as powerful as a chain smoker's need to inhale that first drag in the morning. She resisted for three more straining seconds.

And then she looked.

Their gazes connected. An electric bridge of awareness leaped between them. Crackled and sizzled. Penetrated tissue, blood and bones down to her very DNA.

And then he looked away.

Always he looked away. Always she doubted what she'd seen and felt. Always she told herself that tomorrow, she wouldn't look and put herself through this torture again.

Since the night he'd kissed Donna, Sarah had

watched her friend pursue Jack, watched him sidestep capture yet stay within range. She hadn't interfered in the least. She'd simply died a little each day. Unable to stop the cancerous longing killing her cell by cell.

Shaking off her morbid thoughts, Sarah approached her lunch table. Thank God for these kids. Without their healing presence, there'd be nothing left of her in three months, when she had to appear at John's murder trial.

She set down her tray to a unison chorus of "Sarina!" What had started out as a joke—mimicking the way bar patrons greeted Norm on the classic TV show "Cheers"—was now a daily ritual. As usual, it made her smile.

She sat between Elaine and Kate, and conversations all around picked up where they'd left off at Sarah's arrival.

"Uh-oh," Elaine murmured, eyeing Sarah's tray knowingly. "Anything over five-hundred calories means something's wrong. What happened?"

A month ago, Elaine never would've thought twice about food other than its taste. Now, she removed the last of the cheese, egg and ham cubes from her chef's salad, then added a packet of diet dressing to what was left.

She also waited patiently for an answer, undeterred by Sarah's silence.

"I created a monster," Sarah grumbled, unwrapping her corned beef sandwich and taking a bite. When she finished moaning in ecstasy, she relented. "If you must know what's wrong, on the way to the cafeteria I had a little run-in with Bruce.''

Literally. One minute she'd had her head down moving full speed, the next she'd barreled into his brawny chest.

On her left, the forkful of mashed potatoes rising to Kate's mouth stopped in midair. ''What did he want?''

Sarah faced the girl grimly. ''He wanted to be sure I knew about his little party on Friday. He said you'll be there. And that his parents won't.''

Kate lowered her fork and flushed. ''I told him I would think about it, that's all.''

Sarah bit back a dozen heated protests. ''Good. Then there's no problem. Because if you *think* about it, you won't go.''

She'd grown very fond of Kate in her own right, regardless of the interest she held as Jack's little sister. Sarah hadn't visited the girl's house since that first time, but they talked regularly in home ec class and on the phone.

Elaine spoke up. ''There's something you're not telling us. What else did Bruce say?''

''Oh, just his usual crude macho stuff. Nothing I couldn't handle.'' Sarah took a huge bite to forestall more questions.

Elaine knew Bruce baited Sarah at every opportunity. What the girl didn't know was that his size, hostility and conscienceless eyes rattled her more than she ever admitted. Today he'd defined exactly what kind of fun he intended to have with Kate, and Sarah's stomach had turned.

He was completely capable of using an innocent girl to get back at her, Sarah knew. She vowed to keep closer tabs on Kate in the next week.

"Hey, Sarina?" Janice called from across the table, a welcome interruption. "The prom committee meets after school today, doesn't it?"

Donna was the adult supervisor of the student committee, and had roped Sarah into joining the group. "No, the meeting's tomorrow. Why?"

"I heard Wendy wants to have a Barbie and Ken decoration theme. You'll fight her on it, won't you?" Janice persisted over the loud groans around her. "I refuse to have my picture made next to a cardboard cutout of Ken—with me looking down on his head."

Sarah laughed along with the others, glad the tall girl was learning to relax a little about her height. "I don't know how much influence I have, but I'll do my best."

"I heard Wendy wants to *be* Barbie for the night, with Tony as Ken," Derek piped up. "People who want to can have their pictures taken with them. Sort of like a celebrity impersonator thing."

Kate opened her mouth and made a gagging motion with her index finger.

"I'd rather get my picture taken with a purple dinosaur," Elaine muttered.

"I dunno," Beto protested. "Maybe we're bein' a little callous, here. This is my only chance to snuggle next to a sexy blond babe. Who knows? I might get lucky."

Fred pushed up his glasses. "If I remember my Barbie anatomy, you'll need more than luck to get lucky. She'll need radical surgery.''

The girls groaned, the boys cackled.

Sarah looked Fred in the eye, not easy to do through one-inch lenses. ''We need to work on your social life, son.''

He popped a corn chip into his mouth and shrugged. ''I had sisters. They left their dolls lying around. I did what little brothers do.''

''Yeah, be a little creep,'' Janice said.

Sarah grinned. ''Here's an idea for the prom theme. How about *Guys and Dolls*? Whatd'ya think, Fred?'' She got a chip thrown in her face for her weak attempt at humor. Tasty, with her corned beef sandwich. Maybe she should try another joke.

''Can we forget the doll thing?'' Fred asked in a pained voice. ''Somebody please change the subject.''

''I heard Mr. Morgan is sleeping with Ms. Kaiser,'' Derek obliged, then stuffed an entire Oreo in his mouth.

Sarah swallowed her bite of sandwich unchewed. It hit her stomach like a deadweight.

''Why's everybody staring at me like that?'' Derek asked, his voice muffled by cookie.

Beto snorted. ''Because it's not polite to talk with a full mouth and an empty head. Jeez, man, I really wonder about you.'' He nodded toward Kate, who looked as uncomfortable as Sarah felt.

The lightbulb finally clicked on. ''O-o-oh. Sorry, Kate. I forget sometimes that Mr. Morgan is your brother. You never talk about him.''

"I know. It's okay," Kate said stiffly. "Jack and Ms. Kaiser have dated some, but it's nothing serious. Who told you they were sleeping together?"

Derek's look of fierce concentration was comical. Then his features relaxed. "Lisa Meyer. Tyler Wilkes told Lisa that Karen Polk told *Tyler* that her older sister lives in the same condominium complex as Ms. Kaiser. Anyway, Karen's sister saw a tall dark-haired man leaving Ms. Kaiser's house about 3:00 a.m. this Sat— Well, I guess that would be Sunday. Karen figured it might be Mr. Morgan, since Ms. Kaiser's always flirting with him at school."

Sarah was paying already for eating that heavy corned beef sandwich. Her stomach churned. Voices faded behind the louder buzz of her thoughts.

According to Donna, she avoided Jack at school, knowing administration would frown on any blatant personal relationship. She'd often complained about how hard it was to keep her distance. Only she must not've done a very good job. So much for discretion.

And so much for Sarah's secret fantasy. For weeks she'd nurtured the disloyal wish that Jack would abandon his principles and battle for "Mark's" woman. Now she knew that would never happen. Jack had apparently claimed his own woman this past weekend. In so doing, he'd killed Sarah's last faint hope.

Along with a few hundred million of her cells.

THAT AFTERNOON at the beginning of fifth period class, Jack checked attendance, then rounded his desk to sit on one corner.

He waited until he had everyone's full attention. "The schedule I handed out the first week of school announced a final theme paper due in two weeks." Noting the panic or distaste on most faces, he added, "I want you to take the assignment off the list."

A beat of silence, then an outbreak of smiles and pleased exclamations.

"Whoa, now," Jack cautioned, raising a palm. "Before you celebrate, I have a new assignment to review with you." He slipped off the desk, scooped up a stack of papers from his Out box, then gave students at the head of each row a sheaf to pass back. He sensed an ugly shift in mood, but pretended not to notice.

He'd done a lot of thinking since the day Sarah had criticized his by-the-book manner of grading a multiple choice quiz. What, he'd asked himself, would writing a theme paper on *The Grapes of Wrath* teach his kids? English composition? How to organize their thoughts? A few universal themes, garnered from class notes or good ol' Cliffs?

Maybe. But would they learn anything relating to their lives? Anything they would remember one week after turning in their papers?

He hadn't felt comfortable with the answer. Or with the fact that Sarah was making him question his teaching methods. But if she was right, he couldn't sacrifice what was best for students in the interest of his pride.

When everyone had a copy of the assignment, he reclaimed his desk corner perch. This must be how Coach Clark felt preparing his football players before a big game. Excited. Anxious to motivate good performance without applying too much pressure.

As Jack's "team" quietly read the assignment, he did what he'd wanted to do since the class bell had rung. He looked at Sarah.

Now that his first electric glimpse of her for the day was behind him, he could study her with some emotional detachment. She seemed pale and...oddly subdued. Almost shaken. Had something frightened her? He'd seen Donna Saturday, and she hadn't mentioned any reason to be alarmed for Sarah's safety.

Students began shifting in their seats.

Frowning, Jack dragged his gaze to a more neutral location, his thoughts reluctantly back to the task at hand: explaining the assignment.

"Okay, as you can see, we're trying something a little different, here. A little more interesting, I hope, than the usual theme paper. I want you to look around at your environment—home, school, community—and focus on one person or aspect of society. Then compare your selection with a character or social condition described in *The Grapes of Wrath*."

Ignoring the hostile, bewildered or bored expressions on many faces, he forged gamely ahead. "I've given you some examples of possible ideas, but you're not held to them by any means. I expect you to research your topic and give me your own interpretation, not somebody else's."

He glanced at Sarah, who didn't look up or acknowledge his emphasis on individual interpretation. Somehow he'd thought she would be pleased.

Disappointed, he scanned the other students. "Now, who has questions?"

Did Coach Clark's players ever look like these kids, as if they'd been handed play patterns for hockey instead of football? Somehow Jack doubted it.

He waited grimly, relieved when a hand crept up. "Yes, Jessica?"

"I don't understand," she said, apathy in her tone, in the finger twirling a lock of sandy blond hair around and around.

Patience, he counseled himself. "What don't you understand?"

"Any of it. Can we do the old theme assignment if we want? I understood that." The accusation in her gaze clipped Jack at the knees.

"Yeah, that assignment was better," Tony grumbled.

"This is too hard," a shadow jock agreed.

"Why'd you change it, anyway?" Kim whined, a third body heaped on the pile.

Bruised and deflated, Jack rolled out from under in time to see another hand raise. "Go ahead, Beto," he said wearily.

"I like the new assignment better. If I do it, can I get extra credit?"

The Hispanic boy's air of contained excitement roused Jack's suspicions. "You want to do the new assignment?" he asked, expecting a punchline.

"Yeah. *Mi abuela,* my grandmother, see, she met my grandfather in McAllen when she was picking grapefruit. Her family moved from crop to crop all over the Rio Grande Valley. They were migrant work-ers, just like all those people we've been reading about."

Mentally pushing himself up from the ground, Jack stood and brushed off his backside. "I'm with you. Go on."

"Well, I've been asking her about how her life was. You know, if it was as bad as what the Joads went through? And she has some real cool stories. I could maybe use some of them for this assignment." Beto paused, looking anxious. "That's sort of what you're looking for, isn't it?"

Jack felt like spiking a football and wobbling his knees in a victory dance.

He settled for breaking into a huge smile. "That's exactly the kind of thing I'm looking for! It sounds like the start of a great paper," he said sincerely, amazed at the light of pride in eyes that were normally mischievous. "You won't get extra credit, but you might get the only decent grade in the class."

Jack's challenging gaze swept over Beto's peers. "Come on, people. Someone else give me an idea to bounce around."

He searched out the one person he could count on for lively discussion, the student who *always* voiced her thoughts and opinions. "Sarina, what are you thinking about focusing on for this assignment?"

For the first time since lunch, Sarah looked at Jack directly…and wiped all thoughts of assignments from his mind.

CHAPTER TEN

PAIN DARKENED Sarah's eyes to deep sapphire.

The next instant, Jack wondered if he'd imagined the emotion. Right now her gaze was steady and inscrutable.

"I don't know what I'll write about," she said evenly. "I'm not sure I understand the assignment, yet."

A lie, of course. Jack normally had to stay on his toes to keep up with Sarah. What was going on, here? "Really?"

At least she had the grace to flush.

"Then let me try and make it clearer," Jack said, quelling an irrational sense of betrayal. He forced himself to look away and scan other faces. "Did any of you recognize someone you know, a friend or relative, maybe, in one of Steinbeck's characters? Did a particular scene make you feel a strong emotion? If it did, you're probably identifying with some experience you've had personally."

Jessica's sudden alert expression caught Jack's attention. "What is it, Jessica?" he asked. "Did you want to share something with the class?" *Anything. Please. I'm dying up here.*

"Well…" Jessica twirled that same lock of hair, this time in agitation.

"We're brainstorming. Nothing's a dumb idea," he assured her. "I mentioned identifying with a character through personal experience. Did that happen to you?"

She nodded, her finger still rotating. "My dad, like, lost his job last year? He's working, now," she added hastily. "But when I was reading the book, about how, like, Tom Joad and all the others tried to find a good job and couldn't? And like, how much their pride was hurt? I thought of, you know, my dad. But, I don't think I could write about that."

Jack suspected she was worried about embarrassing her father. "How about exploring the differences in the way the Joads looked for work during The Great Depression, as compared with how your dad eventually found a job? I imagine he didn't sit around waiting for one to fall in his lap, did he?"

"No-o. He mailed out resumés, used the Internet—lots of stuff." Her frown cleared. She slipped her finger out of a long corkscrew curl. "Yeah, I could ask him about that. Hey, this could be kinda cool."

Rich satisfaction fueled Jack's grin. "Yeah, it could be. Sounds like you've got your topic." He looked around with renewed hope. "Anyone else have a question or idea?"

Several hands went up at once.

It was one of those times in a teacher's life that make up for all the useless administrative meetings, the endless hours of filling out reports and grading papers, the frustration of battling student apathy or downright insolence. Once kicked open, the door to these kids' imaginations released a stimulating variety of ideas.

Not everyone vocalized his or her thoughts. Most notably, Sarah, who remained unresponsive. But he knew instinctively that he'd engaged his other students' interest in a way the original theme paper assignment never would have accomplished.

Invigorated, Jack was shocked to check the clock and see only five minutes remained until the bell. "All right, class. Don't let time get away from you on this project. You'll need every bit of the next two weeks to get me your first draft. I'll help with the composition, but *content* better be there. Understand?"

Unlike at the beginning of class, the grumbles now were good-natured in tone. When Tony's hand popped up, Jack smiled and nodded permission to speak.

"I wanted to remind you I'll be out three days next week, Mr. Morgan," Tony said, his dark gaze uneasy.

Jack's smile vanished. He remembered. Tony was visiting several college campuses intent on wooing him to play for their team. Jack hadn't liked agreeing to excuse the star quarterback's absence, but a full scholarship was an opportunity not to be passed up.

"What's your point, Tony?" Jack asked.

"Well, this new assignment will take a lot more time than the old one would've. I've got two other big projects to turn in the week I leave…"

Jack hardened his heart. This kid would have assignments in college that interfered with his football demands, too. "Then you'd better get started right away on this one, huh? I'll expect your first draft on my desk by the end of school next Tuesday."

"But—" Tony darted red-faced glances at his classmates then looked entreatingly at Jack. "Can I talk to you after class—?"

"There's nothing to discuss, Tony. Knowing how to throw a football doesn't give you special privileges in my class. The due date is next Friday. If you can't deliver, you'll accept the consequences."

The shrill bell signaled a discordant ending to an otherwise harmonious class session. Tony sprang up, hoisted his backpack in an angry motion, then stalked out into the hall ahead of his classmates.

Disturbed and guilty, second-guessing his tried and true methods *again,* Jack searched among the exiting students for Sarah.

Trailing at the end of the line, she met his gaze. If looks could do bodily harm, he'd be mortally wounded. Or maimed, at the very least.

Bracing himself for battle, he waited until she passed nearby. "Sarina, could I talk to you a minute?"

She stopped, her chin going up. "I'll be late to my next class."

"I'll write you a note." The next hour was his plan period. No students would be rushing in before the next bell. "Please. I won't keep you long."

Obviously reluctant, she nodded and crossed her arms, the action swelling her hot pink ribbed-knit shirt.

He'd seen larger breasts in his classes, but knowing these were twenty-seven years old made a huge moral difference. And knowing they were Sarah's made them impossible to ignore.

"I'm up here, Jack," she said in a hard angry voice.

He hadn't blushed so hard since his mother had caught him flipping through *Playboy* when he was ten. His gaze lifted.

Her eyes matched her voice. "Tony's the one you should be talking to now. Why wouldn't you have the courtesy to meet with him after class?"

Struggling for composure, Jack slid off the edge of his desk, grabbing even so small an advantage as height with shameless gratitude. "Because he would've been wasting both our time. Sarah, if somebody at WorldWide Public Relations missed an important deadline—say, forgot to confirm a TV talk show appearance—the client wouldn't care *why* he got replaced on the show—only that he got screwed. Tony's been coasting on charm, good looks and athletic ability his entire high school career. I make him work for what he gets."

"You don't think he's worked for that scholarship? You don't think he's spent hours and hours of grueling practice on the field, not to mention study time learning the play book? This trip next week is what he's been working for, Jack. His *dream*. You, of all people, should understand that. Maybe bend the rules a little this one time." She let out a long aggrieved breath.

A fist of outrage squeezed his chest. "What happens if Tony doesn't make the pros and has to earn a living like mortal men? He'll have to manage multiple re-

sponsibilities. No excuses. No fun. No bending of the
rules to bail him out of his obligations."

Jack endured a probing look that seemed to reach
and study his very soul.

Sarah lowered her arms, comprehension dawning in
her gaze. "My God, you're jealous."

Jack flinched. *"What?"*

"You are. You're jealous. Of a kid who's about to
fulfill his dream right out of high school. Like you
never had the chance to do. You're jealous of *all* these
kids, for having the carefree youth, the fun you
should've had, but were robbed of enjoying." She ran
polished hot pink fingernails through clashing red hair,
then spoke as if to herself. "That's what Morgan's Ten
Commandments is all about. That's where this obsession you have with responsibility is coming from."

Jack managed a strangled laugh. "Right. I don't
want them to be prepared for the real world when they
graduate. Everything I do is based on a petty grudge.
Thanks for the free analysis, Doc." He regrouped to
launch a counterattack. "As long as you're at it,
what's your theory on why you clammed up in class
today?"

She couldn't hide her consternation quite fast
enough. "I don't know what you mean."

He charged ahead. "Sure you do. Usually I can't
shut you up. But today, when I could've really used
some blocking protection, you played dumb and let
me get sacked on my ass. What was that all about,
hmm?"

Shrugging, she appeared fascinated with the wall

clock. "I was having a bad day. I didn't feel like talking."

Her pale cheeks reminded him of how she'd first looked in class—subdued and shaken. Jack's offensive direction shifted. "Sarah, did you see something recently that scared you?" A sudden thought lowered his brows. "Has someone been nosing around Donna asking questions again?"

"The only one sniffing around Donna these days is *you*," Sarah snapped, sarcasm dripping in her voice, hurt shimmering in her eyes. She hitched up her backpack straps and headed for the door.

Hurt shimmered in her eyes?

Jack caught up in two strides, passed her in three and turned to block her path. The bell rang shrilly, jangling nerves that had gone into full alert mode.

Sarah tried to move around him. They danced awkwardly a few eternal seconds.

At last she stopped, growled in frustration and flung back her head. "Move out of my way," she ordered, her voice loud enough to be heard from the hallway.

Anyone passing by could come through the open door to investigate. This sure as hell wouldn't look good, considering his reputation. He should let her leave and maybe call her at the guest house later.

"What did you mean, I'm the only one sniffing around Donna?" he asked, catching a whiff of peaches that made Donna's favored perfume seem cloying and heavy.

"Oh, puh-leeze." Violet eyes rolled. Color bloomed

high on pale cheeks. "Let's not have this conversation. Donna deserves better."

His tense muscles grew tighter. "What has Donna told you about our relationship, Sarah?" It was suddenly important—no, *imperative* that he know.

"Nothing. That's between you two. We don't discuss y'all's love life."

"Love life?" He jammed his hands in his pockets so they wouldn't reach out and shake her silly. "There *is* no love life to discuss. We date casually. I've been up-front with her from the beginning about not wanting a more serious relationship. If she's told you anything different, then she's lying."

Confusion clouded those lovely dark-lashed eyes. "But..." Sarah's cheeks matched her hot pink sweater.

"But *what*, dammit! What do you think you know?"

"The sister of a girl who goes to school here said she saw a tall dark-haired man leaving Donna's condominium on Saturday. Sunday, actually, around 3:00 a.m. Rumor says it was you."

"*Rumor* says." Disillusionment cooled his temper and chilled his voice. "And you believed hearsay?"

Her guilty expression said she had.

"I took Donna to a movie on Saturday, then had a cup of coffee and a fat-free donut inside her condo. I left around eleven-thirty. Any man this sister of a student saw later sure as hell wasn't me." He eyed Sarah closely. "You *do* believe me, don't you?"

"Donna's a beautiful woman," Sarah sidestepped

his question. "You're telling me that after all this time, you're satisfied with a fat-free donut at the end of your dates?"

No, goddamn it. But the only woman who can satisfy the hunger I've got is you.

He'd already explained the innocent nature of his relationship with Donna. He lowered his hands and walked slowly to his desk. Where was that pad? Ah, here. Now where was his *goddamn* pen hiding? He'd left the thing—ah, there it was.

Snatching the Bic from under his calendar, he scribbled a quick note, ripped off the top sheet and turned, nearly whacking Sarah in the nose. When had she moved up?

She stepped back marginally, her gaze urgent. "Jack, I'm sorry. I shouldn't have jumped to conclusions. I *don't* believe the rumor, not if you say you're not slee—not serious about Donna. I guess after I saw you kiss her that time, I naturally—"

"Whoa, whoa, whoa." Jack narrowed his eyes. "*What* time?"

Her gaze filled with horrified dismay.

How very interesting. "Sarah, when did you ever see me kiss Donna?"

Shaking her head, she backed away.

He followed. "When, Sarah?"

Her rear hit a desktop and she stopped, her eyes huge.

A step away, he mentally reviewed his dates with Donna. There was only one opportunity Sarah could have seen them. "In Mrs. Kaiser's driveway," Jack murmured. "You were watching us from somewhere behind the gate," he said incredulously, an impossible hope igniting deep within him.

Her chin came up, pugnacious and adorable. "I was taking a walk. You happened to come home as I reached the gate. I didn't want to embarrass us all, so I..."

"Hid and spied on us," he finished for her. The flickering hope inside him steadied into a low flame. "Now, why would you do that, Sarah?"

"I *told* you. I didn't want to—"

"Embarrass us, right." It was all he could do to keep from dropping tiny kisses over the bright pink face clashing with her hair. "So, you saw me kiss Donna and assumed I was sleeping with her. That's quite a leap in logic, don't you think?"

"It was the *way* you kissed her, Jack! Don't play dumb with me. What was I supposed to think after you tried to remove her tonsils with your tongue?" She looked like a spitting orange tabby cat, mad enough to scratch out his eyes.

And he wanted to try to remove her tonsils with his tongue so badly he couldn't see straight. "You're jealous," he stated, grinning.

She paled. "In your dreams, buddy."

Every night, sweetheart. "You are, you're jealous!" He laughed, his heart pumping hot and wild.

Her hand arced out and raked the note from his fingers. Glaring, she gave his chest a great shove, then scampered for the door.

Jack watched her enter the hallway and veer out of sight, his big goofy smile still going strong.

She didn't like him dating or kissing Donna. Didn't like it *at all*. He didn't know exactly what he'd do with the information, only that he'd definitely do *something*. And that the interesting new possibilities wouldn't fill his dreams at night. Uh-uh. No. Not this time.

To dream, first he'd have to fall asleep. There wasn't a chance in hell of that happening tonight.

HER ARMS PUMPING, her stride forceful, Elaine felt her stiff muscles begin to warm and loosen up. In an hour, track team practice would start. A good incentive to push herself faster.

The February day was balmy enough for her gym shorts and T-shirt. Another few minutes in this heat and she'd be sweating buckets. Yet an overnight cold front was expected to drop temperatures below freezing. People in Houston always told visitors, "If you don't like the weather, stick around five minutes and it'll change."

Rounding the first turn, Elaine glanced down at the tousled red-orange hair bobbing beside her on the track. "So, what did Mr. Morgan want to see you about after class today?" she asked breathily.

She didn't wheeze like a cow in labor any more, but she was a long way from being in peak condition. Four steps later she realized her friend hadn't answered.

"Sarina, what's wrong? Did you get in trouble with Mr. Morgan?"

"Trouble?" Sarina's brief laugh sounded a little wild. "Nah, he wanted to know why I was so quiet during the class discussion, is all. Can you believe it? He didn't ask *you* that, and you hardly said a word. But *I* don't tell him how great his new assignment is, and something must be wrong with me. I don't answer you just now, and something must be wrong with me." She slanted up an indignant glare. "Do I talk that much usually?"

Elaine concentrated on the goalpost to her left until her urge to smile passed. "I don't know what you mean by 'that much.' You usually have an opinion, which is good. Class is tons more fun since you transferred here," she said sincerely. "I think it's sweet that Mr. Morgan was worried about you."

"Sweet?" Sarina accelerated from power walk to a near jog.

Elaine watched ruefully as the petite girl surged ahead. Her own top speed—which had increased considerably in a month—was still holding Sarina back. Yet she never complained or seemed disgusted. She never acted superior or treated Elaine like a charity case in need of guidance.

Elaine was the one who'd asked a million questions in the past month. About the seminar that had forced Sarina to focus on her good traits instead of her flaws. About the difference that made in how she'd treated herself. Elaine had asked for specifics, and only then had Sarina proven to be a walking encyclopedia of information on how to look and feel better.

In all fairness, Elaine's parents had told her a lot of the same stuff for years. Only they acted as if they would love her more if she followed their advice. Whereas this way cool girl from California seemed to like her exactly as she was right now. Weird, how that made Sarina's help so much easier to take.

A movement up ahead near the huge tan brick gym building caught her eye. The locker room door had opened, and a boy in sweatpants and no shirt came out to begin a series of leg stretches. Tony Baldovino! She'd know him anywhere.

Sarina immediately slowed and fell back into step beside Elaine. "Okay, don't panic. This is no big deal. We're gonna do the eight laps like we said, right?"

Sarina had suggested they bump up the distance they walked from one and a half miles to two, starting today. Elaine had been kind of excited about the challenge.

Until now.

"I should've worn sweatpants," she said miserably, tugging down the shorts legs creeping up her thighs.

"Tony's no different from the other athletes we see out here. He's only interested in his own workout. He'll barely notice us."

Maybe. But Elaine didn't have a crush on the track team guys who showed up early for practice.

Tony finished stretching and jogged slowly to the track. Catching sight of them, he broke into the white crooked grin that always speeded up Elaine's pulse, which was bad enough when she was sitting still. Right now, her heart was cracking a few ribs and pounding the air from her lungs.

She started wheezing, louder than any cow in labor. Could a whale wheeze underwater? That's what she felt like. A big blubbery whale.

"Elaine, *look* at me," Sarina ordered. "That's right. Now breathe with me. In—" she drew a slow deep breath, her gaze never leaving Elaine's "—now out. In...now out."

Elaine mimicked her friend's breathing pattern, and that awful I'm-gonna-pass-out feeling went away. The sound of thudding feet behind them widened her eyes. Her breathing faltered.

"Don't you dare," Sarina warned darkly. "In... out. In...out."

Tony moved up beside Sarina and matched their pace, his hands fisted, his arms swinging in an exaggerated parody of theirs. "Hi, girls. Am I doin' this right?"

"Only if you're trying to look even more stupid than us," Sarina said, grinning. "Or, if you're trying to work out your frustrations through exercise." She pumped her arms as if uppercutting an invisible punching beg. "Just pretend Mr. Morgan is a half step ahead. Works for me, anyway."

Tony laughed. "Not a bad idea. But a hard run is what usually works best for me. Y'all have fun, though. See ya around."

"Every quarter mile would be my guess," Sarina agreed.

He laughed again and took off with a little wave before Elaine could find the wits to say a word. She watched the muscles in his back ripple, the lean grace of his ground-eating lope, until he rounded the upcoming turn out of her direct line of vision.

"Now see, that wasn't so bad, was it?" Sarina asked mildly.

"Only because *you* were here." Elaine tugged down her shorts legs, then resumed swinging her arms. "If it'd been just me, his teasing would have been even worse."

"Probably so."

Startled, Elaine cast a wounded glance at her friend. Sarina's expression was compassionate, but no-nonsense. "Elaine, you might as well tape a sign on your back that says, Kick Me. You *expect* to be made fun of. You *expect* to be a victim. As long as you feel like that, your expectations will probably come true."

For the first time since she'd met Sarina, Elaine experienced a flash of hot anger toward the girl. "You make it sound as if I *want* to be hurt, as if I have a choice. Well, I don't!"

"Sure, you do."

Elaine's breathing was getting ragged, again, but she didn't give a damn. "You've seen Wendy in action. I haven't done anything to her. I *sure* haven't asked her to treat me like dirt. I don't know *why* she does."

"She treats you like dirt because you let her, Elaine. She's a bully. Bullies trample over anyone who lets them. And yes, sometimes even over people who fight back. The difference is, when you fight back, you keep your self-respect. Trust me, I know what I'm talking about.''

The self-contempt in her voice penetrated Elaine's aggrieved sense of betrayal. Had Sarina ever not fought back? Elaine couldn't imagine such a thing.

After a brief pause laden with tension, Sarina continued. ''But even kind people will treat us—meaning you, me, anyone—as we *allow* ourselves to be treated. Take just now with Tony, for example.''

Elaine stared silently ahead, her eyes stinging, the white lane stripes blurring into red clay. Sweat, she told herself angrily.

''Tony's a nice guy. Cocky—but nice,'' Sarina said. ''Yet he was primed and ready to make fun of us. Who could resist? We *do* look stupid. But see, I admitted it and we laughed together. If I'd gotten all huffy, or acted hurt, I would've allowed him to make me a victim.''

Behind them, the rhythmic thudding of sneakers grew louder. Tony streaked by and lifted a hand in greeting. Then gave them a view of his broad glistening back, his low-riding gray sweatpants already dark at the waist, the fleece clinging to the alternating flex of steel buns.

Elaine sighed. ''I can think of worse things than being his victim.'' She met startled bluish purple eyes and realized what she'd said.

Sarina looked back at Tony, then snorted. ''Good point.''

Elaine giggled.

Suddenly they were both laughing, one peal of hilarity leading to another. They laughed so hard they started weaving in their lanes and had to stop and lean against one another.

Holding on to her side, Sarina asked breathlessly, "Okay, I'm wiped out. Wanna go inside and call it a day?"

The approaching pound of feet pulled Elaine upright. She drew in a steadying breath. "No, let's finish the two miles."

"Really? I'm impressed."

Tony whizzed past on their left, having claimed the inside lane.

"Yeah, I'm a regular greyhound," Elaine said, grinning. "C'mon. First one to catch the rabbit wins."

CHAPTER ELEVEN

THE NEXT DAY Sarah slammed shut her locker, slipped on her jacket and backpack, then headed for the senior prom planning meeting. Three-thirty in the cafeteria. A committee of teens arguing about decorations, refreshments, music and the like. Oh joy. Donna owed her big time for this favor.

No, more like I owe her my firstborn child for everything she's done for me.

Not that Sarah could deliver on that debt, either, she realized, dodging oncoming hall traffic with an ease that had eluded her six weeks ago.

After all, Mark was out of the equation. Or he would be, once she returned to Dallas and told him so. *If* she made it safely to the courthouse on trial day…

Sarah shook off her nagging fear. The point was, motherhood wasn't in her future anytime soon. Maybe never. Funny, how much that thought hurt now.

Before witnessing John's murder, she hadn't wanted children. Hadn't thought she would have the time to nurture a child properly, as a parent should. As her parents never had. She'd been rising up the corporate career ladder, and contemplating marriage to an equally ambitious man. There wouldn't be room for another ego in the family. And Mark had agreed. Another reason he'd seemed the perfect compatible partner, the ideal 4-H prospect...

Okay, 3-H prospect.

Handsome, hardworking, heterosexual males were hard enough to find. She'd never known an honorable one, who wasn't already married. Not until she'd met Jack, who epitomized the word. Who would make a wonderful father for some lucky child, a wonderful husband for some luckier woman.

Sheesh. Trust her to fall in love with the first single 4-H man she met—

Sarah stopped. Someone rammed into the back of her shoulder. She staggered to the right, braced her palm against cold metal. A boy's violent cursing sounded muffled, as if from a great distance.

Dazed, she turned, fell back heavily against the wall of lockers and examined the wondrous emotion filling her heart and mind. Was it really love?

It was much more than admiration or liking or lust. She'd felt those things for other men, although far less strongly than now.

But she'd never felt this craving to have a man's baby, to create a warm home, to surround herself and him and the precious combination of *them* with the proverbial white picket fence she'd once thought delusional. The difference was profound and elemental. It answered her question incontrovertibly.

She was in love with Jack Morgan.

Dear lord, now what?

Sarah had told Donna last night that kids were gossiping about Assistant Principal Kaiser and Mr. Morgan. Donna had wished the rumor was true. Her neighbor was tall, dark-haired and kept late hours. She'd speculated that he was the man who'd probably been spotted, since Jack had left her condo early as he'd said. Not that she hadn't wanted him to stay.

Donna "loved" Jack, she'd confessed. But for some unfathomable reason Jack didn't return her feelings. A heartbreaking situation, but one Sarah's continued silence and lack of interference wouldn't change. Donna had known Jack for years. In all that time, their relationship had remained platonic.

Now it was Sarah's turn.

An exhilarating—and terrifying—decision. To tell Jack how she felt and leave the next step up to him. But at least then she wouldn't let the situation bully her without putting up a fight. She wouldn't wonder "what if" the rest of her life.

Awareness of her surroundings returned slowly. The hallway was almost deserted. Damn. She was late! Grabbing the straps of her backpack, she jogged toward the cafeteria.

All her recent walking paid off. She made it in record time. Pausing outside the main entrance, she tugged down her lavender crushed velvet dress, regained her breath, then pushed through the double doors.

The kids had shoved two long tables together in the middle of the cafeteria and now sat on both sides. Sarah did a quick head count. Seven girls, five boys.

Ugh, there was Wendy, in between Jessica and Tony. The others she recognized, but didn't know by name.

Donna stood at one end of the table holding a clipboard. She looked up and smiled as Sarah approached. "There you are. Glad you could make it. I was about to cross you off my volunteer list."

I may be off your friend list soon, she thought, offering Donna an apologetic grin.

"For those of you who don't know her, this is Sarina Davis. I invited her to join our committee because her school in California has executed some fantastic prom themes in the past."

And I happen to know how to organize gala society events blindfolded.

"Pull up a chair, Sarina. I was telling the committee that our top priority today is choosing a theme. Everything else sort of depends on that."

Twelve pairs of eyes examined Sarah as she dragged a chair from a nearby table, then took off her backpack and jacket. In her career, she'd conducted client presentations, luncheon speeches and multimedia press conferences under watchful gazes. And she was convinced there was no appraisal more thorough, critical or nerve-racking than that of the average teenager.

When she was seated near the head of the table, Donna sat, too, and continued. "Okay, let's start at this end—" she indicated the side opposite Sarah "—and go around. I'll record all your suggestions. Then we'll discuss the feasibility of executing each theme. Catherine, why don't you begin? What would you like to put on the list?''

A plump freckle-faced blonde cast a furtive glance at Wendy, then shrugged. ''Do I have to go first? Can you come back to me?''

Donna nodded understandingly. ''Sure, no problem.'' Her gaze moved to the next volunteer, a stocky black kid with tight cornrow braids in intricate patterns. A football jock, Sarah was pretty sure.

''Russ, how about you? Do you have an idea for our theme?''

He fiddled with the senior class ring on his finger. ''Can I pass, too?''

''Now *that* would be a first,'' Wendy muttered loudly, prompting a few snickers.

Donna glared a warning. ''I'm quite prepared to ask anyone who doesn't cooperate to leave.'' She turned back to Russ, who was scowling. ''It's okay, Russ, this isn't a test. Jump in later if you think of something.'' Her wary gaze moved on. ''Kevin?''

The lanky red-haired boy squirmed in his chair. His buzz cut was so short his head looked pink.

Donna smiled tightly. ''Listen, *somebody* has to start the ball rolling. You can't all pass on your chance to offer a suggestion.''

''Yeah, we're brainstorming, here,'' Jessica spoke up unexpectedly. ''There are no dumb ideas. C'mon, Kevin, give us something to bounce around.''

Two days ago, Jessica would've probably passed on her turn as well. Sarah felt a warm surge of pride in Jack's accomplishment.

"Suck-up," Wendy grumbled, adding "Teacher's pet," in a singsong voice.

Jessica turned on the blonde. "You know, Wendy, I'm really sick of you trying to make everybody else feel stupid. Flunking three subjects doesn't exactly make you class valedictorian. Quit being so callous and give it a rest, huh, Brainiac?"

Whoa! Sarah met Donna's startled glance, then checked out Wendy. The girl looked as if she'd swallowed a porcupine whole. At least six people besides Sarah broke into a grin. She gave Jessica a mental high five.

Forearms on the table, Kevin leaned toward Donna. "Okay, here's an idea. Since last year they did the nostalgia thing, with jukeboxes and a soda fountain and stuff, I was thinking maybe the opposite could be cool this year. You know, Welcome to Future World or something like that."

"Good idea, Kevin! Let me get that down." Donna scribbled madly on her clipboard pad, then looked expectantly at a slim dark-eyed brunette. "Heather?"

"Well…I learned how to scuba dive last summer? And the sea is so totally awesome! It's like a different world when you're underwater. And everybody loved *The Little Mermaid* movie—even if no dude will admit it." Her arch look at the dudes present earned several sheepish grins. "Anyway, I think Enchantment Under the Sea, or whatever you want to call it, would be the Bomb."

"Good, good," Donna murmured while writing. "Okay, got that. Next?"

In general, the girls favored romantic themes, the guys action-adventure. Surprise, surprise. The Barbie and Ken suggestion from Wendy got the sneers and snide comments her "callousness" had reaped. Sarah was thankful the idea didn't have a snowball's chance in Houston of getting selected.

When Sarah's turn finally came around, Donna smiled ruefully. "You've got your work cut out for you being last, Sarina. Is there anything that hasn't been mentioned you'd like to add?"

Only one thing.

"Magic," Sarah said. "Not as in, Enchantment Under the Sea. I mean the David Copperfield kind of magic. There's a lot that can be done with that theme." She should know. She'd done a lot with it for a fund-raising gala in Dallas. The museum client had been thrilled with the results.

They spent the next hour discussing the logistics of coordinating props, food and music with each theme. In the end, the fact that a magic act could be additional entertainment to the standard band swayed the majority vote in its favor.

The committee decided to convene weekly—same time, same place—until all the details were hammered out and subcommittees formed.

The meeting adjourned with everyone in high spirits. Everyone, that is, except Wendy. The queen had been knocked off her throne, and her butt was obviously stinging. Until she climbed back on, Sarah planned to keep out of the girl's way. She put on her jacket and backpack, smiled at Donna—who was surrounded by three lingerers—and headed for the door.

"Sarina, wait," Donna called. She spoke to the threesome, put down her clipboard and walked quickly to Sarah's side. "Thanks for all your help today," she said softly. "Can I drive you home?"

Home. A bittersweet pain lanced Sarah's heart. Would she ever have the kind of home she now dreamed of?

"Come on," Donna persisted. "No one will think anything of me giving you a lift after the meeting. I feel so guilty when you walk in this cold weather."

Time alone with Donna these days meant time listening to her go on about Jack. Sarah couldn't handle that now. "You know getting outside helps keep me from going nuts. I feel enough like a caged monkey as it is. And I didn't get to walk the track. I need the exercise."

Donna frowned, then sighed. "Will you at least agree to use Gram's car on rainy days? It just sits in that garage collecting dust. You're not going to get a ticket driving six blocks, not if you're careful. And walking in the rain makes you stand out, which is exactly what we *don't* want."

They'd determined early on that Sarah's riding with Donna to and from school regularly would create unnecessary speculation. Plus, walking helped her blend in with the flow of kids coming and going—on *clear* days.

"Okay," Sarah relented. "Next time it rains I'll take your grandmother's land yacht to school. It'll blend right in with the pickups and Mustangs and Jeeps,'' she teased, referring to the big American luxury car Ms. Kaiser owned.

"Yeah, yeah." Grinning, Donna gave Sarah's shoulder a little push toward the door. "Go get your exercise, stubborn. I'll call you tonight."

"I'll be home," Sarah said dryly.

With a little wave, she shoved through the door into the wide corridor, then turned right. Their meeting had run long. She'd have to hoof it to get to the guest house before sunset.

Far ahead, and trailing the other committee members, Wendy and Tony strolled hand in hand. He slowed and leaned down for a kiss. She yanked away her hand and ran off, shrieking as Tony followed in hot pursuit. They turned left out of sight at the first hall intersection.

Sarah realized she'd stopped, more alone…and lonely, than before. A locker door slammed somewhere in the building. Two classrooms ahead, a vacuum cleaner whined from within. She began walking, picking up speed with each step. The doors she passed now were closed, their rectangular windows dark.

Suddenly she needed to get out. To get some air. To get to her safe little cage fast before she cracked and either cried or screamed, or did a little of both. Loudly.

She hit the intersecting hallway at a near jog and veered sharply to the left—smack into a brick wall of a chest. Recoiling, she gasped. Bruce?

Sarah lifted her gaze. "Jack!"

The man she'd realized only hours ago she loved reached out and gripped her arms, his hands strong and warm. "Hey, hey, easy now. Did I hurt you?"

No, but you probably will. "I'm all right. I should've been paying attention. What are you doing here?" she asked stupidly. The man did teach here, after all.

"I was waiting for you to get out of the meeting. I have something to tell you." Something major, from the sudden bruising squeeze of his hands, the barely contained excitement glittering in his hazel eyes.

She quelled an irrational flicker of dread. "O-okay. I'm listening."

"I checked my mailbox in the teacher's lounge one last time after school. There was a new message—" He broke off and cocked his head.

Voices. Approaching from the same route Sarah had taken.

"The rest of the committee's coming," she confirmed.

Casting a searching look around, he released her arms, grasped her hand and hauled her toward a nearby door marked Supplies. She didn't realize the door was ajar until she stood—blinking and stunned—inside a brightly lit, very small storage closet. Jack pulled the door shut with a soft click.

"It locks automatically, but not from the inside," he murmured, turning. Then he pressed a warning index finger to his mouth.

As if she could make a sound.

Although he faced her, his gaze was fixed on a shelf

of bathroom supplies, his senses obviously focused on the hallway outside the door. While three exuberant teenagers passed by only feet away, she studied Jack through the eyes of a woman in love. How had she ever thought his features too stern and forbidding?

A palm's width of dark hair brushed his forehead boyishly, the strands glossy and thick, begging to be smoothed back. His nose was large, yes, but straight and noble; his jaw was a bit square, granted, but authoritative and manly. Especially when shadowed with beard, like now. The blue-tinted skin would scrape the pads of her fingers if she dared to touch, to stroke, to feel.

O-oh, what she'd give to feel. His mink soft hair, the lean planes of his face, his hard sculptured mouth...that beautifully formed mouth. Startlingly sensual in such a masculine face.

What would that mouth feel like pressed against her own? Sarah's longing to know was a physical pain. Stupid to torture herself like this. She looked up.

Jack stared back.

Oh-god-oh-god-oh-god.

Busted! Caught red-handed in a grip of lust and love she couldn't control, couldn't hide—because she couldn't look away.

The thread of awareness always between them zapped into a white-hot humming current. Charging the air she breathed, forcing her to take shallower and faster breaths. She watched helplessly as his eye color shifted from khaki to a swirl of green-gold flecks.

Oh-god-oh-god, we're alone in a closet, her heart babbled.

Yes, but why? Think! her mind commanded.

Jack had something he wanted to tell her. Yes, that was it. If she didn't break this unbearable tension soon she'd do something really stupid. Like launch herself at him bodily.

"Wha—" She stopped and cleared her throat. "What did you want to tell me, Jack?"

His eyes clouded, as if he were having trouble processing her question.

"You got a message in your mailbox," she reminded him desperately.

Comprehension lit his gaze, along with the return of that strange earlier excitement that had driven him to seek a private place to talk. "Yeah, a message from Irving Greenbloom to call him as soon as possible. I phoned from the teacher's lounge. And Sarah..."

The result of his call fermented in his gaze, frothing up to spill over in a flow of words. "Two independent production companies want to option *Free Fall*. It could mean an auction! Irving is flying to Houston on Friday to discuss negotiation terms with me. He thinks I have a good shot at doing the rewrites, if I want."

It was Sarah's turn to process words sluggishly. "Rewrites? Isn't the sceenplay already written?"

"Yes, but all directors want changes to scripts. Usually major changes. Usually hired out to one or more established writers the director trusts. This could be a huge opportunity for me, Sarah!"

A thought struck dread in her heart. "Would you have to leave Houston?"

His inner glow dimmed. "I don't know. Maybe. I hadn't thought much past telling you." He frowned at a lower shelf as if taking stock of more than bathroom supplies.

This was his dream come true they were talking about. He'd waited for her in the hallway, knowing the danger of being spotted with a female student. Risking it anyway to share his good news with her first. She'd dampened his joy, when this should be a shining glorious memory.

"You *did* it, Jack!" Sarah said fiercely, drawing his surprised gaze. "I'm so proud of you, I could bust! If I could, I'd take you out for lobster and champagne, my treat. But you'll have to settle for my congratulations."

Gathering all the love and admiration she felt for this man—which was more than enough to smother her selfish disappointment—she poured it into a beaming smile.

For an astonishing instant she saw his throat work. Then he laughed self-consciously and rumpled his hair. *Too* cute!

"I'd settle for a big hug," he said, spreading his hands wide.

She rushed forward gladly. His strong arms aided her burrowing snuggle against his chest. She laid her cheek against his boring blue shirt, absorbed the battering beat of his heart...and would've happily stayed locked in a supply closet for the rest of her life—if it meant she could stay locked in his arms.

She closed her eyes and inhaled his fresh woodsy scent, a combination of clean skin and expensive cologne. Her hands crept around his waist. "You smell so good," she murmured, drowsy and content.

His arms tightened, his heartbeat sped up. He lowered his face and nuzzled the crown of her head.

Her eyes popped open.

"Mmm, even your hair smells like peaches," he said in a satisfied growl. "Did you know that's my favorite food in the world? Is that why you do everything but brush your teeth with the damn things, so you can slowly drive me crazy?"

She was wide-awake now. "No-o. The guest house has a big basket of peach-scented stuff. It's got everything. Soap, shampoo, lotion, talcum powder—even body massage oil."

He grew very still.

"That's the only one I haven't used, yet. Maybe I'll try it soon. What do you think?" She smiled against his shirt.

"I think you like to live dangerously." His thudding heart belied his casual tone.

"Depends on how you define *danger*. I don't like knowing there's a bullet out there with my name on it, if only the gun knew where to find me. But I kind of like driving you crazy. Serves you right for making me jealous."

He drew in a sharp breath.

She didn't smile. She'd crossed the line from coy innuendo to true confessions. There was no turning back now. "Why did you kiss Donna that night like you wanted to take her to bed?"

His breath released slowly. To his credit, he didn't pretend to misunderstand. "It was an experiment. To see if I wanted to take her to bed."

She tensed. "And did you?"

"I've answered that once already."

"*No,* not 'Did you take her to bed?' Did you *want* to? Tell me the truth." A year crawled by.

"No, Sarah, I didn't."

She was so consumed with relief it took her a second to realize he was slipping off the straps of her backpack. "What are you doing?"

"First, I'm getting rid of this thing."

He caught the full weight of the pack with one hand and lowered it easily to the floor.

"Then I'm getting rid of this *damn jacket*—" his fingers were already on the third button "—which, by the way, I really, really hate—" he tugged off the garment one sleeve at a time while she stood as limp as a toddler "—so I can see this short little purple dress of yours—" he tossed her coat over her backpack "—which, by the way, I really, really love. And then, Sarah Davidson, we're going to conduct a little experiment."

"We are?" Her voice came out thready and weak. Lack of oxygen tended to do that.

"Yes, we are," he stated firmly in his resonant Moses voice.

Hallelujah!

He swept a steel forearm around her waist, tilted up her chin with his free hand and lowered his head.

CHAPTER TWELVE

SARAH GLIMPSED the turbulent swirl of Jack's creek water eyes and braced herself for rapids.

But the first touch of his lips against hers was soft, a sliding of flesh into a quiet pool. Silky. Supple. Stunningly sensuous, for all that his mouth barely made contact. One brush. Two. A slight waggle of his head.

Her eyelids fluttered down. She slid her palms over his shoulders and pressed chest to knee against Jack Morgan. Indescribable. A blissful sigh parted lips she kept open—an entreaty that, much to her frustration, he ignored.

For such a hard-looking mouth, his lips were exquisitely gentle. They brushed and plucked and nibbled in careful increments of increasing pressure. As if he had all the detachment, all the patience, all the control of a scientist in his lab. Without her bulky jacket between them, Sarah knew better.

Every male muscle pressed against her was taut and straining, evidence she hadn't misread his eyes earlier. The creek rushed strong and fierce, was in fact rising up the banks of his control by the second. The hard ridge nudging her belly urged her to jump right in. And unlike Jack, she didn't need an engraved invitation.

Sarah threaded her fingers through his hair, sealed their mouths together and recklessly took the plunge.

She stroked boldly, greedy for texture and taste, eager to enter the deep waters just beyond her reach. Three seconds passed. Four. Then she hit the current she sought. The green-gold swirl she loved. The man he hid from the world. Impassioned...and blisteringly passionate.

The powerful arm cinching her waist dragged her in tighter, bending her back. His free hand moved to catch the base of her skull. He swallowed her gasp and slanted his mouth for a tighter fit—the better to sweep her away with his delving tongue.

Being kissed by Jack was hot, rough and wet. The wildest most exhilarating ride of her life. She tumbled against the sleek boulders and banks of his mouth with instinctive pliancy. Yielding to his domination. His sheer maleness. Aggressive, but not bullying. Exciting and natural.

The things he did to her mouth generated a moist billowing heat between her thighs. A tension she recognized, but had never experienced this fast, this tight, this desperate. Twining her arms around his neck, she rotated her hips against his groin.

Sensation rocketed up from the point of friction, sluiced back down in a warm liquid rush.

He reached spread-fingered for her bottom, then lifted her inches off the floor. She broke off the kiss and panted. Dizzy. Shelves moving. *She* was moving. But where? She braced her palms on his bunched shoulders and twisted.

His mouth latched onto her right breast.

Through crushed velvet and pink satin, as if her nipple were bare, he suckled until Sarah clutched his head and wanted him inside her *now*.

She was sliding down, down his body. More friction. More heat. More dampness where she ached.

"I knew it would be like this between us," he said thickly, grasping her waist with both hands. He hitched her onto a tall chair.

No, a stack of boxes. Her legs dangled beside his hips. Wanton. Scandalous. She didn't care.

"Sarah, Sarah, I tried to stay away from you." He palmed her thighs and pushed up crushed velvet, his gaze never wavering from hers. "Tell me you love this Mark guy and I'll stop."

With a roar in her ears like that of water closing over her head, Sarah surrendered to the green-gold undertow, floated and swirled on eddies of desire. "I don't love Mark," she whispered. "I never loved Mark."

Triumph flared in his eyes. His warm hand moved slowly up her inner thigh. "You're so soft. So incredibly soft."

If he stopped now, she would die.

"So brave and fierce and small and—" his fingertips slid under silk "—ahh *Sarah*. You're so wet for me, sweetheart, so responsive—" he anointed her reverently with the evidence of her passion "—so beautiful and good and—" one finger slipped inside her "—hot and tight." He drew in a hissing breath as her hips moved involuntarily. "That's right, sweetheart, let me take you all the way there. I'll keep you safe."

Sarah reached for him blindly. Her hands scrabbled on his shirt, collected fists full of cotton, and jerked him toward her waiting mouth. She kissed him with all the terrible wonderful passion obliterating rational thought, drowning her in fire. She kissed him desperately—whimpering a protest—when he tried suddenly to pull away. She kissed him voraciously—whimpering her need—when he quickened the pace of his busy fingers. She kissed him through a climax that exploded through her body like floodwater through a canyon, sweeping away all previous experiences as if they'd never been.

She might've kept on kissing Jack the rest of her life if he hadn't ripped his mouth away, shoved down her dress and closed her knees. A shocked gasp pierced Sarah's receding passion. She blinked over his shoulder.

A cleaning woman holding a dangling set of keys stood just inside the open door. But it wasn't the titillated horror in her dark brown gaze that made Sarah feel physically ill, although that was mortifying enough. It was the horrified betrayal in the slate blue eyes staring at her from the hallway.

Fighting her nausea, Sarah knew she'd just been crossed off Donna's list of friends.

BY FRIDAY, Sarah's agitation over The Closet Incident had relocated to her chest and become a con-stant ache. Sitting at her sewing machine in home ec class, she found it hard to concentrate on making a silly skirt. Eight other classmates worked with sweatshop fervor on various garments they would model in three weeks. On the opposite end of the room, a wall of computer monitors glowed with colorful graphics, students staring at the screens.

If only she were designing a functional floor plan for a family of four. She envied Fred for having completed his three-week stint at the sewing machine last week. With typical self-absorption at the computer, he was oblivious to her misery. She was on her own. So, what else was new?

According to Mrs. Dent, this skirt pattern was a piece of cake. Ha! As if Sarah and cake weren't synonymous with disaster. Maybe this pattern was simple for someone who had the *slightest* interest in taming this beastly machine from hell.

All she wanted to do was rip out the thing's guts and let them rust in the February drizzle.

Who cared if her stitches were straight when her best friend was hurting? When *she* was the one who'd inflicted the pain? She should've confessed her attraction to Jack long ago. Then Donna wouldn't have been totally shocked by seeing Sarah flushed and replete, her legs spread wide...

"O-o-ohh," she groaned, violently rejecting the mental image.

"Sarina?" Mrs. Dent turned from beside Kate two machines ahead. "You didn't break *another* needle, did you?"

Sarah held the school record, if the elderly home ec

teacher's memory was correct. Several giggles sounded above the electric whir of motors. Kate twisted around, her expression sympathetic.

"No, ma'am," Sarah answered. "I'm okay."

"Well…" Fingering a strand of pearls at her neck, her eyes filled with exasperated affection, Mrs. Dent finally nodded. "I'll be next door in the kitchen if you need me. Ask for help if you think you're getting into trouble."

Too late for that. "Thank you, Mrs. Dent. I will."

Sarah hunched over her sewing machine, pressed the foot pedal and slid black cotton gingerly beneath the jackhammer needle. With her hands busy, her thoughts returned to The Closet Incident.

After her initial shocked glimpse, Donna had recovered her wits enough to hustle the cleaning lady out before Jack turned around and was recognized as a teacher. In her best Assistant Principal voice, she'd assured the woman that appropriate action would be taken.

Of course she'd done nothing since then. Literally. She wouldn't talk to Sarah at school, had barely looked at her all week. Hadn't called at night to check in and make sure she was okay. As dependent as she was on her friend for safety and food, Sarah feared most for the loss of warm camaraderie.

And then there was Jack. Grrr—oops!

"Darn," Sarah muttered, steering her skirt seam back on course.

Jack had retreated behind his rules and regulations as if they would protect him from her brazen influence.

As if he hadn't gone fishing for her tonsils in that closet, or changed her definition of "the little death" to "enormous."

Not that he'd been callous. No, he'd simply...withdrawn. She had the uneasy impression he thought she expected a ring on her finger. Mr. Responsibility *would* think that. Sarah blinked rapidly and scowled down at her sloppy seam. Stupid man.

Well, she was a grown woman, dammit. He wasn't responsible for her sexual behavior, and she wasn't answerable to his moral code.

She could lure the Saturday postman into the guest house for wild sex if she wanted. She could seduce the cute college kid who tended Mrs. Kaiser's garden if she felt like it. For that matter, she could play Lolita for the entire male faculty at Roosevelt High if she had a mind to. Jack could ding his little bell until his finger fell off and there was nothing he could do to stop her—

Clunk.

Grrr. She stared at the balled up mess of black cotton beneath the broken sewing machine needle.

"I *hate* this machine!" she bawled, stopping the surrounding whir temporarily.

Classmates turned and stared in amazement at the sight of Sarina obviously close to a breakdown of some sort.

Kate rose from her chair, hissed at the others to keep sewing, then moved to Sarah's side. "Bad day, huh?"

Sarah managed a choked laugh.

Kate tossed back her long dark hair and smiled

grimly. "I hear ya. My whole week has been the pits."
She held out her upturned fist and uncurled her fingers.
"This should make you feel better."

Please don't be a joint. Sarah eyed the sewing machine needle with a mixture of relief and humble gratitude.

"Thanks, Kate. I owe you one." Standing, Sarah let the girl sit in her place and start the repair work.

Asking Mrs. Dent for another replacement needle was a humiliation Sarah couldn't have borne. She had no desire to make the *Guinness Book of World Records* for Most Sewing Machine Needles Broken by a Home Ec Student.

No, if she went after any record, it would be for something with a little more pizzazz. Like Most Necks Broken by a Woman Posing as a High School Student who Suddenly Went Berserk in Fifth Period English. Sarah smiled to herself. Yeah, that had a nice ring to it. Much more potential for publicity, too.

She'd leave her first victim under his poster of Morgan's Ten Commandments. Poetic justice—

"Wanna know something else funny?" Kate asked, jerking Sarah back to the present. "You remember that algebra test I studied so hard for?"

Sarah nodded, not liking where this was headed. Kate would flunk the subject unless she pulled off a C or above on every remaining test.

"Well, I got a C plus."

"But...that's great!" Sarah grinned delightedly. "I knew you could do it! Did you tell your mom and Ja—your brother?"

"Yeah, I told 'em." Picking up a pair of small scissors, Kate began snipping out errant threads on the ruined skirt seam. "I got a lecture on how Jack's perfect study habits got him a scholarship to USC. And how if I didn't want to be stuck in a rut once I graduated from high school, I'd better shape up and start applying myself now."

Sarah mentally shifted Vera Morgan to the top of her broken neck victim list. Didn't the woman realize the more she compared Kate unfavorably to Jack, the more she pushed the girl into rebellion? Getting into trouble was the only thing left for Kate to prove she could do better than her older brother.

Putting aside her own worries, Sarah frowned sympathetically. "I know that was a bummer to hear. But try not to let it get you down. I'm sure your mom means well." She grabbed at a straw of memory. "You said yourself she tried working outside the home after your dad died, but wasn't qualified for any decent-paying job. She probably wants you to have better options than she did."

Kate looked up, her gaze bitter. "Good theory. There's only one problem."

Sarah waited.

"It wasn't Mom who lectured me. It was Jack."

Jack? Sarah assimilated the information while Kate looked down again and smoothed the skirt material bunched up under the needle. Pausing periodically, she pulled out bits of thread and added them to a growing pile.

"That doesn't sound like Ja—Mr. Morgan," Sarah

finally said. Only it did. At least, the Mr. Morgan she'd first met a lifetime ago.

His sister lifted a shoulder, her gaze still focused on the pitiful excuse of a skirt. "He's been nervous about some meeting he's got tonight with—" She stopped just short of divulging her brother's rendezvous with Irving Greenbloom. "Anyway, you'd think he was having dinner with the president the way he's been snapping and yelling at every little thing."

Sarah winced, suspecting she was as much—if not more—at fault than the L.A. agent for Jack's foul humor. He obviously not only regretted getting caught with his hand in the cookie jar, but also resented the hunger that had sent him reaching.

Kate looked up, her gaze ferocious. "He grounded me *again*, Sarina! For getting a friggin' C on the test. He's *not my father!* He can't tell me what to do. I'll go crazy spending another weekend watching Mom crochet or try some stupid new recipe." Desperation tinged her features. Her focus shifted to an inner vision. "God, I can't *wait* until I'm old enough to drive and can just...I dunno...go anywhere that isn't home."

Sarah remembered the trapped restless feelings of postchildhood, preadulthood all too well. "Hang in there, Kate. If your brother's been nervous about tonight, let him get past it, then talk to him again. I bet he'll be much more relaxed and reasonable."

"You don't talk to Jack. He talks to you. I *hate* him!" Kate spat out.

Classmates were turning around to investigate the

commotion, Fred among them. Even his beloved computer couldn't compete with Kate's distress. He started to rise, and Sarah gave him a fierce look and small shake of her head. Sinking back down, he continued to frown and stare.

Sarah squeezed Kate's shoulder, leaned over and spoke for her ears alone. "Look, I know being grounded stinks. Call me tonight and we'll work out a game plan. But promise me you won't do anything stupid before we talk, okay?"

Shrugging off Sarah's hand, Kate scraped back her chair and rose. Her accusing glare welled with unshed tears. "Now *you* think I'm stupid, too? I'll tell you what's stupid. Wasting my life when I should be having fun is stupid! I thought you'd understand."

"Kate—"

"You'll have to start over on the seam." Kate gestured sharply to the skirt she'd rescued. "Only this time, follow a straight line. You seem to be getting good at that, so it shouldn't be a problem." Whirling, she stalked back to her own sewing machine and sat gracefully, her back rigid.

Reclaiming her chair, Sarah stared at the skirt, then the black threads heaped in a pile. Her life was like that. Unraveled. Nothing even. Nothing solid. Threads of the old Sarah mixed with Sarina in a confusing tangle she tried to sift through now.

She'd intended to serve her time as Sarina with little personal involvement. Maybe have a little casual fun. Relive a painful phase of her life with the benefit of experience and confidence on her side.

Instead, she'd grown to love a group of kids who would take the world by storm—with a little more experience and confidence. The first would come with time. The latter was something she could help them gain now. *Had* been helping them achieve, to a small extent. And her sense of personal satisfaction had never been greater.

What if she stepped up her efforts? Could she really make a difference in these kids' lives? The possibility was exciting. A welcome distraction from— No, she wouldn't think about Jack. She would concentrate on Kate and Elaine and Fred and the others who would welcome her attention and...love.

Sweeping the pile of threads into a small trash basket under her machine, Sarah adjusted the black cotton, lifted her chin and started anew.

WHEN KATE hadn't called the guest house by eight o'clock that night, Sarah had picked up the phone and dialed the Morgan's number. Kate had been sullen and uncommunicative, growing downright uncivil when Sarah had offered to drive over and keep the girl company.

"I don't need a baby-sitter," Kate had said sarcastically, then practically hung up on Sarah's attempt to make amends.

Now, at ten-thirty, sitting at the bar counter with a mug of tea, Sarah still couldn't rid herself of a nagging sense that something wasn't right. Kate had sounded more than rude. She'd seemed...nervous. Yeah, that was what had been bothering Sarah all night. The girl was planning to do something when Jack wasn't home to interfere.

Impulsively, Sarah headed for the phone and dialed the number she'd memorized weeks ago. Someone picked up on the fourth ring.

"Hello?" Vera Morgan said groggily.

"Mrs. Morgan? This is Sarina Davis. May I speak with Kate, please?"

"She's probably asleep. I know *I* was."

Sarah cringed. "I'm really sorry for calling so late, but it's very important. Thank you for getting her."

A disgruntled pause followed. "Hold on."

The receiver thudded onto a hard surface, probably the nightstand. Vera grumbled something about people calling past ten o'clock. Bedsprings creaked.

Silence.

Sarah stared at the kitchen wall clock. How was Jack faring with the hotshot agent from L.A.? They must've taken their business dinner to the next level— drinks at a bar, where negotiation disagreements had a way of smoothing out with good whiskey. Jack Daniel's was one too many Jack's during a discussion of *Free Fall,* in Sarah's opinion.

A muffled fumbling of the receiver recaptured her attention.

"She's not in her room," Vera said sharply.

Uh-oh. "Did you check the rest of the house?"

"Yes, of course. I found a pillow in her bed." Vera released a shaky breath. "She sneaked out. Probably to meet *that boy.* The one Jack told her she couldn't see anymore."

Bruce Logan. Who was having a party tonight without his parents in town. Who'd told Sarah in disgusting detail what he would do to Kate if she showed up. An intimidation tactic at the time. He hadn't expected Jack to unsnap his sister's leash, Sarah was sure.

"Oh, I wish Jack were home," Vera said fretfully. "He'd know what to do."

Sarah had already hoisted up the white pages from under the end table and was flipping to *Logan*. Damn. There must be at least a hundred and fifty. Lots of initial *B*'s, but no Bruce.

"Mrs. Morgan, do you know Bruce's phone number, or his address?"

"That awful boy?" Distress and honest confusion rang in Vera's voice. "Why would I know that?"

Call me crazy, but maybe because you knew your daughter was hanging out with him, probably getting drugs from him. "I think Kate might be at his house. I'll track down his address and go over there. In the meantime, call her friends on the chance she's with one of them. Do you have a pencil handy?"

"A pencil?" A drawer opened and shut. "Yes, yes I have one."

"Okay, take down this number and call me if you find her, or know where she is." Sarah relayed the guest house cellular phone number. "If I find Kate first, I'll call *you*."

"Sarina, do you know something you're not telling me? Is Kate in danger?"

An image of Bruce's ice-blue eyes chilled Sarah's blood. She forced a note of false confidence into her voice. "I'm sure she's fine. But sometimes parties get out of hand, and neighbors call the police. It's still early. If she's there, I'll talk her into leaving with me before that can happen." *Somehow.*

"Oh, I wish Jack would get home. He probably has the phone numbers of Kate's friends written down some—"

"Mrs. Morgan," Sarah interrupted impatiently. "Your son can't think for you all the time. You have a brain. Use it. And remember to call me with any news. Goodbye." She hung up.

Pretty callous, Sarah knew, but she didn't have the time or inclination to coddle Mrs. Morgan like Jack did. His mother might suffer from clinical depression, but she was being treated with drug therapy, according to Kate. If hundreds of others with that condition could lead independent productive lives, so could Mrs. Morgan. Finding Kate was Sarah's first priority.

The next person she called was Elaine, who looked up Bruce's address in a school directory. The girl fussed about Sarah going alone, then made her promise to call back with an update. When Sarah agreed and hung up, she was halfway to Mrs. Kaiser's garage.

Minutes later, the cell phone beside her on the passenger seat, Sarah backed the land yacht out of the driveway and headed to the Logan blowout.

She was not in a party mood.

CHAPTER THIRTEEN

SARAH DROVE BY Bruce's two-story Georgian bricked home at a slow crawl. Gas lanterns flickered on each side of the intricately carved double doors. No interior lights. No loud music. No cars and trucks lining the curb.

Apparently no party in progress.

That's good, Sarah tried to convince herself, even as her hands gripped the steering wheel tighter.

A convertible and a pickup truck sat in the circular driveway. Bruce drove the Mustang. The truck could belong to anyone. She eyed the curtained windows. No telltale movement. *Are you in there, Kate?* No convenient telepathy provided an answer.

The cellular phone had remained silent on Sarah's drive to this prestigious subdivision. Clearly Mrs. Morgan hadn't located her daughter yet. Sarah could phone Bruce and ask if Kate was with him, but she didn't trust him to tell her the truth, not after his promised earlier threats, damn his scuzzy hide. She would have to check out the situation for herself. No problem.

Yeah, piece of cake, her instincts warned.

She parked at the front curb, scooped up the phone and left the car unlocked. If she had to make a quick getaway, she didn't want to fumble with a key in the door. The land yacht didn't have an electronic gizmo on a key chain to do the job for her.

Okay, this is no big deal, Sarah told herself, walking slowly toward the front doors. Bruce's parents were probably in town, contrary to the tall tales he'd told. Kate was probably sulking at a friend's house. This was nothing at all like that night in Dallas when no one had answered John Merrit's front door. No, nothing at all.

But her body wasn't listening. It remembered the black velvet blanket over a sleeping neighborhood, the approach to a silent stately house, the sense of security that had been cruelly false. Her ears strained for the sound of voices arguing, disrupting the peaceful quiet.

By the time she stood on the huge slate-tiled porch, her muscles were coiled for flight. Her breathing was rapid. Sweat misted her forehead and trickled between her breasts. Irrational. Humiliating. Proof of what a wimp she was deep down inside. Her hand shook as she pressed the doorbell.

She listened to the gong of chimes echo inside. *One-Mississippi, two-Mississippi, three-Mississippi.* She cursed herself and Kate and ten other people before she managed to ring the bell a second time. *One-Mississippi, two-Mississippi, three-Mississippi, four-Mississ—*

The door opened.

Sarah stared into ice-blue eyes, all the more creepy for being bloodshot. Bruce propped a raised arm on the frame, the pose lifting his sleeveless sweatshirt two inches above his jeans. His stomach was furry black, his forearms only slightly less so.

"Well, well, well," he said, starting to smile. "I thought it was you through the peephole. Did you come to the party, beautiful?"

She always skipped the ape section at the zoo, and almost told him so. His reptilian eyes changed her mind. "Is Kate here? I need to talk to her."

"Sure, babe. Come on in." He nudged the door open wider.

A drift of pungent smoke hit Sarah in the face. Whew! No mystery how he got those bloodshot eyes. "Ask her to come to the door, please."

"Ask her yourself. She's right inside." Although he didn't move, he suddenly seemed more alert, the way a snake appears lifting its head from a coiled sleep. "Don't tell me Sarina Davis is afraid?"

She was terrified. Walking inside that house would put her at his mercy. *Turn around and leave, then call for help,* her instincts screamed.

And leave Kate like you left John? her conscience sneered.

Sarah flipped open her cell phone, her stomach twisting at the gleam of wariness in his gaze. "What have you done to Kate. Why can't she come to the door? What are you hiding?"

"Hey, Bruce!" a male voice bellowed from inside. "Get your ass in here, or I'm not waitin'."

Bruce swiveled his head. "Keep your hands off until I say so," he roared, then turned back to Sarah with a sly shrug. "Pizza's getting cold."

They weren't fighting over pizza.

"Get Kate out here *now*," Sarah ordered, pressing the phone's power button. "Or I call 911 and report a kidnapping. If the cops sniff around inside your house, what will they find besides Kate, hmm?"

He lurched forward. She skittered back and punched 911.

"Wait!"

She stopped, her finger poised above Send. Bruce swayed on his feet, his hands fisted, his icy glare filled with malevolence.

They faced off in some bizarre modern day showdown. Technology versus brute strength. She could see him gauging the ten feet between them, calculating his chances.

"Don't be stupid," Sarah advised in a hard voice. "Do you *really* want your parents to get a call from the cops? I'll bet it won't be the first time," she guessed—correctly, from the flare of fear in his eyes. "They might take away the Mustang, or who knows what?"

Bruce obviously knew. The threat of his parents' displeasure was the bullet that sent him spinning around to disappear inside.

Sarah's knees buckled. She stumbled and dropped the phone. Plastic casing clattered ominously against the tiled porch. Frantic, she snatched up her "gun" and punched the Power button. Nothing. O-o-oh *no*. She was firing with blanks.

Motion at the doorway captured her attention. She

resumed her finger-above-the-Send-button aim and prayed Bruce wouldn't notice the dark dial digits.

One look at Kate, lying rag doll limp in Bruce's arms, made Sarah wish she held a loaded shotgun, so she couldn't miss once he set down his burden.

"You bastard," she breathed. "What did you do to her?"

"Nothing. She did it to herself. Can't hold her liquor. Where do you want her?"

Running to the car, Sarah flung open the passenger door, then rounded the bumper to the driver's side. While Bruce heaved Kate onto the seat none too gently, Sarah fumbled for her keys and waited until he'd closed the door.

He straightened and faced her over the car top. "This stays between you and me, got that, bitch? Or next time—" he jerked a thumb at Kate "—I finish what I start."

Sarah believed him. Without a working phone. she wasn't about to antagonize him further. Nodding, she slid behind the wheel, locked Kate's door and then her own, started the ignition and got the hell out of Dodge.

One block away, headlights approached at a dangerous speed. Sarah slowed as a station wagon shot past. Idiot drunken driver. She started shaking. A little, at first, then so hard her teeth rattled. Pulling over to the curb, she stopped and turned to Kate. The girl sat slumped against the door, passed out cold. She needed her seat belt buckled, Sarah thought wildly, but her hands shook too much to accomplish the task.

Headlights glared from behind. Blinding. Right on

her tail. The car was stopping. Oh, God, she shouldn't have parked. Sarah twisted and reached for the ignition, checking her rearview mirror. A tall broad-shouldered male got out of the driver's side of a station wagon. The drunk. Her heart raced with the land yacht's gunning engine. She shifted gears, glanced in the mirror again…and made a startled sound of gladness.

Fred was walking toward her door! She shifted back to neutral, cut the engine and rolled down her window. He leaned down and peered inside, his narrow face and black-framed glasses a dear and welcome sight.

"Is she hurt?" he asked without preamble in a voice she didn't recognize.

"I don't th-think so," Sarah said through chattering teeth. "I th-think they slipped her a m-mickey and she's only sleeping it off. But I haven't had a ch-chance to look her over."

"Get out," he ordered gently, a reassuring presence as she obeyed and stood on trembling legs. He slid into her place and checked Kate's pulse, lifted her eyelids, ran his hands carefully over her limbs as if testing for a physical reaction. His movements were confident and efficient, evidence of serious first aid training.

Just watching him calmed Sarah's shakes. She hugged her stomach and waited for his pronouncement. At last he buckled Kate's seat belt and slid back out to stand beside Sarah.

"She's unconscious, but her vital signs are stable, and she doesn't seem to be bruised or hurting. She'll wake up groggy and maybe lose her last meal, but she should be okay. Someone will have to examine her more closely to see if she's…'' His mouth thinned, his jaw bulged.

''I got there in time,'' Sarah said gently, laying a hand on his shoulder. ''Elaine shouldn't have called you, but I've never been so glad to see anyone in my life. Thanks for coming, Fred.''

He nodded, and they shared a look of mutual caring and affection. ''Turn the heater on high in the car. When you get to Kate's, drink something hot. I'll call later to check on her.'' His gaze moved to study the quiet residential street that led to Bruce's house.

Oh, no. Surely not? ''Fred, he's got another guy in there with him—maybe more. Don't you *dare* do anything macho and stupid,'' Sarah ordered. That got his attention.

He flashed his rare white grin. ''I'm not exactly known for being macho, Sarina. And the one thing I'm definitely not is stupid.''

Sarah found herself being handed decisively into the driver's seat and buckled in before she knew what hit her. Giving in to Kate's greater need, Sarah relented and started the engine. She didn't like driving off, leaving Fred behind in this strange mood.

But like he said, he wasn't macho and stupid. Nothing would happen. What could he do?

FRED ADLER HAD beaten the crap out of Bruce Logan.

After five days, Jack was still a little pissed. He'd been deprived of the pleasure of rearranging Bruce's face himself. Leaning back in his creaking chair, he stared vacantly at his closed classroom door.

If the emergency room doctor hadn't pronounced Kate untouched and basically unharmed, nothing would've kept Jack from a brother's revenge. Not to mention acting on the black rage he'd felt learning Sarah might've been hurt. Only her quick thinking and bravery had saved his baby sister, and herself, from becoming victims—

Wood cracked. Jack blinked down at the snapped pencil in his hands. Not the slime bucket's neck, unfortunately. He'd lost his shot at that. But with all due credit, he had to admit the Adler boy kicked damn good butt.

Tossing the pencil pieces onto his open calendar, he frowned at the heaps of paperwork awaiting his attention. Plan period—his last hour of the school day—was normally a time to clear out some of this mess. Yet the clutter in his mind far surpassed that on his desk.

Mentally reviewing the past five days, he sorted through his confused thoughts and emotions.

Jack had talked to Bruce's parents on Sunday, seen for himself their son's swollen face and bandaged ribs. But it had taken Bruce's cohort—an eyewitness to what went down—to calm high tempers on all sides.

The "friend" had squealed about the barbiturate they'd slipped in Kate's beer, then revealed the details of the fight. Bruce's parents had shut up about lawsuits. And Jack had realized Bruce's reputation as a cool stud was history—a fitting punishment. Worse than a jail sentence in the kid's mind.

By Monday afternoon the story had already filtered to the teacher's lounge. Fred, the computer nerd, had challenged Bruce to "try to take someone who doesn't wear a bra."

A smile tugged at Jack's mouth now. Who would've thought Fred was a black belt in karate? Not Bruce, who'd launched into the fight with cocky confidence. And ended it curled moaning on the ground. He wouldn't be bothering Kate again. His parents and Fred would make sure of that.

The damsels-in-distress angle made Fred an even more romantic figure at school. Girls were all aflutter with admiration. Guys were calling Bruce a wimp.

Jack's smile broke free. Sarah was having a field day capitalizing on the publicity on Fred's behalf. Her little band of misfits was slowly evolving into a clique the student body admired, rather than ridiculed. Sarah would go to the top of her profession. He'd never known a woman with her energy, her enthusiasm, her fire...

The memory surged forward again. Sarah, hot and wet beneath his mouth and hand. An electrical storm in his arms, setting off jolts of desire in his own body that took him excruciatingly close to release. If the door to that closet had opened three minutes later, he would've been buried deep where he'd wanted to be for weeks. Where he still wanted to be. Where he didn't dare be, for fear of never wanting to leave.

Letting his head fall back, he closed his eyes. God,

he was hard again. A chronic condition since the episode in the closet. Served him right for hurting Sarah. She knew he regretted his actions, but he doubted she knew why.

In one of life's twisted ironies, the woman who understood and supported his secret ambition most was also his dream's greatest threat. He'd wanted personal and creative freedom for as long as he could remember.

But he sensed that one word from Sarah could bind him to her side. In Dallas, where her dream and opportunity intertwined.

A quick knock brought his head up. The door opened and Donna walked in, graceful and lovely in a white sweater dress. Why didn't the sight of her quicken his pulse? They shared the same traditional values. She would be content putting the man she loved before her own career. She would be content to create a loving home wherever that might be.

She would be boring, the uncharitable thought came out of nowhere.

"A call just came in for you," Donna said, blushing slightly beneath his analytical gaze. "Linda said the man sounded quite urgent. I thought you might like to know." She held out a pink message slip.

His stomach turned over as he reached for the note. Before he read the name, he knew. Irving Greenbloom requested a return call as soon as possible.

"Jack?" Donna hurried around the desk and laid a hand on his arm. "Is it bad news?"

He looked up into her kind eyes. "I don't know,"

he said truthfully. "Would you mind if I use your office to make a phone call?"

"No, of course not. Come on. I'll make sure you're not disturbed."

Jack followed her to the administrative offices in a daze. Irving had warned not to expect news on *Free Fall* until the end of the week. Maybe the interested production companies had backed out. Maybe the auction had bombed.

Donna led him past the curved public reception counter manned by volunteer moms to a private back hallway. As many years as he'd known Donna, he'd been in her office only three or four times. The third door on the left. Orderly, windowless and bland. Like his classroom, he realized, frowning.

He stood jingling his pocket change, feeling awkward as hell while she stacked papers and tidied her already neat desk. She'd saved his job when the cleaning lady had discovered him with Sarah. They hadn't talked about that embarrassing moment, but Jack knew he'd wounded Donna as much as Sarah.

Damn. He should've made this call from home.

"Okay, it's all yours," Donna said brightly. "Dial nine to get an outside line. I'll have Linda hold my calls. Take all the time you want."

"Thank you." He waited. Surely she wasn't planning on staying at her desk?

"Jack…" She blushed prettily, heightening the blue in her eyes.

Damn. He should've made this call from home.

"I know you were honest with me from the beginning about not wanting to…get involved. But…I hope you were equally honest with Sarah. She's pretty vulnerable right now. It would be easy for her to lean on someone strong.''

Sarah? *Lean* on someone? He couldn't hide his skepticism. ''Sarina the Fearless, defender of the weak? Sarah doesn't *want* to lean on anyone. She'd be insulted if I thought she did.''

Donna's mouth pursed. Her eyes grew cool. ''Sarah will fight to the death in defense of someone she loves. The problem is, she doesn't love herself nearly enough.'' Easing out from behind the desk, she avoided his gaze and walked to the door. It was almost closed when she paused, her head poking through the gap. ''You're a good man, Jack. Hardworking. Responsible. Smart. But you don't know shit about women.''

Click!

Jack grimaced at the closed door. He'd managed to inspire the first unladylike language he'd ever heard from Donna. Now *there* was something to be proud of.

And she was dead right, Jack admitted, dragging the phone to a more convenient spot on the desk. He would never understand women. He'd been trying for years to figure out the ones he lived with, and only seemed to make them unhappy.

Maybe it was time to concentrate on his own happiness, for once. Maybe at this time in his life, he could only do that without any females cluttering his mind.

Two hours later, Sarah left the steamy bathroom and headed for the kitchen to make a mug of tea. This was her favorite part of the day. The strain of seeing Jack and Donna at school was over, as was her vigorous walk at the track. She'd washed her hair and felt refreshed and relaxed.

Well, as relaxed as she could feel considering both her best friend and the man she loved avoided her like the plague. There were a few bright rays piercing her personal gloom, however. Kate's remorse and gratitude, for one.

She'd apologized upside down for calling Bruce to pick her up, then entering his house alone. It would be a long time, if ever, before rebellious anger overrode her common sense again. And, of course, there was the story of Fred's heroics to lighten Sarah's spirits.

Grinning, she filled her teakettle and set it on the stove to heat. If ever there was an image consultant's dream opportunity, this was it! When she got through with him, his status at school would rival Tony Baldovino's. Once she convinced Fred to cooperate, that is. Which she would. He would thank her for it one day in his *Forbes* article.

The phone rang, jump-starting her heart.

Mrs. Anderson had delivered the repaired phone the day before. Donna had dropped it off at the main house with a request that Sarah receive it at the housekeeper's convenience.

Was Donna calling to break the ice at last?

Sarah rushed to pick up on the second ring. "Hello?"

"Sarah, it's Jack."

Adrenaline flooded into her bloodstream.

"Look, I've been driving around thinking for the past hour, and the car keeps showing up on your street. I'm at the convenience store by the school. Would you mind letting me in the driveway gate? I'd like to talk to you without having to disturb Mrs. Kaiser."

"All right," she managed evenly. "But let me give you the security code, and you can open the gate yourself."

Her mind was a blank. She could barely breathe, much less think. The code. What was the damn code? Ah, yes. She rattled off the sequence.

"Got it. Thanks, Sarah. I'll be there in two minutes. Bye."

"Bye," she croaked to the dial tone. *Two minutes?*

Sarah raced into the bathroom and groaned at her reflection. Her hair was still wet, her face scrubbed free of all makeup. No time to change from her shapeless gray sweatshirt and pants. Just *once* she'd like Jack to see her in the full war paint and battle garb of a twenty-seven-year old woman dressed to kill.

Grabbing her makeup bag, she did the best she could under pressure. Lipstick, powder and blush brought her back from the undead. She'd just lifted her hair dryer when the sound of the electronic gate froze her arm in midair.

She stared at the woman in the mirror, her face flushed, her lips parted, her eyes lit like Roman candles, and warned her silently not to expect too much. There could be any number of reasons Jack would want to talk to her so urgently after driving around "thinking."

Still, when he knocked, she couldn't prevent the weightless surge of her heart. She put away the makeup bag and hair dryer, walked slowly to the door and pulled it open.

He wore the charcoal gray T-shirt and trousers she'd first seen in his foyer—minus the black jacket. One palm was braced high on the door frame, his other hand shoved deep in a pocket. A pose similar to the one Bruce had struck. Yet *heavens,* what a difference!

"Hi," he said softly, contained excitement in his eyes.

"Hi," she breathed, entranced with the spectacular biceps he'd hidden all this time.

"Can I come in?" Amusement tinged his voice.

She met the matching gleam in his gaze and backed up hastily. "Sure. Sorry."

The whistling teakettle gave her an excuse to regain *some* of her dignity. She bustled into the kitchen. "I was about to have some tea. Do you want a cup? Or I could make coffee?"

He closed the door. "Yeah, coffee would be good. If it's not too much trouble."

"No. It'll only take a minute." Polite small talk. Very small. When his expression said he had something big to say. She turned and filled her automatic drip machine with jerky movements. "So, what's on your mind, Jack?"

"Three-hundred thousand dollars and an offer to re-write *Free Fall.* It's official. I talked to Irving this afternoon from school."

Her hands stilled. Her heart sank. She forced her features into a semblance of pleasure and whirled. "Jack, that's wonderful! Oh my gosh, we should be drinking champagne, not coffee." Hurrying to the re-frigerator, she slung open the door and peered inside, as if a bottle would magically appear. Anything to gain a few more private seconds to compose herself. "The only thing I've got that fizzes is Diet Dr Pepper. Which will it be, Mr. Hotshot Screenwriter? Guess coffee will have to do."

She closed the door and faced him again. Her smile came easier now. Especially when he released his own full-to-bursting grin.

"So, tell me everything," Sarah demanded. "Why have you been driving around thinking for an hour? Why aren't you home telling your mother and Kate the good news? They'll be so happy for you, Jack."

He sobered frighteningly fast. "I don't think so."

"How could they not be?" But somehow she knew. Had known from the second he'd said the word *re-write.*

"Because the director wants me in L.A. ready to start work by the end of next week. If I accept, I'll have to live there indefinitely."

"Oh." *No, no, no, no.*

"What should I do, Sarah?"

CHAPTER FOURTEEN

CRUEL CRUEL QUESTION. Wasn't it enough that the thought of him leaving was an arrow through her heart? Did he want her to pack his bags and wave goodbye with a smile?

His expression was a mixture of eager little boy and conflicted adult. The same as when he'd first shared his dream with her in this very room. He hadn't gone home with his news. He'd come to her first for a reason. Did she dare hope it was because her support, her encouragement, and that of no one else's, was what he sought?

She pulled the shaft out of her heart and prayed for the strength to make it through the conversation. See him out the door and on with his new life. Then—and only then—could she quietly bleed to death.

"What should you do?" she repeated in a scoffing voice. "That's ridiculous. You should go live in L.A."

An emotion she couldn't read flickered quicksilver in his eyes.

"Ask me something that isn't a no-brainer," she challenged.

"Okay." He folded his arms. A stunningly masculine pose in his clinging T-shirt. "How will Mother and Kate manage without me? They can't stay in the same room ten minutes without arguing. What will my kids do when a substitute teacher is thrown at them right at the end of their senior year? Beto and Tony are barely squeaking by. Jessica could go either way, depending on how interested she is in the material—"

"Whoa, whoa, Jack. One question at a time. Why don't you sit at the bar. I'll pour you some coffee and we'll look at the situation objectively, okay?"

Looking unconvinced, he nodded and parked on the stool with his elbows on the counter, his gaze following her as she moved about the kitchen. It was all she could do to keep her hands from trembling, her mouth from blurting, "What about *me?* Don't I rate a question in your life?"

At last she gave him his mug of coffee, carried her tea to the empty bar stool and sat facing him, their knees almost touching. Her best bet for getting through this without begging him to stay was to keep it light.

"All right, Jack. As hard as it is for you to believe, you're not indispensable. No one is. People are amazingly flexible creatures—well, people who don't put commandments on their walls, that is." She offered a small smile, which he sheepishly returned. "Your mother and Kate will miss you terribly. And yes, they'll probably fight a lot without you. But you know what? I think in time, they'll grow closer to each other with you gone."

He lifted his coffee, blew the rising steam, took a sip. His obvious doubt was tinged with hope.

Nothing like a little pressure, Sarah thought. "I mean it. They're *much* too dependent on you, Jack.

You're bound to have realized that long ago, but the pattern was set. It was easier for everyone not to cross over the lines. Without you there to handle every little problem, they'll be forced to think for themselves, maybe even rely on each other for once.''

Slowly, he set down his cup, raised his eyes, studied her face. When he spoke, he did so quietly. ''Not every woman is as independent and strong as you, Sarah.''

She double-checked his expression, but he seemed sincere. He also seemed…something more. Intensely more.

''Women are only as independent as they have to be,'' she said dryly. His expression was *not* going to get to her. ''When the crutch goes to L.A., your mother and Kate will walk. You'll see. And as for your students…''

His frown returned. He really cared about ''his'' kids. A truly honorable man.

''They've had—what? Six months with you at the pulpit? If they haven't learned Morgan's Ten Commandments by now, they ain't gonna find religion in the next three months. The ones that would've passed with you, will pass without you, and vice versa. They'll adapt to a new teacher without being scarred for life. Especially if you take that *damn bell* and lose it some place in L.A.'' She took a sip of tea and smiled into her cup.

''You're going to miss my damn bell,'' he said with mock offense. ''Just you wait.''

He'd decided that so easily. Too easily. She resisted

the urge to press her heart and staunch the flow of blood. He didn't even realize what he'd revealed.

Sarah covered her involuntary wince of pain with another long slow sip, then set the mug on her knee. "Okay, on to the next question. Who else do you think can't live without you?" She almost pulled off a flippant tone. She did manage a flippant tilt of her head.

He studied her thoughtfully, one hand gripping his mug on the counter, the other draped loosely over his knee. His long, thick to-die-for lashes lowered a fraction, filtering a sudden gleam. "You tell me."

He knew!

Humiliation swept through Sarah, followed by a strengthening rush of anger. The cocky son of a bitch knew she loved him and was toying with her deepest emotions! Damn if there really wasn't a thin line between love and hate.

Lifting her chin, she slipped off her stool and played tug-of-war with his unfinished coffee. He was forced to relinquish the handle or get splashed.

She gripped both mugs and headed for the kitchen. "It's been real nice chatting with you, Jack, but you've outstayed your welcome. Run along home and spill your good news, so you can gloat over breaking two more hearts."

A rush of air was her only warning. Jack's arms enclosed her from behind. His hands clamped the top of each mug. He resisted her efforts to pull free with insulting ease, then steered her cargo to the counter beside the sink.

"Put the mugs down," he rumbled in her ear.

A delicious shiver tickled her neck. This was a game two could easily play. "Okay. Let go of them, first."

She saw his fingers start to lift, then he must've sensed her intention. He gripped the mugs tighter than before.

"Sa-arah," he warned, his breath warm, the body behind her warmer. "Don't you dare throw coffee on these clothes I bought to impress you. They cost me half a month's salary."

"You're rich, now, Hotshot. Buy replacements," she snapped, her attention skidding to a sudden stop. What was that he'd said? "You bought those clothes to impress me?"

He shrugged his broad shoulders. "Hey, I was happy with slacks instead of 'trousers.' You could throw coffee on my slacks and I wouldn't care."

She was still tingling from that shrug. She hated that she still tingled from that shrug. She loved that she still tingled from that shrug. Damn.

"Water resistance is nothing to brag about for men's slacks," she assured him.

"Quit impugning my wardrobe and let go of the mugs."

"No."

"Sa-arah."

Somehow letting go had become a symbol of surrender. "Tell me why I should."

"*Because*—" he drew out the word "—I need to turn you around and see your eyes." He sounded gentle and sad. Not cocky at all.

"Why?"

He rested his cheek on top of her head. "Because, you implied I broke your heart, and I don't think I could stand that."

"Why not?" she persisted, feeling him smile against her hair, loving the trapped-snuggled sensation of Jack's body enveloping hers.

"*Because,* Sarah, you have a big grand noble heart, full of kindness and courage and strength. Breaking a heart like that would be a heinous crime."

Her body softened, the better to absorb his words. "It would?"

"It would."

She melted into him more, unable to resist one last, "Why?"

"Because—" he curled closer around her, the movement protective and exquisitely tender "—breaking *your* heart would break *my* heart. Is that what you wanted to hear?"

Sarah let go of the mugs with a clunk.

Jack turned her around, his hands gripping her upper arms, then peered anxiously into her face. She had no defenses left. Everything she felt was in her eyes for him to see. Her heart was breaking. Her heart was rejoicing. Her heart belonged totally and completely to him.

Wonder dawned in his eyes, swelled into a high noon blaze of exultation. His hands tightened on her arms.

"You really didn't know?" she asked, laying her palms on his chest.

He shook his head in a dazed manner, a shadow of trepidation creeping into his expression. He was beginning to understand the awfulness of their situation.

She watched his dream fight for survival with his conscience, saw the exact second Moses won the battle. As he always would with this man. It was one of the main reasons she loved him.

Resolve firmed his jaw. "I'll call Irving and tell him I'm staying here. It won't affect the sale. They'll get someone else to do the rewrite."

"No, they won't," she corrected gently. "Because you're going to do it. Brilliantly. You're going to move to L.A. and accept this incredible opportunity God and your talent have given you." His heart thrummed hard and fast beneath her palms.

He lowered his forehead against hers and rolled from side to side. "Sarah, Sarah. I can't leave now. I can't leave y—"

Two of her fingertips stopped the word. "You can, Jack. You *must*. If you stayed, you'd grow to hate me—and yourself." She managed a weak smile. "I sound like a B movie. A really bad one. Somebody please rewrite this script."

He lifted his head, anguish and an odd anger in his gaze. "All right. You've appointed yourself the director of this story. Tell me how you want the scene to play."

She slid her palms up the hard wall of his chest and rose on tiptoe. "Not with anger or guilt," she murmured against one ear, lowering her heels to string a necklace of kisses across his bobbing Adam's apple, rising again to reach the opposite ear. "Not with regret or pain," she whispered, threading her fingers into his sable hair, pulling back to look into his green-gold eyes.

"This is a love scene, Jack. A man and woman have one night together before he ships out. They don't know what the future holds, so they make the most of the hours they can control. No strings. No promises they may not be able to keep.

"They create a memory to make them ache for each other when they go their separate ways. A memory to make them smile in their old age. *That's* how I want the scene to play." She massaged the base of his skull, sank into his body to tip the scales and prayed he wouldn't sense the heaviness of her heart. "Think you can handle that, Hotshot?"

She got her answer in the form of an openmouthed kiss, so hard and hungry it drove her stumbling back until her spine bumped the kitchen counter. The ride was as wet and wild as before, but escalated quickly to a new level of thrill.

No door would open. No eyes would judge and condemn. They were two consenting adults with time and privacy on their side.

His hands were everywhere at once. Big, gentle and fervent. Just when they seemed to settle on a favorite spot, they moved on to cup or squeeze or stroke new territory.

"You feel so good," he said against her lips. "I can't get enough of you."

"Try," she demanded, her hands equally busy.

His biceps were as hard as they looked, his back a marvel of flexing muscles. His buns of steel filled her palms as nicely as she'd suspected since he'd first turned to write on his classroom blackboard. Her hand wandered to the ridge beneath his belt buckle. He clapped a palm over her fingers and broke their kiss.

"Wait," he rasped out, his erection pulsing once. Twice. When he finally lifted his restraining hand, it was to divest her of sweatshirt and pants with quick efficiency.

In minutes she was standing in her kitchen, wearing pink satin bra and matching bikini underwear, shivering beneath his hot devouring gaze. She moved to cover herself, and his hands clamped her wrists.

"Don't. You're perfect." His thumbs rubbed her frantic pulse, his gaze scorched a path from her breasts to the apex of her thighs. "I've waited too long for this, wanted you too much. I think, Madam Director, it's time to cut to a new location." He bent over and scooped her up against his chest.

She looped her arms around his neck during the dizzying walk, feeling small and feminine and desirable. As perfect as he'd said. It freed her inhibitions as nothing else could. They had all night, but she wanted him *now*.

He lowered her effortlessly to the bed, then started to follow her down.

"Wait," she repeated his earlier order, her palm pressed to his chest. "Get undressed. Hurry."

He obeyed without modesty, his burning gaze never leaving hers, his movements forceful and exciting. He came to her magnificently aroused, a compliment she returned in full. He discovered as much when he unclasped her bra to reveal stiff distended nipples, when he slipped off her panties and brushed his knuckles against her dewy welcome. She lifted her arms and pleaded, "Come here."

At last he covered her with a glorious masculine blanket of heated muscle and hair-roughened skin. She wriggled down to meet him properly. The kiss of intimate flesh was hot and moist. Unbearably erotic.

"Easy, easy," he soothed, as much a warning to himself, she suspected, as a means to soothe her fractious need.

"I don't want easy. I want hard. I love you so much, Jack," she said with ardent agony, hearing his quick intake of breath. "I want you inside me now." She surged up to drive her point home, succeeding only partially. "Jack, please. Let me show you how much I love you."

"I've got a better idea," Jack crooned, threading their fingers together, lifting their hands palm to palm above her head. "Let's show each other."

In one powerful thrust, he drove all the way home.

In her old age, she would remember this moment above all others. Jack gazing down with a branding tender possessiveness while her heart beat joyful and wild.

Then he began the timeless rhythm that, in perfectly matched lovers, was like shooting the rapids in a kayak. They gasped and panted and rolled and laughed, rushing ever nearer to the exhilarating plunge they sensed ahead. She reached it seconds in front of Jack and snatched him desperately to her breast to bring him with her.

She fell into an awesome climax that ripped his name from her throat, convulsed her body in spasms of splendid pleasure. As her ripples of sensation quieted, Jack reached his completion with a choked cry, then collapsed on her chest, his nose buried in her neck.

Deeply content to be uncomfortable beneath his weight, she drifted into calmer waters. The hand that flopped tiredly over his shoulder rubbed light lazy circles on his damp skin.

The hurt would come eventually, she knew. And it would be very very bad. But she had tonight. There were more memories to create.

If she had to let him go, she would make damn sure this was one scene he'd never forget.

HE HAD TO GO. It was almost midnight, and he didn't want to face speculative glances or outright questions from Kate and his mother by arriving in the morning just in time to leave for school. There would be enough questions when he told them about the sale of *Free Fall*.

Rolling onto his side, Jack braced his jaw on a palm.

Moonlight filtered through an oak tree outside the window, dappling the sleeping form beside him in silver and gray. Leached of flamboyant color, Sarah seemed unfamiliar. More like a piece of sculpture than the small red-haired dynamo he'd come to know. He studied her with the appreciation of a museum visitor, his gaze unhurried. Unclouded by the passion hazing his earlier impressions.

She was still perfect.

Half on her belly, one knee drawn up high, she displayed a beautiful swell of hip artfully draped with a sheet. The downslope was sharp, ascending gently up a narrow rib cage into a generous palmful of breast.

His gaze traveled leisurely over her slender arm—hooked over her pillow to frame an immensely pleasing profile—then back down the landscape of her body. He could encircle that tiny waist with both hands, he'd discovered. Slide his palms up to test the weight and yield of rose-tipped flesh. His body stirred strongly.

Unbelievable. Even prolonged abstinence couldn't account for his insatiable response to this woman. He'd known the sex would be good. He hadn't known it would move his soul as well as the earth.

For several contented moments Jack watched the rise and fall of her ribs, listened to the sound of her easy breathing; an entrancing feminine sound he could wake up to every morning—if he moved to Dallas instead of L.A.

Averting his gaze, Jack stared bleakly out the window. An emptiness unlike any he'd known replaced his peace. Was he making the right decision?

His mother and Kate would be well provided for financially when he left, and Sarah was right. They *had* become too dependent on him. His fault. He hadn't held them to the same accountability he required of his students. His departure would be a crash course in survival, but they would pass.

The high school would be in a bind, having to produce a substitute for the remaining three months. He hated that. But teachers had left unexpectedly before due to various reasons. The system would kick in and provide coverage.

As for his kids...man, he *really* hated not being around to see them through their last months of high school. Yet, as Sarah had said, he'd provided them with a good foundation. And maybe—no, probably—Jack corrected honestly, they deserved a break from his inflexibility.

He wasn't proud of the realization that Sarah had been right about something else: his jealousy. Its absence in the face of imminent freedom was noticeable. He might never have admitted experiencing the ugly emotion otherwise.

Responsibility was good, but, like anything else, not in excess. Certainly not at the sacrifice of youthful spontaneity and a time of life that should be remembered with joy.

So that alleviated two of his main doubts in the wisdom of leaving. The remaining one slept quietly beside him. Was she right about him growing to resent her, or worse, if he stayed? He didn't know. But looking back on another "if only" in his life, particularly one of this magnitude, was something he couldn't do. Not and maintain his self-respect.

But would his heart survive? He looked at Sarah.

Her eyes were open and watching him. She yawned, then offered a sweet drowsy smile.

Just that fast he was hard and ready for action. Again. He should ignore the clamor of his body. They'd gotten fairly acrobatic in some of their earlier lovemaking. She was very likely sore.

Her smile faded slowly and the moment stretched, her expression growing more alert. Then another kind of languor seemed to overtake her, this one sensual and heavy with promise.

"You aren't in a hurry to leave, are you?" she asked, her siren's voice stroking his arousal like a physical touch.

Tell her you have to go. "Uhh…" he croaked.

"Wait." With a mysterious feminine smile that had him perking up like Rin Tin Tin for a T-bone, she whipped back the sheet and padded out the bedroom door.

He cocked his head toward the sound of rummaging in the bathroom, then tensed as she appeared in the doorway. And he'd thought he'd enjoyed the view of her leaving. Ha!

She approached with the grace and look-what-I've-brought-you demeanor of a small dainty cat with a proffered kill. "I thought maybe I would try this out, if you're willing to cooperate," she purred.

He was so distracted by the charms her front view presented it took him a second to focus on her out-stretched gift. A small bottle with peaches on the label. He peered closer. Body massage oil.

He looked up with heated anticipation, his grin slow and lazy. "Sure. I'm in no hurry."

CHAPTER FIFTEEN

MANY THINGS about entering high school as a twenty-seven-year-old had been a difficult adjustment for Sarah. The structured routine, the homework, the patronizing attitude of adults. The complex social hierarchy that ruled students' happiness. All these factors, combined with the fear that her new safe house would be discovered, had made January and February stressful, to say the very least.

Yet fifth period English with Mr. Morgan had provided a reason to look forward to each day. At first, because he added nice scenery to her windowless routine. Then later, because he made her brain think, her blood heat and her heart fill to bursting. How could she help but fall in love?

The "scenery," she'd learned firsthand, wasn't simply nice. It was worthy of a calendar. During the two weeks following their lovemaking, she'd spent hours visualizing twelve poses that would do it justice.

She had one spectacular night of memories to design from. It would have to suffice. They'd both agreed a repeat performance wouldn't be wise, although neither of them had specified why.

Sarah's reasons for abstaining had nothing to do with high morals, and everything to do with fear. He'd made his decision to leave. She was bound and determined to honor his choice. Now, when she lay awake in the dark, seconds from throwing back the covers, driving to Jack's house and crawling through his bedroom window, she closed her eyes and conjured up a powerful deterrent: a vision of herself clinging to Jack's knees, begging him to stay as he dragged her along the floor.

On Jack's final day of school in late February, she'd thought she was prepared to let him go. She'd urged him to leave, for Pete's sake. She'd even helped organize fifth period's surprise farewell party.

"His kids" may have griped about Morgan's Ten Commandments, but the messages they'd written on his goodbye card revealed affection and deep respect. To see the stern Mr. Morgan visibly choked up had caused an epidemic of watery eyes and clearing throats.

Even Tony had gotten a little misty. It would've made a great Hallmark commercial if the cameras had been rolling. Almost as poignant as the moment after school when she'd said her final goodbye.

Jack had stood in the hallway holding a box of clutter from the desk he'd just cleared. With kids streaming around them, she'd stared into his beautiful hazel eyes and muttered inane words she'd promptly forgotten.

But she would *never* forget her sense of utter desolation at his curt good wishes for the future, his privately uttered admonition to be careful and send him a note after the trial. Or the premonition while watching him walk out to his car—its interior already half-packed with belongings for his drive to L.A. in the morning—that this was only the tip of her agony. That miles of icy loneliness stretched below. Too many miles to melt in a lifetime.

She'd thought she was prepared to let him go.

But she'd been oh-so-very wrong.

THE FOLLOWING March and April were two of the worst—and best—months of Sarah's life. The worst hours began at sunset, when the rest of the world went home to a family, or a loving pet, or the empty but comforting haven created by individual taste and personal mementos.

Sarah went "home" to the echo of her own voice, in a place decorated by someone else, filled with books left by myriad guests, scattered with framed photos of the Kaiser family. Even the clothes on her back weren't hers—but Sarina's. Or technically, Donna's.

More and more, Sarah longed to go home to *her* apartment and sit in the furniture *she'd* selected, read the books of *her* choice. Gaze at the photo of *her* parents captured in a moment of rare accord.

She wanted to wear her own sophisticated grown-up clothes and go to the grocery store, or the movies. Any place that wasn't the guest house or Roosevelt High School. In that sense she truly empathized with teenage restlessness like Kate's. Sarah's imprisonment, albeit a privileged one, chafed and galled.

Her nightly routine rarely deviated. She would shower with peach-scented soap and *shove back the memory* of large hands slick with oil, gliding warm and appreciatively over her skin. She'd head for the kitchen and pull out a frozen dinner, bought and delivered by a friend only slightly warmer, pop it in the microwave and wait for the *ding!*

Then she'd *shove back the memory* of a small domed bell on a desktop, and stretch the process of eating from five minutes to at least fifteen. On a lucky night she had enough dirty laundry to make a full load, and she'd take it to the main house and kill another hour.

Homework wasn't the chore it had been at first, but a welcome task more diverting than TV. On a lucky night, it would occupy as many as three hours. Four, if she had a test the next day. Her substitute English teacher, a pretty young woman determined to prove her worth, was a firm believer in pop quizzes. Sarah would study for multiple choice questions, *shove back the memory* of her first debate on the subject, and maybe watch a little of Letterman before bed.

At last she would accept the inevitable, brush her teeth and climb between cool sheets, where the memories were hottest, the loneliness coldest. And she would wonder how Jack was doing, was he happy, did he miss her at least a little? Was he dazzled by the beautiful women in his new industry, as they no doubt were dazzled by the handsome new screenwriter in their midst?

She knew he was living in the director's Hollywood home, and that they were working closely—but not always harmoniously—on the rewrites. He hadn't written or called her since he'd left. Her scraps of information were gleaned cautiously from Kate, lest she tell her brother that Sarina had been asking for details.

On a lucky night she didn't toss and turn, or ache and need, or get up to make hot tea. On a lucky night, she fell asleep at a decent hour and woke up refreshed.

Which was good. Because her best hours during that endless March and April began in the morning. At school.

Her role of Sarina Davis had become a comfortable second skin, melding more each day with her old self to form a new identity. An apt process for the season when feathers molted, butterflies emerged from cocoons, and rejuvenation was the order of the day.

The result was a Sarah Davidson who was less cynical. Less quick to assume appearances were only masks for the person one wished to hide from the world. Sometimes that was true, yes. But not always. Not usually.

It had taken a motley collection of Roosevelt High School students to renew her faith in the basic decency of people, to restore her pride in her profession.

If Sarah hadn't had *her* kids that awful spring, she would've surely gone mad.

RUSHING INTO the girls' locker room, Sarah threw her gym bag on a bench and began changing into her "walking" clothes. She was late. Elaine was already outside on the track. Donna had called an emergency wrap-up meeting after school for the senior prom planning committee. With only ten days left until *Abra-*

cadabra—*You're Outta Here!* gave graduating students "a magical night to remember," the committee was jittery about living up to the advance publicity.

With good reason. Ticket sales had gone through the roof once news leaked out that Alan Chaney would make an appearance. The hot new comedian-magician who'd grown up in Houston was on the fast track to stardom.

No one could believe the entertainer who'd recently hosted "Saturday Night Live" would book a lowly high school prom gig. Hadn't he taken that paparazzo's camera and smashed it on the sidewalk? Wasn't his greatest illusion acting charming and sincere when in reality he was a conceited jerk?

Allowing herself a smug smile, Sarah dropped her Nike cross-trainers on the floor and sat to tie them on. She loved it when timing, know-how and luck converged to make things happen. With Donna as her mouthpiece, Sarah had contacted Alan's agent and hyped the benefits of counteracting that nasty wave of negative publicity. Houston media sound bites of the prom would be picked up nationally, and the country would see what a nice man Alan *really* was, sacrificing big bucks to give kids in his hometown a true night to remember.

Sarah was thankful the negotiations and countless other aspects of *Abracadabra* had forced her and Donna to work closely together. Eventually, they'd talked about Jack. In the face of a misery surpassing her own, Donna had thawed, finally admitting she'd had no real claim on him. That he'd been honest, and she'd stubbornly refused to see they had no future.

Tugging up her socks, Sarah stood and headed for the exit leading to the track. Her own future was a big question mark. The Monday following the prom, John Merrit's murder trial would begin. Getting there was no problem. Walking into the courthouse safely was another issue. Since initial efforts to find her had failed, that would be the most likely time for another attempt on her life.

Sarah suppressed a shudder, pushed through the door, and burst into the late afternoon sunshine with relief. Two steps outside she stopped to let her eyes adjust. The scent of fresh-mown grass, sweet with clover, wafted in from the athletic fields. Shrill whistles, barked orders and occasional laughter told of baseball, softball and track team practices in session. A balmy breeze ruffled her hair.

Ah, much better. It was hard to believe in the bogeyman amid such normalcy.

The red track was a happening place. She searched the two outside lanes—the only ones allotted for non-team use at this time of year—and spotted Elaine. Look at that girl go! Arms pumping, head turning occasionally to smile and return a comment from passing runners, she was a far different sight from the shy teen who'd barely made it twice around the track in January.

For one thing, she'd lost all but about ten pounds of her excess weight. As her facial bone structure and nice curves began emerging from hiding, she'd no longer needed a companion to motivate her to exercise or eat properly.

Yet those were only cosmetic changes. Good for gaining acceptance in an appearance-oriented society. But by no means the secret to personal happiness. Sarah had worked with too many slim beautiful women who were also neurotic wrecks to believe otherwise.

Jogging slowly to the track, she experienced immense pride in her young friend's deeper transformation. Elaine was much more assertive and confident than before. Her aura said, "I'm somebody worth knowing," instead of, "Kick me."

Too bad her newfound attitude hadn't given her the courage to ask a boy to be her date for the prom. Elaine refused to attend alone, as Sarah had done for her own senior prom.

What do you expect, after telling her you were a miserable wallflower at your prom? a sarcastic inner voice jeered.

Sarah shook off her guilt and prepared to step onto the track beside Elaine. She was coming up fast with a wide, challenging grin.

Oh-ho! The kid wanted to take on the pro again, did she?

Sarah entered the outside lane and moved into a warm-up walk. Not enough time to do the job properly, but she never ignored a thrown gauntlet. By the time Elaine moved up beside her, Sarah's muscles had loosened enough to proceed as planned.

"Hi there," Sarah greeted, slowly increasing her

speed to match the girl's. "How many laps have you done?"

"Ten, once I hit the mile mark. Want to race my last two?"

Hmm. Elaine was probably tiring.

"Okay, you're on," Sarah accepted, an idea forming. "But if I win, you have to go to the prom."

Elaine's brown eyes flashed. "I'm not going by myself! I already told you."

"And I'm not deaf," Sarah groused. "Sheesh, I'll provide the date. And I promise he'll be presentable."

They thudded in silence, Elaine glowering.

"Well?" Sarah prodded. "We're getting close to the mile mark.

"You're not going to quit nagging me about this prom thing, are you?"

"Nope." Sarah grinned unrepentantly.

"Oh, all *right*. But if I win, not *one* more word about next Friday, is it a deal?"

Yesss! "Deal."

They were almost upon the mile mark now.

"Feet in contact with the track at all times," Sarah recited the rules. "Don't kill yourself trying to win. Stop if you have to."

"Eat my dust," Elaine answered.

The race was on!

Sarah hadn't lost a bet with the girl yet, but it soon became clear this could be a major upset. Damn, Elaine's legs were long. A serious advantage. And of course, her muscles were completely warmed up. Another big point in her favor. Maybe this hadn't been so smart. Maybe— No.

Sarah narrowed her eyes and lifted her chin. She might be shorter. Her muscles might be stiffer. But she was older, tougher and meaner than any upstart eighteen-year-old. She found her stride and bumped it up a notch.

Damn, Elaine's legs were long. She took a single step for Sarah's every two.

At one lap they were neck and neck. Sarah's muscles burned. Her lungs weren't far behind. If she went any faster she'd break into a jog. She'd gone from perspiring delicately to sweating profusely and—oh, swell—they'd attracted an audience. Just what she needed. Witnesses as the pro went down.

Guys from the track team started calling out their names, cheering on one or the other. Elaine, the underdog, received the most encouragement. Sarah tuned it all out and focused on her goal. Pumped her arms. Ignored her burning muscles and lungs. *Damn,* Elaine's legs were long.

Into the homestretch now. This was it. Unless Sarah grew five inches in the next eighth of a mile, Elaine would sit home on prom night and miss all the magic and fun. Miss a dance every girl dreamed of with fairy-tale wistfulness. Not going would make Elaine *feel* like a wallflower as surely as Sarah had been one in fact. She couldn't let that happen.

It was time to eat the can of spinach, to duck into the phone booth and put on a cape, to separate the women from the girls. Sarah reached deep down inside her and found an eighth of a mile's worth of grit.

Then she glanced at Elaine and said, "Eat my dust."

ON SATURDAY, Sarah drove the land yacht for the first time since heading to Bruce Logan's house.

If a killer was out there watching her now, which was highly unlikely, she would simply have to get shot. She'd promised to meet some of her kids at the mall to help with last-minute prom necessities. She'd done all she could using magazine photos and fashion catalogs to show examples of styles she thought would work. But some things needed to be eyeballed. No way was she bailing out on these kids at the critical hour.

Kate wasn't sure about the color of a prom dress she'd put on hold. Fred had finally agreed to have his hair cut, but couldn't be trusted to instruct the stylist properly. Elaine needed a magic wand top to bottom in order to be ready for Prince Charming when he escorted her to the ball. Grinning to herself, Sarah trolled the parking lot for an empty space, more proud of her recent coup than of getting a hotshot entertainer to perform at the prom.

Greg Lake, the cute Rice University student who took care of Mrs. Kaiser's lawn and garden, had asked Sarah last week if the guest house would be available for rent when she left. This morning she'd struck a bargain. She would propose to Mrs. Kaiser the wisdom of leasing the guest house, recommending Greg as a tenant gardener, if he would escort a beautiful girl to a glamorous hotel ballroom next Friday to see Alan Chaney perform.

Both parties were thrilled with the agreement. Elaine was not quite as enthusiastic, since she was nervous about a blind date for the prom, but Sarah *had* won the race. Quite handily, too, as a matter of fact.

Spotting a woman loading packages in a car up ahead, Sarah clicked on her blinkers to stake her claim. Five minutes later, she entered the busy suburban mall.

Freedom! How sweet it was, if only for a day. Sarah stood very still and absorbed the wondrous sights, sounds and smells she hadn't allowed herself in months.

The mother dragging a squalling toddler. What a cute little tyke. The couple clogging traffic outside the jewelry store. Wasn't love grand? The husband sprawled on a bench, guarding his wife's packages with a bored expression—until a pretty girl passed by. She probably reminded him of his daughter, sweet man.

A rap song played in Sam Goody behind Sarah. "When You Wish Upon a Star" warbled from The Disney Store ahead. She got all choked up. It was just so profound. Like the mingled scents of pizza, fried rice and fajitas drifting from the food court.

What a great big melting pot of a country this was! So many choices. So much personal freedom. How had she *ever* not liked going to the mall?

"There you are!" Fred's deep voice broke into her

musing. "You were supposed to meet us in front of the movie theater."

Sarah beamed as he walked up with Kate and Elaine in tow.

"I told you she was probably out here," Elaine said.

The three started squabbling, and Sarah took a moment to simply enjoy them all. She'd decided the rugged outdoorsman look would both suit Fred's build and aid his image the best. The whiz kid had sold some stock from his impressive portfolio, and Sarah had ordered from Abercrombie & Fitch as well as Lands' End catalogs.

He looked tall, broad and hunky in a blue chambray shirt, black jeans and black hiking boots. But the most startling change had occurred when he'd switched from Buddy Holly style glasses to contacts. Man-oh-man! Good thing Kate had seen the light after he'd defended her honor so impressively. Ever since he'd uncovered those Mel Gibson look-alikes, the girls at school had forgotten they'd ever called Fred a geek.

Kate was lovelier than ever, mainly because she smiled a lot these days. In Jack's absence, Fred had been a stable influence. What's more, he adored her, and she blossomed beneath such unconditional approval. She suddenly wanted to look pretty and be smart. Her grooming and grades improved—which pleased Vera, who acted less crabby.

The Morgan women are holding their own, thank you very much, Jack. At least, the two Morgan women who bore his name. Sarah wasn't doing nearly as well.

Elaine's jeans were baggy, as was her T-shirt. A

month ago they'd been snug. When she reached a level weight, her parents would replenish her wardrobe gladly. They were proud and impressed with her discipline the past four months. Her long chestnut hair had been glorious, but the new shoulder-length blunt cut was sophisticated and framed her oval face beautifully. With luck, they would find a dress to bring out the rich red highlights....

"Uh-oh. She's got that look on her face," Elaine warned.

"Which one of us is she working on now?" Kate asked.

"Quick! Last one in to Sam Goody has to be her guinea pig," Fred teased.

"Okay, wise guy." Sarah walked forward and hooked her arm through his. "Just for that, I think we should start with your haircut."

The girls escorted him, moaning the entire way, to Visible Changes, where Sarah spent a good ten minutes telling the stylist how to do her job.

Forty minutes later, everyone agreed Sarah knew her stuff. Fred looked gorgeous. Clipped short—but not buzzed—from about ear level down, his black hair spilled over onto his forehead in a windblown outdoorsy look. Mmm-hmm.

"I am *not* letting you out of my sight," Kate told him as they left the salon.

Fred looked over his shoulder at Sarah and grinned his thanks.

They checked out Kate's dress next. Or, rather, the girls did. Fred was banned from the formal wear section, since Kate wanted to knock his socks off on prom night.

And she would, Sarah declared, seeing the emerald green strapless dress on the girl. His contacts would pop out, too. The color was great with her hair, and it made her eyes seem even greener. Buy it, she recommended.

Two down, one to go.

The lovebirds went off to the movies. Sarah and Elaine set out alone. After two hours and a growing sense of desperation, they hit the jackpot.

An off-the-shoulder gown in shimmery autumn brown. Tight in the bodice and upper waist, flowing fluidly from there to the floor. The color was perfect, as if custom dyed to match a strand of Elaine's hair. For the first time since she'd lost the bet, her eyes sparkled at the prospect of going to the prom.

That's when Sarah knew. Whatever she did in the future would involve helping adolescents feel good about themselves. Her job at WorldWide Public Relations had stroked her ego, not made her happy.

Funny how she'd had to become a teenager again to grow up.

CHAPTER SIXTEEN

JACK POURED a dollop of oil onto his palm and rubbed his hands slowly together. The motion almost looked gleeful. Appropriate. He certainly felt gleeful at the moment.

His gaze traveled hungrily over the woman awaiting his touch. Where to start. So many delectable curves, all of them tempting. Her skin was pale, and as soft as moonlight looked. Would it feel different when slick? He reached out and—

"Yoo-hoo, Jack?"

Jack blinked. Sunlight chased the moonlit vision from his mind. He was back in Los Angeles, eating lunch on an outdoor patio with Gail Powers, executive producer of Swan Production Company, and Daniel Harris, director of *Free Fall*.

"I'm sorry, Did you say something?" Jack asked Gail.

She arched a penciled brow. "I said you really should try one of these peach daiquiris. And then—poof!" She made a little exploding motion with her hand. "You were gone."

Jack's neck heated. The strong scent of peaches was a torment he tried to ignore. "Sorry." He reached for his Corona beer. "I'm back now."

But not totally. Each week that passed, he learned his way around the city a little more, felt a little more of himself drift back to Houston.

Gail looked at him thoughtfully over the rim of her daiquiri glass, leaned back in the wrought-iron chair and crossed her legs. At sixty-something, she still had great gams. "Daniel said you haven't been sleeping well. You do look tired."

Jack shot the silver-haired director a startled glance.

Daniel shrugged. "Consuela's bedroom is next to the kitchen. She hears you moving around. Plus, you look like death warmed over, son." His dark eyes twinkled. "I wouldn't notice. Except everyone in L.A. but you has a tan."

"What's this really about, Daniel?" Jack leveled a don't-bullshit-me look. "I thought you were happy with my work."

The director lifted his palms placatingly. "Hey, you've done a terrific job. That last scene you knocked out is gonna blow the audience away. I was telling Bob DeNiro just last week you're a real comer. He's anxious to read the revised script." Daniel reached for his martini, toyed with the skewered olive. "You're a decent guy, Jack. There aren't many of those left in this town. Something's been eating at you. I mentioned it to Gail. She suggested we all do lunch. No nefarious motive. We get so caught up in the business sometimes, we forget people have personal lives."

Gail picked up the cue. "How's your family? You have a mother and sister in Houston, right?"

A sharp twist of homesickness burrowed in Jack's

chest. "Yeah. They're fine. My baby sister is going to her first prom tonight." He smiled and shook his head. "I'd give anything to be a fly on the wall. But Mother will take a whole roll of film, I'm sure."

"Why don't you take half the roll?" Gail suggested.

Jack's gaze snapped to hers.

She smiled. "I've heard Houston has an airport. You could be there in time if you hustle. Take the weekend off."

"I need Monday, too." The minute Jack said it, he realized he'd made the decision long before today. He simply could not let Sarah go to that murder trial alone. He had no special training, but no matter. He would give up his life to protect her, if necessary.

Daniel snorted. "Well, that didn't take much arm-twisting. Sure, take Monday off. Actually, I don't need you back here until Wednesday, at the earliest."

"You look better already," Gail said. "Who is she?"

Jack paused in the act of lifting his beer. "My sister? Her name is Kate."

Gail rolled her eyes. "Who's the woman in Houston you're in love with?"

He nearly choked on his beer. His insomnia, his distinct lack of enchantment with the freedom he'd been given, the sights and scents that triggered memories more vivid than reality...they all led to a conclusion he'd be a fool to deny.

"Her name is Sarah Davidson. But some people call her Sarina."

"O-O-OH, DONNA. My *clothes*. You brought my clothes." Sarah opened the guest house door and welcomed her garments like beloved friends.

Donna swept through with her arms full. "I told you I would get them, didn't I?" She'd flown to Dallas yesterday to attend a continuing education seminar and had offered to dash into Sarah's apartment for a few items.

"Did you see anyone?"

Donna walked into the bedroom and dropped her load on the bed. "At five o'clock in the morning? Nope. I didn't bring all that much. Theoretically, on Monday you'll have access to all of your clothes. Is this the dress you were talking about for tonight?"

Sarah looked at the sleek fire-engine red halter dress, floor-length with a slit to the thigh. "That's the one."

"It's hot. You'll look fabulous." Donna spread the silk carefully on the bed. "Sorry, but your ficus tree and spider plant are history. You'd think as long as the justice department pays your rent, they'd send someone in to water the plants occasionally. Nice apartment, by the way."

"How did it look?" Sarah asked piteously.

"Lonely. A little dusty. Nothing Molly Maid can't handle when you get back." Donna peered closer at Sarah, who'd pressed a hand to her throat. "Hey, don't fall apart, now. You're so close to being home free."

Sarah nodded. "I know. It's just…you've done so much for me already, and now this." She gestured vaguely to the clothes.

Donna caught Sarah's hand in midair and squeezed. "*You've* done so much for Roosevelt High, Sarah. Getting Alan Chaney for the prom, taking the kids under your wing and making some positive changes in their lives. We're all going to miss Sarina when she leaves." Donna's eyes lit with mischief. "How would you like to send her out with a bang, tonight?"

What in the world?

Releasing Sarah's hand, Donna rummaged through the purse half buried among the clothes on the bed. "I picked up one more thing for you before I left Dallas." She pulled something out. "Catch!"

Sarah snatched the rectangular box of hair color. Not Outrageous Red, but Midnight Black. She broke into a slow and increasingly delighted grin. To be Sarah Davidson again, from the top of her head to her floor-length Givenchy gown!

"You really think I should?" Sarah asked.

"Go for it, kiddo. I'm tired of that ho-hum hair you've got now." Donna wriggled her fingers and breezed to the front door. "See ya at seven. Don't make me wait. And don't expect a corsage." The door closed on the sound of her chuckle.

Sarah made the most of the next six hours. The first task was a no-brainer. Oh, the glorious moment she toweled dry her Midnight Black hair! But when she stared at her reflection, she was a little freaked. Her old self seemed like a stranger. Sheesh, she'd be lucky not to come out of this experience seriously schizophrenic.

Moving on, she painted her nails a bright red to

match her dress. She shaved her legs, ate a late afternoon sandwich, then pulled a *Gone with the Wind* fragile Southern belle act and took a nap before the night of magic and dancing.

Not that *she* would dance, Sarah thought groggily two hours later. But she was eager to see all her young friends hit the floor. Oh, God, what would they think of her hair? A little late now for second thoughts.

Shrugging, she splashed her face with cold water, then began applying her makeup. For the first time as Sarina, she used a full arsenal of cosmetics. When she finished, she looked twenty-seven. On prom night, it didn't really matter.

Most of the teenage girls there would look twenty-eight.

She spent more time than usual on her hair, experimenting with mousse and a curling iron. Blowing her hair dryer in short spurts to tousle the curls. The end result was a sophisticated just-got-laid look she had to admit was pretty great.

When she realized she would have to go braless—her halter style bra was in a dresser drawer in Dallas—Sarah began to get a little nervous. There was a fine line between too much, and not enough. But Sarah was a pro at creating images.

When she checked herself out in full war paint, she looked exactly like what she'd planned: a very classy slut dressed to kill.

Her "date" agreed. On the drive to the hotel, Donna kept sneaking peeks.

"For Pete's sake, watch the road," Sarah finally scolded.

"I shouldn't let you loose around all those raging teenage hormones tonight. You look illegal," Donna muttered.

"Did you get dressed without a mirror tonight? Assistant principals do *not* wear strapless gowns and look like you."

Donna had the grace to blush. "You remember that tall dark neighbor I mentioned? The one who keeps late hours? Well, he might stop by to check out the magic act. I sort of said there would be a ticket for him at the entrance."

"Ahh." Sarah grinned. "*Love* the dress."

The rest of the drive passed in harmony. They valet parked and caused quite a few male heads to turn on the way to the ballroom. Inside, it truly was magical. A girl's dream.

Silver and black helium balloons clustered everywhere. Table centerpieces featured silver-and-black-sequined top hats and chocolate bunnies, the latter to be eaten or taken home as souvenirs. Silver stars of all shapes and sizes dangled from the ceiling. And a photo setup standing the girl in a magician's open black box, with her date outside holding a magic wand.

The faces of all the arriving teens at their first glimpse of the room was worth every hour of planning, gluing sequins and haggling with an agent. Sarah's altered appearance caused a sensation, as well.

Wendy's dropped jaw, followed by a venomous

gaze was particularly gratifying. Especially when it turned on Tony, who was sending Sarah a rakish grin.

"Her kids" first gaped, then heaped praises—the girls more than the boys. Beto, Derek and Fred hovered around her like three glowering big brothers.

"Guys, what's going on?" she demanded. "Your dates are getting irritated."

"Well, hell, Sarina, we can't leave you alone looking like *that*," Fred spoke for them all. "The stag line is pawing the ground already."

Sarah glanced at a group of obviously dateless boys. She wouldn't have been human not to preen a little.

"I appreciate your concern, but I can take care of myself. Now go have fun. Oh—has anyone seen Elaine?"

No one had, and Sarah's stomach twisted. Had something gone wrong? She spent the next fifteen minutes anxiously watching the door. And then— boom! There they were, causing quite a stir. As well they should. They looked spectacular together.

Greg's blond good looks set off by formal black. Elaine's beauty at last striking her classmates, who'd only seen her in baggy clothes. Greg had *College Man* written all over him, which raised Elaine's social status considerably. Best of all, he appeared truly besotted with his "bargain" date. When Elaine caught Sarah's eye across the room and broke into a happy belle-of-the-ball smile, she counted the evening a complete success.

Alan Chaney's act brought on the TV cameras, which in turn brought out the best in Alan. Press would be good. Another worry put to rest. She noticed Donna's tall dark neighbor had showed up. Yep. He earned the full cliché—he was handsome, too.

Sarah's euphoria lasted through the first of the dancing, which was fast and fun. She accepted a few invitations to the floor, but declined when the mood began to shift. Things got slower. More mellow and romantic.

And suddenly it wasn't fun.

There were Fred and Kate, locked in a gentle loving sway. Wendy and Tony were in bed standing up. Prince Charming held Elaine as if her glass slippers would break. And if that wasn't Ms. Kaiser being extraordinarily neighborly on the floor, Sarah was a pumpkin.

Chained to her post by the punch bowl, where she'd volunteered to make sure it remained pure, she felt a powerful tide of melancholy rise. Was there anything worse than being alone in a crowd of couples? Anything more heart bruising than knowing your perfect mate existed, but had chosen not to be with you? If there was something more painful, she hoped never to experience it in her lifetime.

A magical night to remember became an occasion to be suffered.

She wanted to leave, but asking anyone right now to take her home would spoil the poor devil's fun. Like an idiot, she hadn't thought to bring cab fare. She would have to wait. And watch. And hurt.

Turning her back to the dance floor, she poured herself a glass of punch. Pretended to admire the decorations. Endured the crooning music. Yearned for a man thousands of miles away. She set down her cup and strolled to the wall, drawn by the perverse irony of everything being different, yet everything being the same. She would always be a wallflower.

Slowly, reluctantly, she faced the dance floor again. Her gaze wandered in search of solace. She looked at the stage where Alan had performed, found proof of her professional savvy. Looked toward the kids she'd helped gain confidence, found deep gratification. Looked around the ballroom, found the satisfaction of a job well done. Still…it wasn't enough. The clawing emptiness remained. Until she glanced at the door.

And found her mate.

"Ah!" her involuntary cry matched the leap of her heart. It was Jack! Jack, standing just inside the door! Everything in her thrummed to life. He wore faded jeans, a black T-shirt and black biker boots. And he outshone every formally dressed male in the room.

His gaze roamed intently. Searching… searching…*connecting.*

The electrifying bolt of awareness struck. Harder than ever. Fueled by ten weeks of yearning. Crackling with an additional element Sarah dared not analyze, for fear she might be wrong.

He walked slowly toward her.

She listened to her rampant heartbeat. The world fell away. There was only this man. There would only be this one man. Forever. He stopped a foot away. Handsome, hardworking, honorable, and one hundred and fifty percent heterosexual.

His hand stretched out palm up. "May I have this dance?"

She placed her palm in his, and her heart exulted. "I thought you'd never ask."

Mr. Ruler-Up-His-Ass Morgan walked through his tuxedo-clad students wearing ragged jeans, heedless of the whispers and avid glances, leading an "eighteen-year-old" girl onto the parquet wood floor. Clasping one of her hands to his chest and draping the other over his neck, he pulled her into his arms and the swaying dance. And he made them a couple, in front of God and Roosevelt High.

Questions and answers could wait. For right now, the feel of his muscular arms around her was enough. The woodsy male scent of his skin was enough. The sight of his swirling green-gold eyes was enough. She believed that with all her heart.

Until he lowered his mouth to her ear and said, "I love you, Sarah."

JACK SIPPED the last of his punch and set his empty cup next to the crystal bowl. Another forty-five official minutes were left on the prom clock, but when Sarah finished her drink, *Abracadabra*—they were outta there!

He turned to Donna, who was containing the buzz of his scandalous conduct to manageable levels by her hovering presence and tacit support. When the entire story came out on Monday, she would be a heroic part of a school legend.

"Sarah said she came with you," Jack said. "I'll

see her home. I think it's best we leave now and let things settle down here."

Donna huffed wryly. "I don't know if that's possible at this point, but I agree you should both leave." She moved forward and grasped his forearm, her gaze fierce. "But if you haven't learned any more about women since you left the first time, Jack Morgan...I'll come after you with a shotgun. Is that clear?"

As a bell. "I was an idiot. Thank you for keeping her safe. I'll take over from now on. *If* she'll let me." Donna's obvious relief dissolved a little of his guilt over hurting her in the past. He leaned forward, bussed her cheek and pulled back, grinning. "You're quite a woman."

A tall dark-haired man appeared out of nowhere to lay his palm briefly on her naked back. The barest touch only, but Jack recognized the male-to-male signal—and Donna's immediate flustered pleasure.

He backed away with a lighter spirit. Suddenly everything he'd experienced since leaving the restaurant in L.A. swelled to a breaking point.

The frantic packing at Daniel's house, the crazy rush to the airport, the building frustration as his flight was delayed. The insistent beat of his pulse drumming *come-on-come-on-come-on* throughout the endless hours until touchdown.

The urgent compulsion to see Sarah propelling him straight to the hotel instead of home, pushing him into the formal ballroom wearing jeans and his heart on his sleeve.

When he'd spotted the stunning raven-haired

woman standing alone by the wall, no power on earth or in heaven could have kept him away.

He turned now and moved to take Sarah's empty cup. "Do you mind too much if we leave early?"

"If we don't, I'm going to drag you underneath there—" she indicated the skirted table "—and have my way with you," she threatened, her voice and gaze sultry.

When his eyes uncrossed, he set down her cup, gripped her elbow, and steered her forcefully toward the exit. Whispers followed their progress, but he was past hearing, much less giving a damn.

They entered the wide hallway outside the ballroom at a near jog. She stumbled and he caught her up against his side, the feel of her a sweet torture.

"Slow down," she gasped, straightening. "I can't walk that fast."

But he grabbed her hand and pulled her on at the same pace, unable to slow his ramming heart, his frenzied need to get her alone, anywhere alone. His rental car was outside where conference visitors parked. He veered from the valet entrance and strode down a narrower side hallway.

"Jack," Sarah pleaded, stumbling again.

He stopped, his gaze searching up and down the empty hallway, landing briefly on the women's bathroom door, dismissing it and spotting another alcove near the exit outside. Insane. But he was wild for her. He hauled her forward and tested the door marked Supplies. *Abracadabra!*

The door opened under his yank. He thrust Sarah

inside, followed and closed them into complete darkness.

He couldn't see her. But he could hear her quick, arousing little breaths, smell her warm peaches-and-woman scent. He closed his eyes in near pain.

"Sarah," he said raggedly, a plea for forgiveness, a plea to absolve him by making the first move.

Fingertips, advanced probes in the dark, touched his chest lightly. Two small palms settled firmly. A vibrant feminine body pressed into him full length. "I changed my mind, Jack. I want the babies and house surrounded by a white picket fence. It doesn't matter where—as long as you're inside, too."

Nothing she might've said could've inflamed him more.

"Come inside, Jack. Come home."

Except that.

His mouth lowered and found hers open, hot and ardent. She tasted of fruit punch and the spicy spitfire he loved. He gulped her thirstily, unable to get his fill, his body and soul parched from two and a half endless months of drought. This petite bundle of energy was all the excitement he needed in his life. His creativity would flourish, his heart would rejoice, his life would be happy with this woman.

He would devote the rest of his days to loving her, the rest of his nights to showing her how much.

Her skin rivaled the silk that clung to breasts he had to taste now, or die. He unfastened the clasp at her neck, peeled down the fabric and drew one pebbled tip into his mouth. Spicy sweet, like her smell. He kneaded the resilient flesh pillowing his mouth and thought about a baby—the one they'd make some day—doing the same. His drive to mate grew indomitable. Her fingers dove into his hair and swam in circles, then clutched and directed his mouth to her other breast.

The small sounds coming from her throat made him crazy. Needing her more than air, he worked the floor-length skirt slowly up her legs. No panty hose, bless her wanton little heart. Only a scrap of silk, which he managed to slide down instead of rip off.

He lifted his head, unbuckled his belt and lowered his zipper. When he sprang free, her fingers were waiting to caress and stroke. Now it was Jack making pleasured noises in his throat. He stretched out his arms, hitting shelving on his left, empty air on his right. Gripping her shoulders, he turned her toward, please God, a wall, and moved her backward. Her spine bumped smooth plaster. Yes!

"Put your arms around my neck," he ordered, lowering his hands to her backside and lifting. She didn't need further instructions. Her thighs wrapped his hips and she welcomed him home.

They mixed words of lust and poetic love in a feverish language known to only soul mates. The rise to climax was swift for them both, and shattering in strength. He lowered his mouth and drank in her cry of fulfillment…and was quenched at last.

Darkness. Slow breathing. His body pinning another's to the wall. In a supply closet, for cripe's sake. No way to treat the woman he loved. He withdrew and helped her slide slowly down until her feet touched the floor.

What should he say? What was she thinking?

That you're an animal, asshole.

She reached up and ran her fingernails lightly along his jawline. "Well, Mr. Morgan," she said, her voice rich with satisfaction and amusement. "I'd say you've learned to loosen up since you left. You're an animal, lover—" one finger tapped his chin twice "—and don't you ever forget it, either."

Jack chuckled, gathered her into a bear hug, and rocked her briefly next to his heart. No, he would never feel tied down by this woman. Just the opposite. She set him free.

They restored their appearance as best they could in the dark, then Jack opened the door and peeked around. No one in his line of sight. He ventured farther, and waved that the coast was clear.

She came out warily, looking mussed and sated and so sexy he considered leading her back inside the closet. But she was already heading for the bathroom halfway up the hall.

"I'm going to freshen up a little," she said over her shoulder.

Jack nodded, admiring the sway of her hips, as content as he'd ever been. He didn't know what made him look beyond her at a dark-suited man turning into their hallway. A businessman on the way to his car. Nothing remarkable. No reason for Jack's skin to prickle, his blood to freeze, his sixth sense to shout that something was wrong. Sarah was about ten yards from the bathroom now. His feet moved, cement blocks weighing him down. She was too far away. Too close to the man. The man who reached under his coat jacket in trite slow-motion action. *Cut!* Jack's mind screamed to the director.

"Sarah, get down!" he roared, even before he saw the gun.

Oh, God no! She wasn't reacting. He couldn't reach her in time. No house, no babies, no white picket fence. He launched himself in a desperate flying tackle. A gunshot exploded. His shoulder hit Sarah. He wrapped his arms around her and twisted, taking the brunt of their impact.

She lay motionless, half on his chest, half on the floor. Too late. Too late. He hadn't saved her. His life was over.

A sharp little elbow dug into his ribs. "You're taking this animal thing a little too far," Sarah grumbled shakily, rising to a sitting position.

Jack whooped, then scrambled up and in front of her on the floor, his gaze riveted on the figure sprawled facedown on the carpet ahead, one hand clutching a pistol with silencer attached.

Fingers pressed against the killer's neck, a second dark-suited man shook his head grimly and rose.

Jack did, too, then helped Sarah stand. They leaned against each other as their rescuer approached, flipping open his ID.

"U.S. Marshal Walt Stone. You folks okay?" His blue gaze assessed Jack quickly, moved to Sarah and took a lot more time.

Jack frowned. "You want to tell us what just happened, here, Marshal?"

Teens and adults were moving hesitantly into the hallway now, drawn morbidly toward the scene of violence. The marshal glanced toward the gasping crowd and back.

"Security will be here soon. You'll get a full report later. Basically, we suspected Lester Jacobs had gotten to a second officer besides Mike Clancy. As the trial got closer, I watched to see who sweated the most. See, no one knew whether or not Mike had told you who his accomplice was before he died, Ms. Davidson."

"Not by name. Mike only referred to 'an amateur.'"

Her sad tone tugged at Jack's heart. He ran his palm slowly up and down her bare arm.

"Deputy Marshal Kelch, there—" he jerked a thumb at the dead man "—is a rookie. When he started staking out your apartment in Dallas, I knew he was getting desperate."

"Donna," Sarah breathed, looking up at Jack to explain. "Donna went to my apartment and brought back this dress and some other clothes. He must've followed her to me." Sarah turned to the marshal. "And you followed him. But…why did he wait until tonight to make his move?"

"He must've spotted me at George Bush Intercontinental," Marshal Stone admitted, his embarrassment fascinating. "Led me all over Houston. Lost me somewhere in The Galleria. By the time he found out about this shindig, you were already inside. Good thing. It bought me some time to track down where you were.

"When I got to the ballroom," he continued, "Kelch had just come out of this hallway looking frantic. Like maybe he'd lost sight of you. He would search outside the ballroom a little, and then come back to this hallway. When he saw you two, he practically lifted his leg and pointed."

Just then two security officers came running up, and everything got hectic.

Jack pulled Sarah aside, his arm locked around her tight, and met the horrified amusement in her gaze. She obviously realized, as he did, that their rendezvous in the closet had probably saved her life.

"Jack, what will we say if they ask where we were?" she whispered urgently.

The enormity of their good fortune hit him. Two disparate personalities forced together by fate, their relationship tested by separation and adversity, strengthened by respect and love. He knew they would both consider this night as binding as their future wedding ceremony.

"If they ask where we were, we'll tell them the truth." Jack's smile spread outward from a full heart. "That we came home."

EPILOGUE

One year later

SARAH GRIPPED Jack's fingers, glad he blocked her from the crowd's view, and rose from the back seat of their limousine. She should've worn something more practical. The shimmering white evening gown that molded her figure to advantage also shackled her ankles.

Their stroll down the red carpet to the movie premiere of *Free Fall* would no doubt show up on Houston's ten o'clock news. Probably in the morning paper, too. And unless Jack cooperated, she would be captured mincing behind her long-legged husband like an obedient geisha.

Before he moved aside, she pleaded, "Go slo-o-owly."

His gaze swept her from head to toe, and came back up glittering with promise. "Don't I always?"

His intimate growl conjured memories of warm slick hands gliding leisurely over her skin. Just that morning, she'd noticed a new bottle of peach-scented massage oil in the medicine cabinet.

"Hold that thought until we get home," Jack ordered.

Tucking her hand in the crook of his elbow, he turned and stood by her side. High wattage camera lights hit their faces, exposing their flushed anticipation. Eight months of marriage had only heightened their desire for each other.

She forced a smile and sensed Jack do the same. Up ahead, about halfway to the movie theater entrance, an attractive blonde waited between velvet swag ropes to intercept them. Her microphone bore the "Entertainment Tonight" logo.

A national audience. Great. Sarah mentally cursed her gown and headed forward, trusting Jack to keep her from entertaining America with a literal interpretation of *Free Fall*.

Not that the reporter would have noticed. The blonde's appreciative gaze was fixed on the impressive male specimen who did great things for a tuxedo. The one who was most definitely unavailable.

Jack leaned down and murmured, "Easy, Sarina."

Duly cautioned by the rarely used nickname, Sarah resumed her false smile, added a beauty pageant wave and reveled in Jack's deep chuckle.

They slowed to a stop in front of the reporter, now speaking to a nearby remote TV camera.

"Here comes Jack Morgan, the creative genius behind *Free Fall,* and his lovely wife, Sarah. Jack, I understand you wrote this screenplay while teaching high school English. You've come a long way since then. How does it feel to be one of the hottest new screenwriters in Hollywood?" She tipped her microphone his way.

"You'd have to ask a hot new screenwriter in Hollywood. I'm still an English teacher living in Houston."

The reporter sent him an arch look. "You're too modest. Advance reviews on *Free Fall* are predicting an Oscar nomination for best screenplay. Rumor has it Matthew McConaughey and Claire Danes have been cast as leads in your next movie, *Hide and Seek*. I can't imagine it's necessary for you to continue teaching at this point in your career."

"I can't imagine anything more necessary or rewarding than teaching our country's future leaders good communication skills," Jack countered, his sincerity unmistakable. "I have no plans to resign from Roosevelt High School."

He'd confided to Sarah that he felt Hollywood could really screw up a person's priorities, and that teaching kept him humble and true to his values.

"*Go, Mr. Morgan!*" a contingent of his current students cheered from behind the velvet ropes.

Sarah experienced an upsurge of pride so fierce her chest hurt.

"Well," the reporter said laughingly, "it sounds as if you've made a popular decision. And apparently it hasn't hurt your writing—or your personal life." She flicked a sly glance at Sarah before speaking to the camera. "For those of you who haven't recognized her, Sarah Morgan was the key witness in John Merrit's murder trial last year. In fact, it was while hiding under cover as a high school student that she met her future husband, and nearly lost her life."

Only hermits wouldn't remember the nationally publicized trial and Sarah's unique participation. Jack's arm tensed beneath her fingers. Lester Jacobs was safely behind bars, but Jack still battled misplaced guilt over her close call with death in a hotel hallway.

"Tell us, Jack, is it true that the strong female character in *Hide and Seek* was inspired by your wife?"

"Inspired, yes. But my wife is far more courageous and complex than a hundred and thirty-five minutes of screen time can convey." He tugged Sarah gently into motion.

The reporter recognized her dismissal and stepped back. "Nicely said. Congratulations on your success, and enjoy your evening." She looked toward a newly arrived limousine. "Ah, here comes Gail Powers, executive producer of Swan Productions, with someone I don't recognize..."

Sarah walked as quickly as her damn dress would allow away from camera lights and into relative privacy. "Slo-o-owly," she reminded Jack.

He immediately reduced his strides. "Sorry."

"No problem. And thanks for the compliment. It *was* nicely said."

"I had a lot of inspiration."

Sarah basked in the warmth of his respect. How blessed she was to love—and to be loved by—this man! How perfect that she could share her good news on his night of triumph...wasn't it?

He cupped her elbow and began the climb up three levels of steps toward the movie theater entrance. "I hate to think that was a taste of what to expect from

now on. The school has had its fill of the media spot-
light.''

"Bull corn. Everyone from the superintendent on
down has enjoyed and benefited from rubbing elbows
with a celebrity teacher, and don't let them tell you
differently. They love the attention.''

A year ago, she'd made a point in every media interview to praise the quality of education at Roosevelt
High, as well as the heroism of Assistant Principal
Kaiser and Mr. Morgan. Firing Donna, or refusing to
rehire Jack, would've set off a spate of negative publicity the school district could ill afford.

"Donna and Jim called earlier to send their regrets
and love," Sarah remembered suddenly. "She had a
false alarm last night and he's making her rest."
Donna's confirmed bachelor neighbor had fallen hard
and fast. Married seven months, she was seven months
pregnant.

"The honeymoon's really over," Jack said dryly as
they reached the glass doors, held open by a uniformed
attendant. "Sarah, what's wrong?''

Quickly hiding her dismay, she summoned a bright
smile. "Nothing. Would you look at this turnout."

The majority of people milling about the huge lobby
had arrived through a side door reserved for guests of
the movie executives and celebrities.

"Do you see Mother and Kate anywhere?" Jack
asked, scanning the crowd.

Being short was a pain. "Look for the hors
d'oeuvres table," Sarah suggested.

Since starting her small catering business, Vera

Morgan never passed up an opportunity to scope out the competition.

Jack tightened his grip on Sarah's elbow and steered her toward an unseen destination, stopping several times to greet teaching staff or school district officials. Sure enough, they finally found Vera and Kate standing beside a majestic swan ice sculpture, nibbling from plates filled with a variety of hors d'oeuvres.

"Taste this," Kate ordered Jack without a preliminary hello, stuffing something into his mouth. "Mom's crab cakes are ten times better, aren't they?"

"Oh, Kate—" Vera made a shooing motion "—you say that about everything I make." Obvious pleasure belied her protest.

Jack finished his bite. "Everything you make *is* great."

Kate shot her mother a triumphant look before turning to Sarah. "I keep telling Mom it's time to expand her business—you look *awesome*, by the way—and go after bigger jobs than the monthly Garden Club meeting. With me handling promotion and sales, she can double her business."

Sarah raised a brow. "How much commission did Fred tell you to charge your poor mother?"

"Twenty percent," Kate admitted, grinning. "But I'll be worth it. I've already got her booked for Larry Epstein's bar mitzvah next month."

Vera set down her plate and circled an arm around Kate's waist. "Enough about us, this is Jack's night. I'm so proud of you, son."

A year ago Vera wouldn't have embraced her

daughter. A year ago Kate would've been wounded by her mother's words. Watching their easy camaraderie now, Sarah swallowed past a lump of emotion. She reached for Jack's hand and squeezed.

The noisy arrival of the rest of "their kids" saved her mascara from streaking.

"See, I told you they'd be next to the food," Elaine crowed.

Beto scoffed. "Lucky guess. You just wanted some boiled shrimp."

"My sister found a toenail in her shrimp salad at the country club," Derek piped up. "She thought is was a piece of shell at first, but then she looked closer and—"

"*De-rek.*" Fred's gaze sought Kate's, his pained expression melting into a silent loving hello.

The lump in Sarah's throat reappeared.

After the trial, she'd returned to Houston and talked privately with each of her young friends. Apologized for having to mislead them. Asked them to forgive her. Their willingness to do so had reinforced her commitment to change the focus of her career.

Three months later, she'd founded Inside Out, her image consulting and counseling service for adolescents.

"Sarah, you look gorgeous!" Elaine complimented, looking svelte and beautiful herself. "You, too, Mr. Morgan."

"Jack," Sarah corrected, amused at everyone's averted gaze.

"It looks as if they're letting people in the theater

now," Jack said, breaking the awkward moment. "Sarah and I are sitting in the reserved section, but you all go in so you can get a good seat. We'll catch up with you again after the movie."

"I still can't believe you wrote part of it during my English class," Beto said. "Thanks again for the invitation, Mr. Mor—um, Mr. Morgan," he finished lamely.

Jack laughed along with the others. Although the kids had resumed their easy familiarity with Sarah, it would take a few more years before they could address her formidable husband by his first name with any level of comfort.

When the final thanks and excited parting smiles had been given, and the lobby had thinned to a handful of people, Sarah looked up at Jack. "Honey?"

"I'm scared," he confessed bluntly. "Everybody I care about and respect is in that audience. What if they don't like it?"

Her heart twisted at the vulnerability in his beautiful hazel eyes. "Oh, Jack, they'll *love* it, just like the test audiences did."

"But what if they don't? What if they get bored, or laugh when they're not supposed to, or boo at the end?"

There was no telling how long he'd suppressed these irrational fears. He didn't need platitudes right now.

"Okay," she said, thinking rapidly. "Let's say they do hate your movie. They hate it so much they spit at the screen. What's the worst that could happen?"

He looked a little sick.

"Would they stop production on *Hide and Seek*?" she persisted.

"No."

"Okay, then you'd still have a second shot at a hit movie—and we both know that script is damn good. But would you stop writing your current script?"

He gave the matter some thought. "No."

"Well, would you get fired from teaching? Would the neighbors egg our house?"

His color was better, the panic in his eyes receding. "I don't suppose so."

"Would I stop loving you?"

"God, I hope not," he said fervently.

"Would our baby stop loving you?" she whispered, her heart hammering with her own irrational fears.

"Our..." His eyes widened. His jaw slackened, then snapped shut. He grasped her shoulders and searched her expression, his gaze a green-gold river of joy. "We're pregnant?"

Relief and happiness spilled over in the form of a laugh. "I wish *we* were. Unfortunately, it'll be me having contractions sometime around January 10. I was going to save the news until later tonight, but you needed shaking up right n—"

His kiss cut off her babbling, expressed the powerful love she returned in full measure. When he lifted his head, they were both breathing hard.

"Are you still scared?" she asked, mesmerized by the tenderness softening his features.

"Terrified. What if I'm a rotten father?"

She pulled back, reached for his hand and tugged him into a walk. ''Handsome, hardworking, honorable men don't make rotten fathers. Come on.'' She dragged him toward the theater's double doors, now shut, their window panels dark. ''At this rate, we'll be lucky to catch the closing credits.''

''Sweetheart, I'm already the luckiest man alive. And you can take all the credit.'' Jack grasped a door handle and paused. ''Watch your step until your eyes adjust.''

Lit from within by love, Sarah followed her husband confidently into the dark theater.

Head Down Under for twelve tales of heated romance in beautiful and untamed Australia!

Here's a sneak preview of the first novel in
THE AUSTRALIANS

Outback Heat **by Emma Darcy**
available July 1998

'HAVE I DONE something wrong?' Angie persisted, wishing Taylor would emit a sense of camaraderie instead of holding an impenetrable reserve.

'Not at all,' he assured her. 'I would say a lot of things right. You seem to be fitting into our little Outback community very well. I've heard only good things about you.'

'They're nice people,' she said sincerely. Only the Maguire family kept her shut out of their hearts.

'Yes,' he agreed. 'Though I appreciate it's taken considerable effort from you. It is a world away from what you're used to.'

The control Angie had been exerting over her feelings snapped. He wasn't as blatant as his aunt in his prejudice against her but she'd felt it coming through every word he'd spoken and she didn't deserve any of it.

'Don't judge me by your wife!'

His jaw jerked. A flicker of some dark emotion destroyed the steady power of his probing gaze.

'No two people are the same. If you don't know that, you're a man of very limited vision. So I come from the city as your wife did! That doesn't stop me from being an individual in my own right.'

She straightened up, proudly defiant, furiously angry with the situation. 'I'm *me*. Angie Cordell. And it's time you took the blinkers off your eyes, Taylor Maguire.'

Then she whirled away from him, too agitated by the explosive expulsion of her emotion to keep facing him.

The storm outside hadn't yet eased. There was nowhere to go. She stopped at the window, staring blindly at the torrential rain. The thundering on the roof was almost deafening but it wasn't as loud as the silence behind her.

'You want me to go, don't you? You've given me a month's respite and now you want me to leave and channel my energies somewhere else.'

'I didn't say that, Angie.'

'You were working your way around it.' Bitterness at his tactics spewed the suspicion. 'Do you have your first choice of governess waiting in the wings?'

'No. I said I'd give you a chance.'

'Have you?' She swung around to face him. 'Have you really, Taylor?'

He hadn't moved. He didn't move now except to make a gesture of appeasement. 'Angie, I was merely trying to ascertain how you felt.'

'Then let me tell you your cynicism was shining through every word.'

He frowned, shook his head. 'I didn't mean to hurt you.' The blue eyes fastened on hers with devastating sincerity. 'I truly did not come in here to take you down or suggest you leave.'

Her heart jiggled painfully. He might be speaking the truth but the judgements were still there, the judgements that ruled his attitude towards her, that kept her shut out of his life, denied any real sharing with him, denied his confidence and trust. She didn't know why it meant so much to her but it did. It did. And the need to fight for justice from him was as much a raging torrent inside her as the rain outside.

DEBBIE MACOMBER

invites you to the

HEART OF TEXAS

Join Debbie Macomber as she brings you the lives
and loves of the folks in the ranching community
of Promise, Texas.

If you loved Midnight Sons—don't miss
Heart of Texas! A brand-new six-book series
from Debbie Macomber.

Available in February 1998
at your favorite retail store.

Heart of Texas by Debbie Macomber

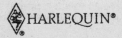

HARLEQUIN®

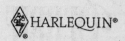 HARLEQUIN®

Not The Same Old Story!

 HARLEQUIN PRESENTS®

Exciting, glamorous romance stories that take readers around the world.

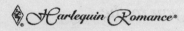 Harlequin Romance®

Sparkling, fresh and tender love stories that bring you pure romance.

 HARLEQUIN® Temptation.

Bold and adventurous—Temptation is strong women, bad boys, great sex!

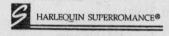 HARLEQUIN SUPERROMANCE®

Provocative and realistic stories that celebrate life and love.

 HARLEQUIN® AMERICAN ROMANCE®

Contemporary fairy tales—where anything is possible and where dreams come true.

 HARLEQUIN® INTRIGUE®

Heart-stopping, suspenseful adventures that combine the best of romance and mystery.

 LOVE & LAUGHTER™

Humorous and romantic stories that capture the lighter side of love.

Look us up on-line at: http://www.romance.net   HGENERIC